D1044991

CRYSTAL DOORS

BOOK II
OCEAN REALM

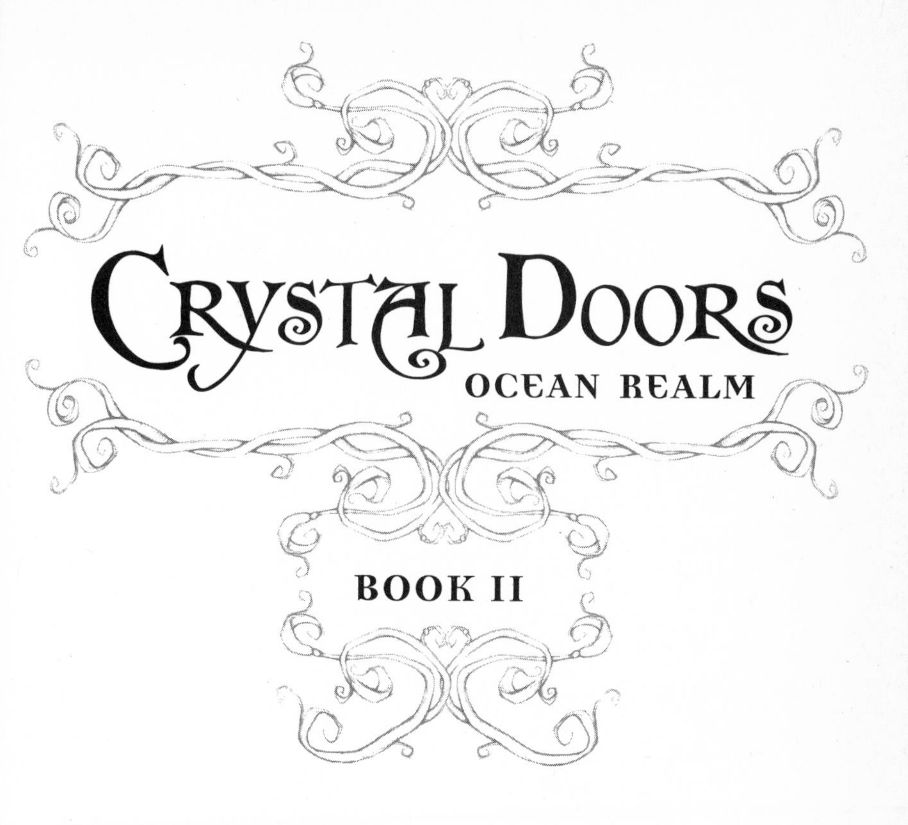

REBECCA MOESTA

AND KEVIN J. ANDERSON

LITTLE, BROWN AND COMPANY

New York Boston

Also by Rebecca Moesta and Kevin J. Anderson:
Crystal Doors #1

Little, Brown and Company

Hachette Book Group USA
237 Park Avenue, New York, NY 10169
Visit our Web site at www.lb-teens.com

First Edition: June 2007

ISBN-10: 0-316-01056-1
ISBN-13: 978-0-316-01056-6

10 9 8 7 6 5 4 3 2 1

Q-FF
Printed in the United States of America

This book is for

JANET BERLINER & BOB FLECK

Acknowledgments

We'd like to express our special appreciation to John Silbersack and Robert Gottlieb of the Trident Media Group for supporting this project from the beginning.

Jennifer Hunt and Noel De La Rosa for their enthusiasm and insightful editing.

Diane E. Jones, Catherine Sidor, and Louis Moesta of WordFire Inc. for their long hours and invaluable comments; Megie Clarke, Paul and Lacy Pfeifer, Jonathan Cowan, and D. Louise Moesta of Word Fire Inc. for keeping things running smoothly in the office.

Our families for putting up with our eccentric schedules and for introducing so many new people to our books.

Igor Kordey for brillant concept artwork and imaginative designs that helped to shape our ideas of Elantya.

Sarah and Dan Hoyt and Rebecca and Alan Lickiss for local cheerleading.

Kristine Kathryn Rush, Dean Wesley Smith, Debra Ray, Lisa Chrisman, Max and Erwin Bush, Letha Burchard, Janet

Berliner and Bob Fleck, Leslie Lauderdale, Kathy Tyree, and Ann Neumann for their decades of long-distance encouragement and keeping us sane in an insane world. Dave and Denise Dorman, Denise Jacobs, Cherie Buchheim, Mary Thomson, Brian and Jan Herbert, Maryelizabeth Hart and Jeff Mariotte, and Brad and Sue Sinor, for their friendship and support.

Crystal Doors

BOOK II
OCEAN REALM

1

AFTER FENDING OFF THE attack of the merlons and their battle kraken on the island, everyone in Elantya pulled together to save the city. Sages performed powerful magic. Ship captains and their crews helped dock workers extinguish burning wrecks and salvage the damaged ships wallowing in the water.

"Sheesh, this looks like the day after Pearl Harbor," Vic Pierce said.

Students from the Citadel — a magical and scientific training center for young people from diverse worlds — threw themselves into the recovery efforts. Although putting out fires, assessing the damage, and restoring the island city were immense tasks, each challenge gave the students a practical way to apply the new skills they were learning.

Hands wet with warm seawater, Vic tried to wipe soot

from his cheeks, though he succeeded more in smearing than cleaning himself. He was tired and sweaty. His strange Elantyan clothes were soaked. "Hard work now, *more* hard work later," he said with a groan, then grinned at his cousin Gwen. "On the other hand, it sure beats *home*work. Back home on Earth, Mrs. Dorman is probably handing out Sentence Structure worksheets right now." Vic and Gwen — born on the same night to mothers who were sisters and fathers who were identical twins — were in the same grade at Stephen Hawking High, back in California.

Gwen waded out from the shore up to her knees and wrestled with a floating beam blasted from a sunken cargo ship. Tossing her blond hair back, she nodded. "Probably. And Mr. Christensen would be assigning us a term paper on Prince Henry the Navigator."

The island of Elantya, magically raised up from the ocean floor thousands of years earlier, served as a hub at the center of an arrangement of crystal doors that linked fantastic worlds. The native merlons, however, had long resented the presence of this unnatural island in their world. They considered it a blemish on their perfect ocean.

Recently, merlon aggression had grown extravagant. The aquatic creatures had attacked and sunk several cargo ships, including the *Golden Walrus,* a vessel used for training students. Vic, Gwen, and their friends had barely survived the ordeal, and Vic suspected there was much more to the merlons' behavior than simply being unfriendly neighbors.

Vic helped Gwen carry the splintered wooden beam to shore and add it to the growing pile of debris removed from the turquoise harbor waters. "I wish my dad were here," he couldn't help saying. Dr. Carlton Pierce had been left behind in California when Vic and Gwen accidentally plunged through a crystal door to this magical world, where the Elantyans were embroiled in a struggle against the fierce undersea merlons.

Vic caught the quick expression of sadness that filled Gwen's dramatic violet eyes. Her own parents were dead, killed in a car accident, which the cousins now knew had probably not been an accident. Vic and Gwen's coming to Elantya hadn't been a complete accident, either. Since their arrival they had encountered too many clues — about their mothers and the potential Vic and Gwen seemed to have inherited from them — to be certain anymore what was coincidence and what was destiny.

Mystery surrounded much of what had happened to the cousins since Vic's father had warned them of a strange danger. Cap Pierce had been arranging crystals in the solarium of their California home when Vic and Gwen had unintentionally stumbled through a crystal door and found themselves here in Elantya, with no obvious way home.

Smoke rose in dark plumes that the sea breezes dissipated, leaving the sky a clear blue that seemed almost too cheery for the exhausting work they all faced.

As Vic and Gwen started back into the water, a shadow passed overhead. Vic looked up to see a purple rectangle trimmed in gold tassels: the magic carpet ridden by their friend Ali el Sharif, a young prince from the flying city of Irrakesh.

Sharif called down to them, "That battle kraken caused a great deal of damage. At least most of the fires are out now." He held the clear eggsphere of his nymph djinni Piri over the edge of the carpet, so that she could get a good look, as well. The tiny fairylike creature glowed blue with earnest concentration. Sharif brought the carpet down closer to his friends. He rolled Piri up and down his arms, contact juggling, while the diminutive feminine figure inside the globe twinkled pink with enjoyment. Sharif grinned at his small friend. "Piri and I have a good view from above. I count sixteen sunken war galleys, fishing boats, and cargo ships, including two large vessels near the mouth of the harbor. Those will need to be moved first."

Sunken ships posed a significant hazard. Many types of sailing ships came through the crystal doors from other worlds. While some had shallow drafts, others had hulls that extended so deeply into the water that they would scrape the wreckage and possibly sink themselves.

Gwen nodded. "In other words, if fishing and cargo ships can't use the main harbor, Elantya might not get enough food and supplies."

"I will circle around once more, then report to the sages and help them decide what to do next," Sharif said.

"Can't they figure that out for themselves?" Gwen said. "I'm pretty sure they already know about the ships blocking the harbor, and we could use another hand down here."

"I am sorry, Gwenya, but my observation duties are too important." After playing with Piri a little more, he tucked her back into the mesh sack that hung around his neck and flew off to circle the harbor again.

Vic groaned. "I guess he'd rather stay above the mess than get his hands or his pantaloons dirty." Although Sharif avoided referring to the fact that he was a prince, his pride frequently reminded them.

So they did the work themselves.

Out in the water up to her chest, a lean brown-skinned young girl from Afirik was wrestling with a tangle of ship debris much larger than she should have been able to handle. Tiaret turned her amber eyes toward them and motioned with a hand. "I could use your assistance, my friends. Together, the three of us can manage this and I . . . I am reluctant to move out into deeper water. I believe the other end is caught in something."

Vic scratched his nose. "Sure, how hard could it be?"

"The question is, will it be as easy as you think?" Gwen said. "But naturally we'll help." They dove in and swam past Tiaret to scope out the intertwined beam, ropes, and broken boards she was trying to retrieve.

Tiaret had never learned to swim. On the dry savannahs of her world, the rainy season was short, and for most of the year watering holes were little more than shallow ponds. When she left Afirik with her master Kundu, her ship had been attacked by merlons en route. Vic and Sharif had arrived on the flying carpet to save Tiaret as killer sharks closed in. No one else had survived.

Because she was a strong girl and an excellent fighter, Tiaret never liked to admit to any weakness. Although she meant to become proficient when the harbor restoration was finished, for now she still couldn't swim. Since her arrival in

Elantya, however, she had learned to enjoy wading in the surf, so she was becoming more comfortable in the ocean.

While Gwen and Tiaret struggled to pull the floating wood loose, Vic dove under the water, keeping his eyes open to see what had snagged the wreckage. The harbor water was murky with silt, stirred up by the recovery operations. Feeling as well as seeing his way, he found a mammoth scooplike object dragging on the floor of the harbor. Its jagged edge had dredged up sand and mud, then lodged in a cluster of rocks. He felt with his hand, located where the wooden rib was connected, then swam a little deeper. The thing felt like a giant seashell, coated with something slippery.

Lungs aching, he swam back up and gulped a deep breath. "Yup, it's stuck on something. Hold on, let me get it unhooked." Puffing his cheeks, Vic blew out his breath before taking another lungful of air. He dove under again, swimming down directly this time. Now that he knew where he was going, he found the snag and began to push aside rocks, disentangling the thing.

The object shifted abruptly, pulling on the snarled ropes attached to the floating wood and jerking Tiaret forward into deeper water. Vic saw his friend's legs kick and thrash as she realized she could no longer touch the bottom. Her head went under and she began churning with furious movements of her arms, as well. As Vic pushed himself upward, dodging the agitated motions of Tiaret's legs, he saw Gwen submerge herself and breast-stroke toward the girl. The cousins reached her at the same time, and together pulled their struggling friend back to the surface.

Coughing and choking, Tiaret let them tow her back into shallower water, then she waved them away. "Thank you for your assistance. Now, let us complete our task." She grasped another piece of the tangled wreckage as if nothing important had happened.

Knowing that this abruptness was Tiaret's way of covering her embarrassment, Vic flashed his cousin an eyebrow shrug, dove again, and started back to work on the snagged object. As soon as he nudged it loose, he realized what it was: the scalloped canopy that had sheltered the two merlon generals riding and goading the battle kraken during its terrible attack against Elantya.

Both merlon commanders had been killed when Sage Polup's magical cannon blasted the kraken. Vic resurfaced as the two girls strained together to pull the wreckage free. He dragged the shell canopy into shallow water where they could see it better.

"I bet this'll make a nice monument or addition to a museum," Vic said.

"The Elantyans will indeed build a memorial to this battle," Tiaret answered in her gruff voice. "However, this chapter in the Great Epic is unfinished. The war continues."

When they brought their prizes to the shore, Vic was proud of the sizable pile collected on the beach. "Look at all this wood — just think of the bonfire we could build. We could roast marshmallows and hot dogs. . . ." His stomach growled. "It's been so long since I had a hot dog."

"Wood must be dry before it can burn, Viccus," Tiaret said.

Vic brushed that aside. "We could find a drying spell."

Gwen gave an exasperated sigh and punched him on the shoulder. "There aren't enough trees on Elantya for us to waste wood by burning it. It's way too useful."

Vic felt sheepish for having forgotten such an important detail. On isolated Elantya, most supplies, including wood, arrived by ship through the crystal doors.

Gwen waded back out into the water and looked down, startled and pleased to see a strange swimming creature. "Look, Vic — an aquit!"

He had always thought of aquits as living mermaid Barbie dolls. Elantyans frequently asked them to carry messages to and from ships across the ocean, just as skrits carried messages and scrolls over land. Stroking with its tiny arms and flapping its fish tail, the creature surfaced and spoke to Gwen and Vic. "Map, please."

"Of course." Gwen bent over to scoop up the little swimmer and cradle it in her hands. The sages had dispatched numerous aquits to scout out the harbor floor, including possible merlon booby traps left in the wake of the recent attack. Carrying the aquit, she sloshed back to shore and headed up the sandy slope. Tiaret and Vic followed.

High up on the beach, their copper-haired friend Lyssandra and several other students had spread out a large chart on which they were making a detailed map of the submerged hazards in the harbor. Lyssandra looked up as they approached. When Vic saw her cobalt-blue eyes, his heart did a little flutter. Lyssandra was ethereal, petite, and very smart. She was the first girl they had met in Elantya, and with her telepathic powers she had helped the cousins understand the language spoken here. Lyssandra's gifts also included frequent prophetic dreams, many of which were alarming or horrific and robbed her of sleep. Recently, she had been haunted again by the strange dream about Vic's and Gwen's xyridium medallion — the one where it spun and danced above sparkling water, splashing like a porpoise in the waves until, at the end, something pulled it to the bottom of the ocean. She'd also had a series of nightmares about blood and drowning. No wonder she didn't want to wade out into the harbor, Vic thought.

Seeing the aquit in Gwen's hands, Lyssandra said, "Good. We need more accurate information. We are compiling a better picture of the undersea wrecks. It is possible that there is no clear path for a ship to get close to the docks."

"There aren't many docks left for them to tie up to," Vic pointed out.

The sounds of construction — shouting men, creaking ropes, clattering pulleys — came from where the largest work group labored to get the main wharf reconstructed.

The aquit's form shifted to mimic Gwen, so that she seemed to be carrying a perfect copy of herself. When she set it down, the small creature picked up tiny pebbles from the beach and walked across the spread-out map. The imitative creature looked down at the drawn lines and bit the edge of its lower lip exactly as Gwen did when she was thinking hard. Vic chuckled at the performance.

The aquit set the small rocks down as markers. "Large ship here. And here." The two pebbles represented vessels Lyssandra had not yet marked on the map.

"Can you tell me what kind of ships they were?" she said.

"War galley. Fishing boat," said the piping voice.

Lyssandra nodded soberly. "Those are also blocking the deep passage to the docks. The sages plan to concentrate on the mouth of the harbor first. Sage Polup and several members of the Pentumvirate are about to try something unusual."

"Let us hope it succeeds," Tiaret said.

"Cool," Vic said. "Maybe they'll, uh, use a disintegrator spell. That would take care of everything."

Gwen gave him one of her oh-grow-up looks.

At the smashed end of one of the docks, Sage Polup stood with all five brightly robed members of Elantya's ruling council, the Pentumvirate. Polup was easily recognizable, for he was an anemonite, a many-frilled jellyfishlike creature, highly intelligent but without much of a body. His people had been enslaved by the merlons because of their scientific and magical genius. When Polup escaped and requested sanctuary in Elantya, some of the island's most brilliant sages and engineers had constructed a head-tank and a clanking walker body powered by steam and spells. Vic thought the contraption looked like a clunky robot from an old science fiction movie.

Vic identified the members of the Pentumvirate by their robe colors: red, blue, green, yellow, and white, each color symbolizing one of the "five elements." This classification annoyed Gwen, who contended that there were well over a hundred elements on the periodic table, but Vic was happy to have that much less to memorize. The Virs each unrolled a spell scroll and began to read aloud. The spells were printed in powerful aja ink, which bound magic to the parchment.

"Look. Out in the water," Tiaret said. The three friends ran closer to the teetering wharf on which the sages had gathered.

Where the largest sunken ship blocked the mouth of the harbor, a frothing, churning storm appeared beneath the water. The broken masts and splintered hull of the large fishing vessel gradually rose to the surface.

"That ship isn't exactly floating, is it?" Gwen said. "There's something . . . swarming around it."

"Looks like maggots," Vic said. "Thousands of little things chewing at the wood."

"Eww." Gwen, who had always wanted to be a marine biologist, quickly assumed an appropriate scientific interest. "Probably sea worms, burrowing parasites. Normally, they're considered a threat to wooden ships, since they can tunnel through the hull planks, like termites."

"They're certainly tunneling now," Vic said. "Looks like they're starving."

Tiaret put her hands on her hips. Droplets of seawater still glistened on her skin. "Sage Polup knows the creatures of the sea. He and the other sages must have called these worms and invited them to have a feast."

As the friends watched the sea worms devour the floating ship hulk, Vic was reminded of how goldfish in ornamental ponds would swarm whenever he tossed a handful of food pellets into the water. Within only a few minutes the wrecked vessel dissolved before their eyes. The broken masts and curved hull planks fell apart into toothpicks. All along the shore, Elantyans cheered, seeing one of the primary obstacles now gone from their harbor.

"Maybe those things'll just eat all of the sunken ships and the floating wreckage and save us a lot of work," Vic said. The water calmed at the mouth of the harbor. The last remaining bits of the sunken fishing vessel drifted out, spreading toward the open sea.

Gwen shook her head. "Number one, that ship was blocking the harbor, so they had to get rid of it quickly. Two, ships and their contents are too valuable to waste like that. Especially wood. And three, I think those little worms have gorged themselves."

"Nevertheless, it is one more thing to celebrate," Tiaret said. "I am already practicing to tell the story."

"And I'm ready for a big celebration banquet," Vic said.

"Provided the merlons don't attack again first," Gwen added.

2

WEEK AFTER WEEK, THE work continued. It was a long time before the Elantyans felt they could pause for an evening of recognition and celebration. They had survived the battle, though the war was far from over, and diligent watchers continued to guard the coasts, alert for any sign of merlons.

On the evening of the celebration, thousands upon thousands of inhabitants gathered in the main governmental rotunda. The meeting chamber was made entirely of polished white stone marbled with gold veins. Shimmering crystals in the alcoves glowed with warm rainbow light, like prismatic torches.

On a low dais at the center of the rotunda, the five robed members of the Pentumvirate waited for the room to come to order as the noisy citizens found their places. Seating themselves in the ornately carved stone chairs arranged in a semicircle on the dais, the members of the Pentumvirate gripped the rose and turquoise decision crystals on the right and left arms of the chairs.

Nibbling the edge of her lower lip, Gwen stood near the exit of the Pentumvirate Hall with Vic, Lyssandra, Tiaret, and Sharif, waiting to be called forward. "Everybody fought the merlons," Gwen whispered to her companions. "Why would the Virs make such a big deal out of what we did?"

Vic gave her a mocking smile. "Don't overanalyze, Doc. It's cool. Just go with it. Celebrate now, contemplate later."

In a low voice Tiaret said, "From the Great Epic, I have learned that false heroes risk others' lives for their own glory and demand to be honored. True heroes, however, risk their own lives for others, because honor demands it."

Agreeing, Sharif leaned toward them with a satisfied smile and added in a hushed voice, "My people have a saying: A land without heroes is easily conquered."

The white-robed Etherya, her dark hair caught up in ringlets high at the top of her head, raised her arms and said in a rich, melodious voice, "We stand in unity."

"In unity is our strength," responded the apprentices, along with the rest of the crowd.

"We who gather here share a belief in order over chaos, justice over uncontrolled power, and good over evil." Etherya lowered her arms.

"We sit together in peace," the crowd replied in unison, and they all took their seats on the tiered benches that ringed the meeting chamber.

Etherya once again raised her voice: "Today we gather to

celebrate our freedom, and our victories in several battles over the merlons. On behalf of the Pentumvirate, I thank every citizen who fought to protect Elantya. We also wish to recognize those essential individuals without whom the victories would not have been possible."

The first ones to be called forward were Sage Rubicas and the anemonite Sage Polup. Ever since the merlon attack, Rubicas had been working on his large protective shield spell, trying day after day to recreate the barrier he had successfully tested — before his treacherous assistant Orpheon stole and destroyed much of his work.

"Before I present the Council's gifts of thanks to Sage Polup and Master Sage Rubicas," Etherya continued, "I have asked our anemonite friend to tell us his story, that we may better treasure our freedom and understand the nature of our enemy." The crowd murmured its approval.

Sage Polup turned toward the crowd in his heavy, clanking body and adjusted something in the twin horn-shaped speakers at his chest. "Many years ago, my people lived at peace in a beautiful reef, sharing the oceans with all creatures and dwelling in harmony with them. We swam free on the currents and rode on spiny kraega steeds, assisting them as they assisted us.

"Then the merlons captured my people. They clipped our swim fronds so that we could not escape, and they forced us to invent weapons for them — something we had no desire to do.

"Because any resistance on our part resulted in torture or death, at last my people gave in. The merlons made many of us work in a place called Lavaja Canyon, where thermal vents spew out molten lava which, as it hardens, releases great magical energies. We anemonites are capable of molding those energies for the merlons' magic.

"When I could no longer compel myself to do the bidding of the merlon king Barak, I resolved to escape. With hope and desperation, I cast myself into the thermal currents rising from a bubbling lavaja vent. Though the water burned me terribly, the hot currents carried me higher and higher, whisking me away from my captors.

"The merlons did not follow, believing me already dead in the hot jets of water. I lost consciousness until a stream of cool water struck me and jetted me out of the thermal currents. I rode that stream for more than a day, not caring where I went, as long as it was away from the merlons. Near some reefs, where the water became shallow and turbulent, I spotted a kraega steed and persuaded it to carry me to Elantya, where your engineers and magical sages worked together to create this amazing body" — he lifted one thick arm to show off its gliding pulleys and bubbling lubricants — "so that I could live among you on the land. That is how I became an instructor at the Citadel. I long for the day when all of my fellow anemonites can be free, but until then I choose to live among you and work toward that time." Polup turned back toward the Pentumvirate.

Etherya thanked him and presented him with a surprise. "We Elantyans made your walking body, and now we offer you a means to travel swiftly and safely in the ocean as well." Engineers came forward carrying a shiny object from their construction laboratories. Polup swiveled his clanking body toward it.

To Gwen, the gift looked like a cartoon version of a flying saucer — a clear basketball-sized submersible bubble with a thick, teardrop-shaped metal base, which boasted a pair of extendable grappling arms and two quarrel launchers. Two magic sages explained the machine to Polup, murmuring words like "utility appendages," "water circulation," and "propulsion systems."

"Cool!" Vic whispered. "A mini-sub made just for Polup."

Gwen smiled. "Now he'll be able to scoot around in the water again, much faster than any regular jellyfish could swim. I'd really miss it if I couldn't swim."

Tiaret glanced at her. "I intend to become an excellent swimmer."

"Don't worry," Vic assured her. "We'll start those lessons soon."

Next Etherya addressed Rubicas. "Master Sage, the Virs have no gift befitting a sage of your skills, knowledge, and courage, save this: the Pentumvirate hereby appoints you Ven Sage Rubicas, the most revered sage in Elantya, Director of the Citadel, and Advisor to this Council."

Though he was gray haired with a long beard, Rubicas grinned like a child. Applause rippled around the room. Lyssandra blinked in astonishment and whispered, "There has been no Ven Sage in Elantya since Qirteas died ten years ago."

Etherya raised her hand again for quiet. "And now, Ven Rubicas, we should reward your apprentices." She beckoned the five friends.

All eyes turned toward the students. Gwen felt distinctly uncomfortable as they walked forward. The others seemed so composed: Vic grinning and waving at the crowd, Sharif walking with straight-backed regal dignity, long-legged Tiaret taking it all in stride, and Lyssandra nodding calmly at everyone. Of course, Gwen had spoken to groups during her time on the debate team in high school, but those audiences had consisted of dozens, perhaps even a few hundred people, not . . . *thousands.*

From the dais, Etherya motioned for them each to stand in front of one of the Virs. "Again, mere words can never express our gratitude toward you. All of you showed surpassing ingenuity and courage in the face of repeated attacks, first at the reefs of Ophir" — here she nodded to Sharif, Vic, and Tiaret — "then aboard the *Golden Walrus.* Later you thwarted a merlon invasion from beneath the very city itself, protected Ven Sage Rubicas from a murderous spy, and chased the traitor down to wrest some of our defensive spells from his grasp. You also fought the battle kraken with spell scrolls, sunshine bombs, and magical cannon fire — and kept the merlons at bay in hand-to-hand combat. Each Vir has chosen a gift in token of our appreciation."

First, Protective Vir Helassa spoke to Tiaret, who stood directly before her holding her teaching staff. Helassa had dressed in a fluttering, floor-length crimson gown in a Grecian style that revealed a good deal of skin. Her hair was a striking mixture of raven streaked with gold that cascaded in beautiful ringlets down her bare back.

"Tiaretya of Afirik, warrior and storyteller and keeper of

your master's staff, for you I chose a special rune to be etched into your staff. Once it is carved into the wood, your staff will become unbreakable. Use it wisely to protect yourself and Elantya."

Vir Parsimanias, who faced Lyssandra, spoke next in the precise, clipped manner he always used. "Lyssandra of Elantya," he said, holding up an emerald-green pendant on a xyridium chain, "for you I chose one of the ancient treasures of Elantya. This crystal vial — carved from pure water aja — is filled with medicinal greenstepe." He twisted off a tiny cut-crystal stopper as the crowd mumbled in confusion. "It appears to hold only a drop. But do not be deceived: no matter how much you drink, the vial will always remain full. You may use the stepe to quench thirst or for its medicinal properties. Use your gift wisely, for yourself and for Elantya."

Lyssandra whispered her thanks and hung the pendant around her neck.

Vir Pecunyas spoke to Sharif. "Sharifas of Irrakesh, for you I, too, chose a rune — one that will be embroidered into your carpet with sun aja thread. The rune will ensure that when you call your carpet, no matter how far apart you are, the carpet will eventually find you. Use it wisely for yourself and all Elantya."

Sharif bowed his thanks. Piri, in the mesh sack around his neck, glowed pink and twirled in spirals of delight. He absently stroked the curve of her crystal sphere.

Questas, the Vir of Learning, looked at the two cousins. "Gwenya and Viccus of . . ." His voice trailed off. "Of Earth? As apprentices to Ven Rubicas, all of you have much work to do, and much that you may wish to record about your experiences here. Therefore, I entrust this gift to both of you." He handed her and Vic small leather-bound booklets no bigger than the palm of a hand and as thin as a book of matches. The miniature volumes — not scrolls, but *books* — were identical, like twins.

"Thank you."

Vic opened his book and flipped through it. All of the pages were blank. Gwen plucked a slender gold stylus from the spine of her book. It was clear that her cousin was feeling a mixture of amazement and faint puzzlement at the marvelous gift. After all, if it wasn't science fiction, a book wasn't necessarily Vic's first choice.

"Is it a diary?" he asked.

"Perhaps. Or a notebook, or a communication device," Questas explained. "Its uses are limited only by your imagination. Books and writing are powerful tools and invincible weapons, and the book you hold is very rare. No matter how many notes you take, how many drawings you make, how much you write or what stories you see fit to put into it, there will always be more blank pages. Use the stylus with it, and the words you write can never be erased."

Gwen flipped the pages, eager to start writing.

"Even more special," the Vir continued, "these two volumes are twinned. Anything one of you writes in your own book will be reflected in the other."

"I guess I won't put all my secrets in it, then," Vic said in a low voice to Gwen. "'Dear Diary, I think I'm being watched.'"

She rolled her eyes and murmured, "I wouldn't want to

snoop in your journal anyway. But I might use it to remind you of things you need to remember. We could send messages."

Vic did not seem excited by the prospect, though he was thoroughly intrigued by the twinned book.

At the end of the presentations, Lyssandra's father Groxas, a pyro sage, put on a stunning fireworks show *inside* the dome of the rotunda, using safety explosives he had devised especially for the occasion. The honorees and the crowd were delighted. Sage Polup was so enraptured with the special demonstration that Gwen heard him murmur with excitement, "I never guessed that pyrotechnics could be so precise as to be used inside a building. Perhaps I could develop something similar that would work under water."

3

THE FOLLOWING MORNING, THE five friends were taking a praktik in quillmanship. They sat on surprisingly comfortable stone chairs pulled up to long, narrow tables arranged in a vee, so that the instructor could help any student without walking too far. Astonishingly, the quillmanship sage was a thin blind man with long salt-and-pepper hair and drooping mustaches. Even though Sage Tyresias could not see, he drew perfect letters and runes on a scribing board, and seemed to know when his students made mistakes.

Vic stared at the gray marble columns that held up the high ceiling of the airy room. He wished that they were all in another martial arts praktik, like the one they'd had yesterday. Sage Jun Li had drilled them in bare-handed offensive skills, and asked the twin cousins to share some of the *zy'oah* techniques their mothers had taught them. When the praktik ended, the whole class had stayed to watch the sage spar with Tiaret in a presentation of staff and spear maneuvers.

Quillmanship was far less exciting. Beside Vic, Lyssandra wrote her assignment in an even, flowing hand. Instead of doing their specific lessons, he scribbled messages to Gwen in his new book, knowing that the words would appear on her own pages. Sitting on the opposite side of the vee of tables, Gwen frowned at him, glancing at his words. Using her gold stylus, she jotted, PRACTICE YOUR QUILLMANSHIP!

When the words appeared on his page, he grinned and wrote back, I AM. I'M PRACTICING BY WRITING TO YOU!"

Vic knew that quillmanship must be important, especially to Elantyans, since every drop of precious aja ink was both valuable and magical. But he wasn't terribly interested in the class and was glad for the interruption when a skrit flew in, its gossamer wings beating hummingbird-fast, and deposited a scroll on the table in front of the instructor. The fairylike messenger flitted off, leaving the blind man to pick up the scroll, which bore the seal of the Pentumvirate.

Sage Tyresias turned to the class and broke the seal on the scroll. "We have received an important message." With his blind eyes turned toward the sky, the sage ran his fingers over the symbols printed on the parchment in aja ink and spoke. "As a show of courage and unity, in spite of the ever-present threat of further merlon attacks, the Pentumvirate announces that the Elantyan holiday of Guise Night will indeed be celebrated this evening."

Excited conversation bubbled through the students. Hardly able to believe that the quillmanship instructor was "reading," Vic stared in fascination while the sage continued.

"The Virs regard this occasion as an opportunity for the people of our island to inspire each other and demonstrate the strength and resilience of Elantyans. Despite the damage done by the battle kraken and merlon warriors, we cannot postpone community life indefinitely. The festivities — observed with all due caution — will do much to lift the spirits of Elantya's people."

The students cheered, as if to prove the statement. Vic looked around at the beaming faces then gave Gwen an eyebrow shrug. Neither of them was familiar with Elantyan holidays, but he figured this must be a good one, since everyone seemed so happy about it.

Gwen, never timid, asked aloud, "What is Guise Night, exactly?"

Sage Snigmythya, who had heard the cheering out in the hallway, poked her head into the quillmanship room just in time to hear Gwen's question. The woman had owlish eyes and a perpetual expression of befuddlement. "Ah, what a wonderful story! Sage Tyresias, would you permit me? A wonderful story."

The old blind man nodded to her patiently. "Please, be my guest."

"Oh, wonderful, wonderful." Snigmythya seemed harmless and good-hearted, though a bit scatterbrained. Vic, who was often accused of being scatterbrained himself, rather liked her. "Guise Night is a traditional celebration of a victory by

Therya, one of the greatest warrior sages who ever lived. One of the greatest! The constellation Therya's Bow is named for her. Sage Therya traveled with a small band of trusted warriors through one crystal door after another, searching for dark sages who misused their power. *Misused,* mind you. Therya believed that these evil men and women were trained by Azric himself.

"You all remember Azric, don't you? The powerful dark sage who created vast immortal armies, which he intended to unleash upon all the worlds linked by crystal doors."

"We all met his henchman Orpheon," Tiaret said, frowning at the memory.

"Oh yes, yes, of course. Orpheon. He and Azric managed to escape when the sages of Elantya imposed the Great Closure, sealing the crystal doors to those worlds — along with a good many others — and trapping Azric's immortal armies forever. Trapping them." With a smile, she tapped her fingers together as if she had finished her story.

"So, how does Therya fit in to Guise Night?" Gwen prompted.

"Oh, yes! Sage Therya sought out dark sages converted by Azric. We do not know why, but after the Great Closure Azric lost his ability to perform the blood rite to create immortal armies. Perhaps the bright sages Qelsyn and Aennia restricted his power somehow in the Closure — we are not certain. Nevertheless, Azric was able to train new dark sages, and they were dangerous. Yes, dangerous, but not immortal. They could be stopped — and stop them Therya did, in world after world.

"But one day the warrior sage stumbled upon hundreds of

dark sages preparing to invade Elantya. They chased Therya and her band, slaughtering anyone who stood in their path — *slaughtering* them! Therya and her bright sages escaped only by disguising themselves, running from one village to the next, and hiding in the homes of such kindhearted folk as would take in weary strangers. Weary strangers." Snigmythya gave an emphatic nod.

"And not one of the people who sheltered them came to any harm, you know. Not one. Finally Therya's band reached the crystal door and returned to Elantya, just in time to warn the other bright sages. When the evil ones arrived, our island was ready and defeated the invaders in a great battle. To this day, we observe the victory by celebrating Guise Night. To this day. That is when we honor those we respect and admire." Snigmythya sounded choked up with her own story.

"But why's it called Guy's Night, when Therya was a woman?" Vic asked.

Lyssandra touched his hand to draw the thought from his mind. She laughed. "I see the confusion. The translation in your head sounds like another word in your language. It is Guise Night, as in *dis*guise. Students in disguise visit adults they admire, and the adults give them presents to help them on their way."

"Cool," Vic said. "It's like Halloween and Christmas all rolled into one."

"For those of you who have never participated," Snigmythya explained, "you may dress as any person or animal you choose."

"Anything? Well, it probably wouldn't be a good idea to dress up like a merlon," Vic pointed out.

The female sage held up her hands. "Oh, no! That would be a very bad idea. For safety's sake. A bad idea."

Gwen shuddered. "I'm not ready to see another merlon, anyway. Even if it is just my cousin in disguise."

"Agreed," Tiaret said. "Yet we *will* face them whenever they come. We must remain watchful."

"This is a rather abrupt announcement," Sharif said. "Where can we find costumes before tonight?"

Blind Sage Tyresias answered. "The Citadel maintains a wardrobe of donated items. Lyssandra can show it to you. Perhaps I should end our quillmanship praktik early?" He received no argument from the students.

VIC, GWEN, TIARET, AND Sharif followed Lyssandra to the wardrober's hall at the Citadel, a place used for both lighthearted and serious disguises. Sages going to other worlds often outfitted themselves here so that they could travel unnoticed. The five apprentices, along with other apprentices, novs, and journeysages, spent the better part of two hours trying on hats, robes, animal skins, masks, wigs, beards, and so on, laughing and joking.

Gwen suddenly grew sober. "It feels weird, doesn't it?"

Vic groaned. "Come on, Doc, don't spoil the mood. What feels weird?"

His cousin gave an uncomfortable shrug. "It's barely been a couple of months since Orpheon was Rubicas's apprentice, and apparently he was in disguise the whole time."

Vic frowned. "Well, we know he was a spy, but we don't

know if he was in disguise — unless you mean that he pretended to be an apprentice at the Citadel."

"He did turn into a merlon when he dove off the cliff to escape us," Sharif pointed out. "But he claimed to be human."

Lyssandra pursed her lips. "Orpheon said he was one of Azric's original generals, trapped with him outside the conquered worlds in the Great Closure. According to legend, Azric and any of his immortal followers have the power to change their shape."

Vic frowned. "So he could come back at any time. He could be disguised tonight, just like we are. He could be anyone or anything, and we wouldn't know it."

Tiaret rapped the floor with the end of her teaching staff, which was now virtually indestructible because of the rune carved on it. "If he shows his face, he will not escape again."

Over the course of the afternoon, they assembled their disguises. Sharif was dressed in swashbuckling splendor as the captain of a trading ship. Tiaret was robed as a Cogitarian, a keeper of Elantya's library, and carried a bundle of scrolls under one arm. Gwen looked for all the world like a djinni who had just popped out of a bottle or a magic lamp.

Sharif, who had helped Gwen with the outfit, raised Piri's eggsphere high and said, "You see, Piri, that is how you will look when you are all grown up." When the nymph djinni's orb started flickering a bright jealous green, Sharif quickly tucked Piri back into her mesh pouch. "Do not worry, little one, no one could ever match *you*." The tiny djinni seemed mollified.

Partly because he was inspired by Sage Polup, and partly

for his own amusement, Vic had chosen an anemonite costume. The rippled mass of the voluminous coral-colored outfit looked like a cross between a sea anemone and a jellyfish. A frilly ridge surrounded the brainlike lump, studded with a ring of eye protrusions, beneath which hung a long fringe of thick gelatinous strands.

Vic found himself most surprised by Lyssandra's disguise. Tonight the petite telepathic girl was warrior Sage Therya herself, wearing a short leather skirt and bodice, a bow and a quiver of arrows slung across her back, and a pair of knee-high walking boots. Her arms were bare and her copper hair hung over one shoulder in a thick, heavy braid. Vic was glad she couldn't see his mouth fall open beneath his anemonite outfit.

As the apprentices set out, the sun was just sinking toward the horizon, saturating the wispy clouds with hues of orange and pink and lavender. The air was balmy, and the light breeze was scented with flowers, moist earth from a late afternoon shower, salt from the ocean, and the tantalizing odors of evening meals being cooked.

By tradition, the groups visited one respected adult after another, with each student getting at least one choice. Some students were disguised as fisher folk, others as Virs, weavers, carpenters, metalsmiths, or military officers. Each group could consist of up to ten students, but because of its magical significance, five was the average number.

"We will give these gifts to our hosts," Lyssandra said, handing each of them a pair of small poem scrolls. "They are inscribed with an ancient Elantyan blessing: Power and grace, protect this place."

"Thanks. So, uh, who should we visit first?" Vic asked, hopping up and down in his anemonite outfit, so that his frills jiggled. The apprentices stood at an intersection of roads, deciding where to go. The streetcrystals winked on. Water gurgled in the magical canals that ran along the streets and a sense of excitement and anticipation hung over the island city.

Lyssandra answered, "If I might be so bold as to make a suggestion, there is a sage who is renowned throughout the city and even in some of the crystal door worlds for . . . culinary expertise. I believe we might be wise to start by visiting that sage. It would not be proper for me to make her my choice, but one of you could —"

Gwen chuckled. "In other words, your mother?"

In her Therya costume, Lyssandra smiled and gave a small bow. "My father is taking my brother Xandas and his group out on their Guise Night rounds, and mother has been cooking all day."

Tiaret tapped her teaching staff on the cobblestone street. "Sage Kaisa is more than just a masterful cook. She is also an excellent sailor and a fearsome warrior. I approve of doing her this honor. I will make her my first choice."

As if on cue, Vic's stomach grumbled loudly. "Hey, you won't get any argument from me."

"It is settled then," Sharif said. "My people have a saying: First fill the army with food, then fill the armory with weapons."

Lyssandra led the way to her home, which was on a hill above the harbor. Tiaret, dressed as a Cogitarian, stepped forward and rapped lightly with her staff on the door. A beaming Kaisa faced them and gave the traditional greeting. "May friends take heart and enemies beware. What brings you to my door?"

Together, they gave the customary response. "We flee dark powers that mean us harm. Will you help us?"

Kaisa's indigo eyes sparkled with enjoyment. "Well, I cannot allow the dark powers to get you, can I? Would some nice hot food help?"

She ushered them into the house to a long table near the kitchen. As soon as they were seated, she began bringing in baskets of freshly baked bread, platters of steaming meat, bowls of savory broth, plates of sliced fruits, and pitchers of cool mos ale and fresh-squeezed sussu juice. As they ate quickly, sampling the various dishes, Kaisa told the apprentices which fruits and vegetables had medicinal properties, how to cure meat for long trips, what leaves and herbs went into greenstepe, how to make greenstepe poultices to heal wounds, and any number of other useful bits of information.

To his surprise, Vic found that he learned exceedingly well while eating.

Two more groups of students arrived and Kaisa sat them all at the long table and continued sharing nuggets of wisdom as if there had been no interruption. When Vic and his friends were finished, Kaisa urged them on their way to see other respected adults; she would not hear of them staying to clear the dishes, as she expected to have many more "fugitives" visiting this night. They thanked her kindly for her help, and Tiaret presented her with a poem scroll as a token of their gratitude.

The evening passed in a pleasant blur. Out in the streets, students in colorful costume impersonated healers, animal herders, minstrels, masons, and various sages and historical figures. Warm light streamed from the windows of every house. Some students stopped beneath streetcrystals and gave impromptu speeches or musical performances in keeping with their characters.

The apprentices visited the anemonite Sage Polup, who offered the "fugitives" small suntips he had designed that could be strapped to a finger for lighting their way in the darkness. Questas, the Vir of Learning, gave them each a small leather pouch for holding currency, little spell scrolls, and crystals. Stern Helassa gave a small, sharp crystal dagger with a xyridium hilt to each of them for personal protection.

Vic then surprised his friends by suggesting that they call on Sage Snigmythya. Though few students took the enthusiastic and somewhat distractible sage seriously, Vic found he could relate to her.

"Oh, dear!" she exclaimed, surprised and startled to find the disguised apprentices at her door. Looking as if she might cry, she gave them the traditional greeting; apparently, no one else had visited her on Guise Night. The owl-eyed sage scrambled around in her cabinets and trunks and finally found each of them a handkerchief, which she offered as her gifts to help them on their way. "Now do not for a moment think these handkerchiefs are just silly or useless. Not useless. You never know, of course, when you might need to wipe your nose, but these can be used for almost anything. Almost anything: a napkin, a face cloth, a small flag to signal someone at a distance, even a bandage in a pinch."

They all assured her that her presents were quite wonderful and tucked them into their new leather pouches. Lyssandra gave her the small blessing scroll, at which the sage teared up again and dabbed at her eyes with her own hankie. Then she gave a flick of the white cloth. "Well, hurry. You must be on your way before any dark sages manage to catch up with you. Hurry!"

Just before midnight, they headed back toward Rubicas's laboratory. When they reached the entrance to his main experimental chamber, several groups of students were saying their farewells to Rubicas. The Ven Sage had apparently been popular tonight.

At the doorway, the Ven Sage offered the five friends the customary Guise Night greeting, and they responded with the traditional request for aid. With a twinkle in his eye, he invited them in. "I can offer you each a comfortable bed and a good night's sleep, safe from evil sages."

"Good, we're really tired," Vic said. Tromping around the steep streets in his floppy anemonite costume had become burdensome very quickly. "Like most good costumes, the concept sounded better than the reality of wearing all this stuff turned out to be."

The companions went inside. "I think that you are likely my last guests for tonight," Ven Rubicas said. "May I offer you some gemberry mead before we all retire?"

They accepted and he poured them each a small glass of the sparkling ruby liquid. "I could really use a soak in the hot springs pool," Gwen said in a hopeful voice. The warm pool was her favorite part of their new quarters.

The Ven Sage grinned. "I, too, have had a long day. It does sound enjoyable." He led them into the communal area of their chambers, and they sat on the stone benches ringing the hot spring pool at the center.

Weeks ago, after becoming the Ven Sage's apprentices, Vic, Gwen, Sharif, and Tiaret had moved from the Citadel dormitories to rooms of their own near the laboratory, and Lyssandra had left her parents' home to take up residence with her friends.

The master sage's main laboratory was a broad oval room, with marble walls and floors, open windows, and support columns flanking the entryway. At one end of the oval, a staircase spiraled up to an observation tower on the roof. Arched doorways on either side of the stairs led to the sage's private chambers, and on the opposite end of the laboratory, another archway led down to the apprentices' quarters.

Vic and Gwen were both delighted with the individual quarters, which were larger than those in the nov dormitory, with a sink and privy in each. The apprentices' rooms were arranged around a shared living area, at the center of which was a circular bathing pool fed by hot springs from beneath the island. The pool reminded Vic of the large Roman baths he had seen in some old sword-and-sandal movies. Now that was luxury!

After shedding their unwieldy and uncomfortable costumes,

the friends donned their brevis — the minimal garments Elantyans wore for swimming — and met back in their communal area by the circular hot spring pool. Rubicas was already there with fresh towels for each of them. Several tiers of concentric ledges provided seating in the steaming pool, while warm stone benches ringed the bathing area. The air had a moist, mineral tang that Vic had found strange at first, but now found soothing.

Rubicas eased his bony body into the water with a long contented sigh. Wasting no time, Vic and Gwen stepped down into the pool and sat on the submerged ledges, followed by Lyssandra, Tiaret, and Sharif.

"Hmm, tell me what you learned on this Guise Night," the old sage said.

Lyssandra answered first, obviously thinking of Snigmythya's emotional reaction. "I learned that showing respect to a teacher can mean a great deal more to them than I ever imagined."

A smile quirked Sharif's full lips. "I learned that running up and down the hills of Elantya is much more difficult than riding a magic carpet."

"Try doing it in a full anemonite costume," Vic quipped.

"I thought you did a great job acting the part, Taz," his cousin teased, using the nickname she had given him years ago. "You almost had me convinced that you were a real anemonite. And wearing disguises and staying in character is a lot harder than it seems."

Tiaret absently swirled her hands through the warm water.

"I found that the people of Elantya are as generous as they are wise."

Pensive, Vic nodded. "And I learned that I'm really starting to think of everybody here as friends and family. If I ever have to escape from a bunch of bad guys, I can't think of anyone I'd rather be with."

The Ven Sage raised his glass. "I give you learning. I give you family. And I give you a good night's sleep."

They all raised their glasses in the toast, drank, and set their glasses back down. With a satisfied sigh, Vic smiled at his cousin across the hot springs pool. "What could be better than this?"

Just then, a commotion came from Rubicas's laboratory. Someone pounded on the door, called out, and rushed inside. The old sage had left the door unlatched, just in case other visitors came for Guise Night. Rubicas climbed out of the therapeutic water and wrapped a towel around himself. "I am coming. Who visits us so late on Guise Night?" He was distracted enough by the interruption that he forgot to use the traditional phrases for the holiday.

Before Vic and his friends could get out of the springs to join him, a neosage rushed down the stone stairs into the warm and steamy room. Vic recognized the curly-haired man from the Crystal Doors Center. "This is not a Guise Night visit, Ven Sage." He used his hand to swab sweat from his forehead. "A small ship has just arrived in the harbor. Out in the ocean the captain found a castaway of some sort — a strange man in an even stranger boat. We felt it was important to come to you right away. No one can understand his unusual words." Other footsteps came down the hall as two strong sailors assisted a bedraggled, sunburned man, who appeared so tired he could barely hold himself up. "Look what we found adrift on the sea."

Gwen gasped. Vic could hardly believe his eyes. Both of them splashed out of the pool and raced forward. This wasn't a trick of Guise Night, but the greatest surprise Vic could have imagined.

"Dad!" Vic cried. Dripping wet, he and Gwen threw their arms around the man.

Dr. Carlton Pierce squeezed the two as if he had just gotten a new burst of energy. "So I really made it to Elantya!"

5

FROM THE HOT SPRINGS, a geyser of questions erupted. In barely coherent mumbles, Gwen and Vic kept saying, "You're here. I can't believe it. You made it. You're here!"

Their friends and even Rubicas looked confused. Vic turned to them, grinning excitedly. "This is my father. We left him back on Earth when we accidentally came through the crystal door."

Gwen added, "The last time we saw him was when we opened that magical window on top of the laboratory tower and just barely got a message through."

The sailors guided the exhausted man to one of the stone benches. Although he looked ready to collapse, he seemed too excited to let himself rest now that he was with Vic and Gwen. He was sunburned, with shadows beneath his eyes, as if he hadn't slept in days. His left knee was bruised and scabbed beneath a tear in his pant leg.

"What happened? How did you hurt yourself?" Gwen asked.

Dr. Pierce brushed at his knee. "I banged it up getting my boat in the water. It's sore, but nothing serious."

"How can you be certain he is not a shape-shifter?" Sharif asked warily. "My people have a saying: Familiar faces —"

"Do not be foolish." Tiaret's words cut him off. "Can you not see the Great Epic unfolding?"

Lyssandra seemed troubled, and then amazed. "Now I understand some of my recent dreams. I had nightmares of many things — of drowning, of underwater fire, of the island shaking, of fleeing from tongues of flame, of ravenous sharks, of indescribable sorrow, of a small sun being swallowed by a burning pit of light, of three-pointed spears red with blood. And yes, of a man you and Gwenya would greet with joy. It is the one dream I have had this month that I truly hoped would come to pass. But I am seldom certain of what my dreams mean. I did not want to raise your hopes."

Despite his amazement, Vic felt somewhat betrayed. "You had a dream about my father coming to us, and you didn't tell me?"

Her cobalt eyes avoided his. "I did not know it was your father, Viccus. I had never seen him before."

Dr. Pierce looked back and forth at the people speaking, his face full of confusion. "What language are you all speaking? I don't understand it."

The cousins turned to their companions and saw similar

incomprehension there. Rubicas said, "Viccus and Gwenya, did you realize you have been speaking mostly in your own language since this man's arrival?"

Apparently, only Vic and Gwen could understand Dr. Pierce. Vic grinned sheepishly. He concentrated on speaking Elantyan. "Lyssandra, we need your help for a moment." Then to his father Vic said, "Sheesh, you're gonna love this, Dad. Just let her touch your head for a couple minutes and see what happens."

Lyssandra placed her fingertips at the center of Dr. Pierce's forehead and prepared his mind to understand Elantyan. He was clearly too weary to do anything but sit still, and before long the coppery-haired girl stepped away, smiling. "There, that is better."

Dr. Pierce heaved a long sigh. "Ah, quite an improvement." He smiled his thanks at Lyssandra. "The guys aboard the ship that picked me up gave me dry clothing and a blanket. Of course, I couldn't understand anything they said, but it was obvious they meant to help. Before I tell my story, may I please have something to drink?"

"You could probably use some greenstepe," Gwen said. "It has healing properties."

Vic brightened. "Lyssandra, what about the greenstepe in the vial the Pentumvirate gave you? Could we try that out?"

"An excellent idea, Viccus." The girl lifted the tiny crystal vial on its xyridium chain from around her neck. She pulled out the small stopper and offered the vial to his father, who with a questioning look tilted it up and tapped the bottom lightly, as if to coax out a drop or two. Instead, fresh warm greenstepe gushed into his mouth in a steady stream, surprising him so much that he coughed and sprayed the liquid all over himself.

He shook his head in amazement. "I wasn't expecting magic!" He laughed and took a good long drink, this time without spilling a drop, then returned the vial to Lyssandra with a nod of thanks. The greenstepe seemed to revive him somewhat, and he sat up straighter. Vic quickly made introductions all around.

"All of this is most intriguing," Rubicas said. "How did you get to Elantya? Are you a Key? Did you open a crystal door yourself?"

Vic and Gwen both sat eagerly next to him on the stone bench. "He's right, Dad. How *did* you get here?"

"Not that we're complaining, Uncle Cap," Gwen said, her voice catching with uncharacteristic emotion. "We're just glad you got here."

Sharif said, "Are you a sage?"

"Were you embroiled in a great battle?" Tiaret asked.

Vic's father chuckled as the questions bubbled around him.

"Did you have assistance?" Rubicas said. "What spell did you use to open the door, Sage, ah, hmmm . . . What shall we call you?"

"Cap would be fine, or Carlton, or Arthur, or Pierce. Any of those will do."

Rubicas's eyebrows raised a notch. "Pierce. You have a sharp mind, and for many other reasons, I like this. I shall call you Sage Pierce."

"Oh, I'm not a sage."

"Of course you are, Uncle Cap," Gwen said. "You're a professor. You're a museum curator. You have a PhD — probably the equivalent of three PhDs, by now."

"Okay, enough with the introductions already." Vic squirmed on the bench next to his father. "Tell us what happened!"

Summoning up the energy the greenstepe had given him, Dr. Pierce began his story. After his attempts to open a door between the worlds — which had mistakenly sent Vic and Gwen through without him — he had worked in vain for weeks with the crystal array in his home solarium, until he decided that he needed to return to "first principles."

"Over the years your mothers both gave my brother and me a good inkling of where they had come from — and the type of danger they were in," Dr. Pierce explained. "But we didn't really understand as much as we should have. For a long time your mothers convinced us that the less we knew, the safer we were, so Rip and I never pushed."

"We already figured out that our moms probably came from one of these crystal doors worlds," Gwen said. "I wouldn't have believed it before, but Vic and I have seen some pretty amazing things in our time here."

Dr. Pierce hung his head. "You'll probably blame me for not preparing you two ahead of time. But Fyera and Kyara felt it was safest for you kids to know nothing until the time was right, which" — he hastened to add before they could interrupt — "they believed would be on your fifteenth birthdays."

He put an arm around Gwen. "After your parents died, Gwen, Kyara and I knew it wasn't an accident. Kyara figured it wouldn't be long before Azric came after the rest of us. Vic, your mom believed she could lead Azric away from you kids and keep your existence a secret. She told me to urge you to keep your medallions with you at all times."

"Still have them," Gwen said, fingering her strange, small pendant, identical to her cousin's. Since using the medallion to ignite the cannon's fuse during the kraken attack, Vic had also begun wearing his on a leather cord around his neck.

"But . . . why?" Vic asked.

"When you were ten years old, Kyara wrote a detailed letter and sealed it away. She told me that if anything ever happened, I was to read the letter thoroughly and then burn it. After she disappeared and I realized she wasn't coming back, I dug out the letter and read it. Her words told me so much that I hadn't known about your mothers, about the two of you, even about me and my brother. She quoted some lines from a poem in the letter. I never much believed in prophecies . . . until now."

"What did the letter say?" Gwen asked, her heart swelling, with the hope that she was about to receive the answers to all the mysteries that surrounded her family.

In the letter, Vic's mother had explained that she and Fyera came from a world called Z'lyss, but were descended from Elantyans. She told how she and Fyera had "broken the seal" to the crystal door leading to Earth, but that such a feat had drained them of their powers for five years. They were helpless when they walked out of the jungles in the Yucatan, where they found the brothers, Cap and Rip. Seeing the twin men,

Kyara and Fyera had known instantly that the brothers were their destiny.

"So, years later, that strange incident at Ocean Kingdoms Amusement Park convinced me that Azric was on to us after all, and I had to do something to keep you two safe."

"And somehow you managed to send us here to Elantya. Sheesh, were we surprised!"

"But I meant to come with you. I guess I messed something up and got stranded. I never could figure out my mistake, so I went back to first principles and reviewed the letter in my mind. In it Kyara had said that if we were ever in danger, to *remember where she came from.* I'd been combining my own science with everything she had told me about crystal doors, trying to use logic and physics and mathematics. I thought she wanted me to create a new crystal door."

"As far as I know, each world only has one crystal door, and all crystal doors lead to Elantya," Rubicas said.

"Huh." Dr Pierce looked bemused. " I realized that I was doing it all wrong. I wasn't remembering where she came from."

Gwen understood. "You mean when they first came out of the jungle?"

"Yup. I knew that's where I had to go: the Yucatan, where Rip and I had excavated an archeological site. I figured the crystal door that she and Fyera had come through to get to Earth must still be there, if only I could find it.

"So I packed up my crystals and left the house in the care of our neighbor, Dr. Alami — you know, the one whose pool you two used to swim in late at night when you were supposed to be asleep? Next day, I flew to the Yucatan, where I bought a top-notch speedboat. I found a purple one — Kyara's favorite color — and thought it was a good omen. I stocked it with a couple of weeks' worth of fuel, water, and food supplies. Even bought some warm-water scuba gear.

"First I started in the river outlet near where Rip and I had our archeological dig. I launched the boat myself —" He rubbed his injured knee, as if suddenly remembering his scrapes and bruises. "I arranged the crystals, prisms, mirrors, and scaffolding in the speedboat as best I could. I searched every waterway — streams, rivers, ponds, mud puddles — to no success. All I got was sunburned. A few times, I put on my wetsuit, fins, mask, and scuba tank, and dove, but I didn't find anything under the water, either. I tried praying, tried making up rhymes. Nothing happened.

"Next, I explored the coast until I came to the Maya ruins at Tulum. I was out past the breakers, so I stopped the boat across from the cove where your mothers had married Rip and me. Did you know Tulum was a walled city on a cliff, and at one point it was probably only accessible by sea? It was considered a magical and sacred place.

"While I was out there drifting, thinking about Kyara and the two of you until well after dark, I started to talk, just whispering things: how much I missed you, how much I wanted to be with Kyara again, how I wanted to protect you. Suddenly something seemed to materialize on the water in front of me. It looked like someone had lit a spotlight behind a clear kaleidoscope that was two stories high. The air sparkled and rippled with constantly changing patterns. Something clicked inside me, and I knew what it was. I knew it couldn't be a mirage or fog or the moon hitting the waves. It was a crystal door.

"And I didn't waste a moment. I wasn't entirely sure whether I could get through, or if I would slam into it like a car hitting a brick wall, but I revved up the boat engine and shot straight forward, closing my eyes just at the last moment.

"When I opened my eyes again, there I was, still on warm waves. There was still a moon shining down, but the night seemed darker than before. I couldn't see the shoreline anymore, even though I'd been cruising parallel to it. In fact, there were no lights anywhere, other than the moon and stars. I couldn't make heads or tails out of any of the constellations, and that's when it hit me: I had done it. I was somewhere else, *in some other world!*

"And I had no idea where to go. So after studying the stars for a while to get a few points to help me gauge my direction, I headed forward, hoping I would just bump into something. I kept going for three days, until the motor ran out of gas, and I just drifted, like a castaway. I didn't even have a sail to get me moving again."

"Elantya is the only speck of land on this whole world," Gwen said. "It wouldn't be easy to find."

"Finally, I spotted a huge three-masted wooden ship. I shouted and waved some colored towels. I tried to get the engine started again, and it coughed and sputtered a bit, but even the gasoline fumes had run out. Then I shot a signal flare into the sky. Someone saw it, and the sailing ship turned and came to rescue me. Nobody understood what I was babbling about, but when I said the word Elantya, they nodded and smiled. Elantya. Elantya. I had to use sign language and a bit of pantomime, but I got them to tow my speedboat behind the ship — they'd never seen anything like it before."

"And now you're here," Vic said. "Finally."

Dr. Pierce scratched the back of his sunburned neck and yawned. "I think I've been running on sheer adrenaline for days." Just then, he wavered and would have fallen off the bench if Gwen and Vic hadn't caught him. "Sorry. Too much excitement, I guess. Just a bit tired. And too much . . . sun. I'll be fi —" His head nodded forward, and he was sound asleep.

Rubicas broke in. "There will be time to talk further in the morning, Viccus. Your father needs to rest and recover. I suggest that we take him to the healers and let them attend to him. Sage Pierce must regain his energy and his spirit."

"Sure thing, but I'm staying with him," Vic said.

"Me, too." Gwen would not be separated from her uncle now. "Even if we have to sleep on the floor."

Sharif got out of the hot springs pool and proudly spoke the rune-command that brought his purple carpet sailing to his side. "I could swiftly deliver all three of you to the Hall of Healers on my flying carpet."

"Cool. Do you have a flashing red light and an ambulance siren?" Vic asked.

Gwen grabbed her cousin's arm. "Come on, I'll get some blankets and pillows. That way we'll both be right next to your dad when he wakes up in the morning."

6

FILLED WITH ANXIOUS ANTICIPATION, the cousins spent an uncomfortable night in the Hall of Healers. Uncle Cap slept deeply, probably more relaxed and content than he had been in months. He still didn't know about all the troubles with the merlons. Gwen sat cross-legged in a chair, trying to sleep, while Vic sprawled out on the stone floor beside his father's bed.

Uncle Cap had explained a lot, but Gwen's mind still overflowed with questions. In the morning, though her eyes felt gritty and her throat scratchy, she was glad to see that Vic's dad looked much improved. The plump chief Healer indulged them by letting the two stay for breakfast with Dr. Pierce, but then she shooed them out.

"The man needs his rest, and we will take good care of him here." She crossed her arms over her chest. "And are you not two of the new apprentices to Ven Sage Rubicas? I am certain he has important work for you."

Uncle Cap gave them each a hug. "Don't worry, you two. I'm here now. I'll come and see you as soon as they let me out of here."

Feeling relieved, tired, and excited all at the same time, Gwen left the Hall of Healers with Vic and headed off to join their three companions in Rubicas's main laboratory.

Seeing Uncle Cap had reminded her of all the things that had changed for them since coming to this watery world full of magic and danger. Sure, she missed her friends from Stephen Hawking High. She missed being able to choose from dozens of tops, shorts, slacks, dresses, and skirts in her wardrobe. She missed her tennis shoes and sandals. She missed shopping, cinnamon buns, In-N-Out burgers, and school dances.

But there were plenty of things she didn't miss: heavy traffic on the freeways, earthquakes, smog, computer viruses, tedious homework assignments, irritating commercials on TV and the Internet, junk email, having to explain to teachers why her parents couldn't come to parent-teacher conferences. . . .

Now that Uncle Cap was here in Elantya, Earth no longer held the draw for her that it once had. She had good friends in this new world, the mystery of her family's background to solve, and the opportunity to learn more than she could possibly absorb in a lifetime — and an obligation to help in the war against the merlons. In an odd way, Gwen actually belonged here.

As they arrived in the communal area of the apprentice

quarters, Tiaret trotted in from her morning run, glistening with perspiration.

Without pausing, she bounded through the archway, down the stairs into the communal area, and jumped feet-first into the hot springs pool, throwing up just the barest hint of a splash. She submerged herself completely, then sprang back out onto the rim of the pool all in the space of a few heartbeats. She stood there dripping, in the short outfit of animal leathers and furs that she wore day after day. Tiaret brushed droplets of water from her skin.

Sharif entered, carrying his rolled-up carpet under one arm. He stashed the carpet in his adjoining quarters and strutted back out wearing a look of surprise, as if wondering why the others hadn't already started work without him. "Ven Rubicas is waiting for us. As my people say: A day wasted is never regained."

"Where's Lyssandra?" Vic asked.

"Coming." She emerged moments later from her quarters looking tired and pale but otherwise ready for work.

At the same time, Vic and Sharif asked, "Nightmares?"

Lyssandra produced a faint smile. "You know me well. Drowning again, and explosions, fire and water — and sea monsters." She shook her head. "I do not wish to think of it."

They went together into Rubicas's primary experimental chamber, where the racks, shelves, and tables overflowed with scrolls and equipment. Bright morning light streamed through windows and the skylights in the domed ceiling, drawing attention to the giant aquariums built into the curved wall.

The first task that the preoccupied Rubicas assigned his apprentices for the day was to refill the wall-sized aquariums at long last. The great tanks had stood empty for many weeks, ever since his apprentice Orpheon had tried to kill him, smashing the glass fronts of the aquariums in the process. The aquits that once inhabited the tanks had been living in a deep urn waiting for their home to be repaired. A few days ago, a ship had arrived carrying the crystal replacement panes, which workers had immediately installed.

The Ven Sage himself sat on a tall stool at his high marble writing lectern, busily compiling a single scroll from all of the most successful verses and spell fragments he had collected so far in his efforts to reconstruct and expand the shield spell for Elantya. He looked as if he had a headache.

Before Orpheon betrayed Elantya and fled to live among the merlons, Rubicas had crafted a complicated spell for a powerful force field that he hoped would one day protect the entire island. But the assistant had stolen key parts of the work, and now the old sage worked to reproduce it from scratch.

A thick pile of unfurled spell scrolls lay beside him on the sloped desktop, and the sage used his elbow as a paperweight. Each time Rubicas finished with one of the fragment scrolls, he lifted his elbow to allow it to reroll itself, then dropped the scroll gently to the floor beneath the desk.

Gwen sighed, knowing she would have quite a job of reorganizing the scrolls. She was aware, however, that the shield spell was crucial to defending the island and its inhabitants from the merlons. So absorbed was Rubicas in his work that he never looked up once after giving his apprentices their assignment for the morning. His only sounds were an occasional "Hmm" or "ahhh" and the furious scritching of his quill.

Gwen turned to look at the empty aquariums, biting the edge of her lower lip as she pondered her approach to the problem. "The aquits prefer seawater, and I think that the creatures the Ven Sage plans to collect live in salt water, too."

Tiaret nodded. "What is our closest source?"

Vic cocked an eyebrow at her. "You mean, *other* than the ocean?"

Piri, who seemed to find this funny, twinkled a bright pink through the mesh of the net that hung at Sharif's neck. The boy from Irrakesh looked dubious. "Yes, the ocean is close, and we could use buckets and my flying carpet, but it would take a very long time. Thousands of buckets. There is a saying among my people: A wall may be built one grain of sand at a time. But a supply of large rocks speeds up the process."

Vic laughed out loud. Ignoring her cousin, Gwen mused, "So the question is, how do we get a large supply of water here faster than in buckets?"

"We could fill barrels and move them here on a sail cart," Lyssandra said. "But the barrels would be very heavy."

"How about a garden hose?" Vic suggested.

Lyssandra put out a hand to touch his arm and drew the image from his mind. "Yes, we have such things."

"We can't really run the hose all the way down to the harbor and then make the water run uphill, can we?" Gwen said.

Vic snapped his fingers. "Water runs both up- and downhill here. We just have to find the right spell."

Sharif looked relieved. "Indeed it does, Viccus. Most of the canals that line the streets in Elantya carry seawater. When I first came here, I often allowed Piri to ride in a small boat in the canals beside me while I walked from place to place, getting to know the city." The nymph djinni gave off a yellow glow of contentment at the memory.

"I would have thought you'd just use your magic carpet to explore every street without getting your feet tired," Vic teased, though the prince did not seem to find it amusing.

"I did that as well, but I do not wish to become fat and lazy, refusing to use my own muscles or my own mind as some sultans have done." His voice was haughty, his olive green eyes full of pride.

"Good," Gwen broke in. "Let's use the canal along the street outside the tower."

Vic stroked his chin with a thumb and forefinger, pretending to be very thoughtful. "Nothing simpler then. If Lyssandra can get the hose for us, we'll rig it so it enters the canal beneath the surface of the water so we won't block any deliveries, maybe flare the opening a bit so that it gathers more water. Then we face the end of the hose into the current — and let gravity or magic do the rest of the work."

Lyssandra's father always kept a hose at the ready while designing his pyrotechnics, so Sharif flew the petite girl home on his carpet to fetch it. Meanwhile, Gwen busied herself rearranging Rubicas's discarded scrolls, and Vic and Tiaret went outside to survey the canal and make plans. When Lyssandra and Sharif returned, the five of them set to work together.

Vic admired the vivid spring green color of the thick tubing. "How do they make this?"

"We do not make it. We collect it from the sea. It comes from doolya, a type of seaweed that can grow up to a hundred times as long as I am tall. We use the sap-stalk as tubing, and the fronds make excellent rope. Thick jungles of doolya grow in many places beneath the water, and we harvest what we need."

Gwen found herself fascinated by this explanation. The doolya stalk was as tough as bamboo, yet nearly as flexible as a boiled noodle, and translucent. Working together, they ran the hose from the main aquarium tank through the experimental chamber, down the hallway, out to the street, and into the canal. When all was ready, Gwen waited by the canal holding one end of the hose and sent Tiaret and Vic inside to hold the other end steady where it ran into the aquarium, so that the flow of water would not accidentally dislodge it.

When they were ready, Tiaret signaled from the top of the tower above Rubicas's laboratory. "You may begin!" she shouted down, then disappeared again.

While Piri "supervised" the operation through her egg-sphere wall, Sharif and Gwen fed the tube into the canal and Lyssandra weighted it down, securing it at the bottom of the canal with rocks. Water gushed into the tubing, filling the hollow space and making the hose twitch and buck. The three went back into the laboratory to watch the tanks fill.

Vic greeted them with elation. "See? No problem. Works like a charm." Water gushed from the end of the sap-stalk at a satisfying rate. The hose squirmed in his hands, so he held it in place with a precariously balanced chunk of rock. When he had secured the tube, he let go and climbed back down the copper wall ladder to the floor. "Easy enough. How long do you think it'll take?"

"Many hours," Sharif concluded.

"Even so, we should remain close by," Lyssandra said.

"Or we could go visit my dad, see if he's all right," Vic said anxiously. "What could possibly go wrong here? It's just a water hose and a tank —"

As if in response to his words, the floor beneath their feet rumbled and trembled and the water in the tanks sloshed wildly. "Earthquake!" Gwen said at the same time Vic cried out, "Stand in the doorway!"

Before they could head for the safety of the door arch, the rough stone chunk weighing down the doolya hose tumbled to the floor. The sap-stem slipped out of the aquarium and, writhing like a snake, sprayed water every which way around the laboratory. The floor still shook from the quake, and now the stone tiles were slippery.

At his worktable, Rubicas did not look up from his scrolls.

Vic and Sharif dove for the wild hose, but both missed as it squirmed away from them. Vic landed on the floor and slid like a penguin on ice.

Gwen ran to salvage the scrolls beneath Rubicas's desk, but she slipped and landed squarely on her rear end. Lyssandra too landed on the floor with a delicate yelp. Tiaret, proving her agility, darted back and forth in pursuit of the snaking water tube; though she did not catch it, neither did she land ignominiously on the floor as the others had.

As suddenly as it had started, the earthquake stopped. Water continued to spurt from the hose. Sharif got to his feet, wringing water from his dripping, billowy sleeves. "What was that shaking and rumbling?" Of course, a boy from a flying city would never have encountered seismic shocks.

"It was just an earthquake," Gwen said a split second before the serpentine stream of water hit Sharif in the face, completely drenching him and Piri, who flickered alternately pink and orange, obviously vacillating between amusement and alarm.

Gwen and Vic and even Tiaret laughed. The friends ganged up on the rogue hose and, after a merry chase with a good deal more sliding and laughter, tackled it. Vic trapped part of the hose with his foot, and Tiaret grabbed the end. Sharif took the end of the tube, climbed quickly to the top of the aquariums, and fed the hose back into the partly filled reservoir, where he anchored it much more securely this time.

Gwen groaned and sat down on the wet floor with a plop. "It's going to take forever to clean up this mess." She nudged Lyssandra, who sat in silence beside her, then realized with concern that her friend had not moved since falling there. The ethereal girl sat stiff and still, her face as pale as milk. Her eyes did not blink. Was she in shock? "Hey, Lyssandra, it's okay." She put an arm around the girl's shoulder, hoping to comfort her. "It was just a short earthquake."

"No. I — I saw that in my dream. The whole island shaking. And in the next part, I kept seeing myself drowning, being pulled under the water, unable to breathe."

Vic sloshed over to them, also concerned. "Well, this water's not very deep, and you're not going to drown here. The quake is over now, just a little one. Nothing like the temblors we had in California."

Lyssandra's voice was barely above a whisper. "But Elantya was formed by magic, anchored to the foundation of the world itself. We have never experienced this shaking of the ground. Never."

Rubicas finally got down from his stool and joined the conversation. "She is correct. In the history of this island, an earthquake has never been recorded. It is somewhat disturbing." As he talked, he climbed a ladder to reach some high shelves, rummaged briefly among the paraphernalia there, then retrieved the scroll he'd been looking for. Still high on the ladder, Rubicas opened the scroll, murmured a few words, and said "S'ibah." Magically, a drain opened in the marble floor, and the water began to gurgle away. "Mmm. That should do nicely."

LATE THAT AFTERNOON, WHEN Dr. Pierce was thoroughly rested, fed, cleaned, and bandaged, he came to join the companions down at the partially rebuilt Elantyan harbor, where his purple speedboat was tied up to a half-restored dock. The crew that had rescued him out in the middle of the ocean had taken care of the boat, which sparkled in the slanted sunlight.

Vic stood by his father, admiring the design of the speedboat. Gwen stepped down into it and took a seat. "This would have been fun to have back home," she said.

“It starts to feel a little cramped after you’ve sat in it for several days in a row,” Dr. Pierce said.

Tiaret, Sharif, and Lyssandra marveled at the sparkling amethyst color, the sleek lines. “A beautiful vessel, Sage Pierce,” said old Rubicas, nodding to himself. He and Sage Polup in his mechanical body had walked together to the end of the half-pier.

“She may be pretty, but she’s not going anywhere,” Vic’s father said. “No fuel left, and I don’t think Elantya has any filling stations.”

The anemonite swimming in the water-filled tank that formed his “head” turned his ring of eyes, and words came out of the speakers. “There are other ways to propel a boat, Sage Pierce. Elantyan engineers and I might come up with some suggestions.” Sage Polup raised one of his heavy, artificial arms. “If they created this body, they can power a small boat.”

Vic climbed in beside Gwen and opened up the storage cases, revealing Uncle Cap’s flopping wetsuit, a full face mask, and air tanks for his scuba rig. “This could be useful,” Vic said. “I’ve always wanted to go diving.”

“It’s not as easy as it looks, Vic,” Dr. Pierce said. “There’s a lot to learn first, but I’ll teach you if you like.”

Rubicas scratched his beard. “Sage Pierce, I remain highly intrigued by how you managed to open a crystal door without training. Were you aware that you yourself must be a Key?”

“I never thought so and was never trained. I always figured that science could solve any problem that magic could. I certainly did a lot of trial and error.” He looked at Gwen and Vic.

"Besides, I had a great deal of incentive. Since these kids made it through by accident, I was sure I could do it on purpose — if I just tried hard enough and got myself to the right place. I applied science to what little my wife had told me about the way your magic works."

Polup turned his bulky body toward the Ven Sage. "I suspect that Sage Pierce could be of great assistance to us in our preparations against the merlons."

Dr. Pierce looked down at the cousins. "I'm not sure I can match what these two have already done for you. But I'll certainly do my best."

"I look forward to hearing your ideas," the Ven Sage said.

Lyssandra hung back, gazing at the water with a troubled expression.

Tiaret, watching Lyssandra, tapped her teaching staff on the dock and nodded to herself. "A good warrior also learns new skills when necessary." She looked to her friends. "The time has come. I would like you to teach me to swim."

7

UNLIKE THE NORTH END of Elantya, with its sheer cliffs and crashing waves, the cove on the lee side of the island was sheltered. Inside a protective breakwater wall of neatly stacked boulders, past which the sea bottom dropped off to much greater depths, the water was calm to the point of being glassy.

Vic and Gwen decided the isolated cove was the perfect spot for Tiaret to learn how to swim.

When the five apprentices walked to the empty beach, gray clouds began to gather, promising an afternoon thunderstorm, and the sea beyond the breakwater looked stirred and choppy. Lyssandra was uneasy to be in such a quiet and deserted area of Elantya. "What if it should rain?" Apparently she was still troubled by ominous dreams she couldn't understand.

Vic chuckled. "Rain? If we're swimming, it doesn't matter how wet we get. As long as there's no lightning." He thought about the time his parents had taken him for a day at the beach in San Diego. It had rained briefly that morning, but the day had been perfect anyway. His father had read on the beach for most of the day, while Vic and his mother swam together. She loved the sea and seemed to shine with happiness when she was in the warm waves. She belonged in the water. Not only were the fish not afraid of her, they seemed drawn to his mother, letting her touch them as they swirled around her.

Gwen hurried down to the edge of the calm water, delighted. "Remember a few years ago when our parents took us to Disney World, and then afterwards we stayed on the Florida coast? The water in Tampa was so warm and calm we just floated and splashed around all day."

Of course he remembered. The thoughts were bittersweet for Vic. Since the day she left, every minute he remembered spending with his mother seemed precious. He tried to divert his mind from the pain of not knowing where she was or if she was still alive. "Yup. I remember you got sunburned as red as ketchup, too," Vic said, coming up beside her and dipping his foot into the water.

"Ketchup? Eww." Gwen punched him in the shoulder. "Anyway, my point is, *it was fun.*" Together they walked back onto the dry sand.

"Point taken. I'd rather swim for pleasure than try to dodge merlons, clean up messes from battles, or worry about a ship sinking beneath me." Vic removed his outer clothes and sandals, tightened the brevi he wore for swimming, and dashed down the sandy beach. Giving his medallion a tug to make sure its cord was secure, he said, "Come on! Last one in is a kraken egg."

Gwen shed her tunic, so that she wore only her medallion on its leather thong, and a white brevi that consisted of a cropped tank and briefs. She raced him to the water.

Tiaret showed no trepidation. Dressed in her tight animal skins, the girl from Afirik thrust her teaching staff into the sand so that it stuck up next to Vic and Gwen's clothes. With lithe movements, she bounded into the water.

Since he would not need it while swimming, Sharif had left his flying carpet rolled up and stashed beneath the sleeping pallet in his quarters. He stripped down to his loincloth while considering whether or not to leave Piri behind on the beach. The nymph djinni could survive perfectly well under water in her eggsphere, and she enjoyed teasing the fish by blinking in tempting colors to lure them closer. He put the mesh bag that held Piri back around his neck.

Lyssandra, wearing a short, snug-fitting chamois brevi that tied over one shoulder, pulled her long coppery hair back in a ponytail so the strands wouldn't get in her eyes, and joined the others. She waded in up to her knees, then her waist, turning around to look at the empty beach.

Vic wanted to start by teaching Tiaret his favorite stroke, the butterfly, but Gwen argued that they should begin with floating and kicking. Vic splashed his cousin.

"Treading water is also a useful skill, especially for a beginner," Lyssandra pointed out. Gwen surprised her with an impulsive splash.

Sharif, getting into the spirit of the occasion, said, "Perhaps we should work on holding your breath first." While he was looking at Tiaret, Lyssandra's hand skimmed the surface of the water, sending a spray into Sharif's face.

"Teach me everything," Tiaret said. "I will master the skills quickly."

Since she sounded so serious, everyone responded by splashing her. Soon they were all laughing and shouting in a friendly water fight. Sharif took Piri out of her pouch so that she could join in the fun, and they all played catch with the twinkling pink eggsphere for quite a while before Sharif tucked her back into the mesh pouch around his neck.

Tiaret looked up at the darkening skies and grew serious again. "Although this is most entertaining, should we not begin my actual lessons?"

When it came to athletic endeavors, the girl from Afirik was a quick study. From Gwen, she learned floating and three types of kicks. Sharif added breathing techniques, and Lyssandra showed her how to tread water. Vic demonstrated several types of arm strokes. Trying the dog paddle first, Tiaret thrashed awkwardly halfway across the cove before pausing to tread water and wave at her friends.

The first shark fin pierced the calm water of the cove like a sacrificial dagger. The sharp, triangular fin cut through the water with barely a ripple. Vic cried out, "Shark!"

"Not funny, Taz," Gwen said. "Anyway, we're in a protected cove."

A second shark fin surfaced closer to Gwen, out of her view. An intricate design was branded onto the side of the fin, some sort of magical symbol. Somehow the sharks had gotten inside the rocky breakwater barrier.

"Escape now, argue later," Vic yelled.

Seeing the danger, Tiaret immediately thrashed toward the shallows.

Within a few moments six large aquatic predators circled the other four friends, who were too far from the beach. One shark streaked after Tiaret as she sloshed toward the beach where her teaching staff stood in the sand.

Gwen splashed furiously at the circling sharks, trying to get rid of them.

Sharif tried to break through the menacing circle. Two of the sharks shot toward him like underwater torpedoes, churning the water to a froth as they bumped him with their rounded snouts. Kicking out, he struck one, but as the shark spun away in pain, another one came to take its place.

Lyssandra called out for help, but no one was near the isolated area to hear them.

Tiaret reached the safety of shore, though the other four companions were trapped in the deeper water of the cove. She raced toward her teaching staff.

The predators weren't in a feeding frenzy; they did not attack. Instead, the sharks seemed to be corralling the friends, preventing them from escaping to shore — as if they were being guided, somehow. That made Vic even more nervous.

With a wild yell, Tiaret bounded back into the water, swinging her staff. She struck one of the sharks with a mighty splash, smashing its snout with the round dragon's-eye stone. She threw herself in among the circling predators, but fighting in the water was different from fighting on land. She couldn't move as swiftly and smoothly as she expected; the water made swinging her staff sluggish.

Then something worse than the sharks arrived. Swimming forms approached like shadows, emerging to show hideous fishlike faces with smooth skin, large eyes, and spiny frills around their heads. They raised clawed, webbed hands.

"I should have known the merlons would arrive sooner or later." Gwen glared at them.

Tiaret continued to thrash with her teaching staff. Using its pointed end like a spear, she injured another one of the sharks; but the angry merlons soon reached her. They overpowered Tiaret, seized the teaching staff, and wrenched it out of her hand.

One of the six merlons blurred his features, shifting until the face and body became recognizable as human: a handsome yet sneering face, dark hair, dusky skin, and cruel eyes. "Look at the little guppies our sharks caught," said Orpheon, Rubicas's treacherous former apprentice. He took Tiaret's teaching staff from one of the merlons.

"It's too bad you didn't hit your head on a rock when you jumped off that cliff," Gwen said in a cold voice. She and Sharif had chased the traitor from Rubicas's lab to the edge of the island, where he had transformed into merlon form before leaping into the sea.

Sharif glared at him. "You were afraid to face us. You are a spy and a minion and a coward."

As if responding to an implied threat, three of the sharks curved up to the surface like dolphins, splashing, showing their wide mouths filled with sharp teeth, then dove again. When the merlons hissed, their gill flaps opened like raw wounds on their necks, fluttering in the air. They extended their claws.

Orpheon said, "Take these two." He pointed to Vic and Gwen, then smiled wickedly as an idea occurred to him. "In fact, take them all. That one with the copper hair, Lyssandra, can understand merlons. The other two" — he looked dismissively at Tiaret and Sharif — "may provide some sport. I don't think the flying piranhas have fed recently."

Merlons grabbed the friends with their slimy hands. Vic gagged at the strong reek of decaying fish that clung to them. He fought back, desperate to get away, thinking of how he and his father had just been reunited. They couldn't be separated again so soon.

Orpheon muttered some sort of incantation in the merlon language. His eyes glowed green. Crackling sparks flashed around him.

Suddenly remembering, Vic cried out, "Sharif! Use the summoning spell. Call your carpet."

But the boy from Irrakesh did not hear Vic. A merlon had seized the prince by the hair and pushed his head underwater. Tiaret had never stopped fighting, even after her teaching staff was taken away. Vic thrashed, then slapped one of the merlons on the sensitive tympanic membranes that served as the aquatic creature's ears. As the hissing merlon reared back, another came forward to grab Vic, extending claws, which dug into his arms.

Out of the corner of his eye, he saw the merlons pull

Sharif's head out of the water and rake their curved claws along the base of his throat, digging deep into the skin. The prince cried out. The aquatic warriors yanked Lyssandra's head back. Gwen made a gurgling sound as the merlons also grabbed and slashed parallel lines in her throat.

Vic struggled against the pointed talons pressing into both sides at the base of his own throat. Through the searing pain that pierced his skin, he saw blood staining the calm water around them in the cove.

Then the powerful merlon abductors yanked all five of their captives under the water.

8

IT WAS THE FIRST time Gwen had ever truly believed she was going to die — whether it would be from drowning or from having her throat slashed made little difference. The merlon that dragged her under the water swam with powerful strokes. Unable to breathe, she struggled feebly, feeling the raw pain of the salt water on her torn throat, knowing she was bleeding. Trails of bubbles streamed from the gashes on her neck.

Orpheon's glimmering green magic infused the water surrounding them. Gwen didn't understand what was happening.

Other merlons pulled Vic, Lyssandra, Tiaret, and Sharif along. The sleek, branded sharks streaked alongside like prowling guard dogs.

They went deeper, stroking toward the rock barrier that blocked off the cove from the rest of the sea. Farther from the surface and breathable air, Gwen became frantic. The merlon held her in a vise grip. Ahead of them through the dim, turquoise water she could discern that a tunnel had been melted through the breakwater wall, forming a secret passage through which the merlons could whisk the five of them out to the open sea. But that hardly mattered. Gwen and her friends would all perish before long.

She remembered Lyssandra's frightening dreams of merlons and drowning. It was too late now to heed the prophetic warnings.

Strangely, Gwen felt the long claw-mark gashes in her throat fizzing, bubbling . . . improving somehow. Her lungs ached. Right now her greatest need was for air. Gwen tried to endure just a minute longer as the merlons tugged their five captives through the hole in the undersea wall.

She was going to black out in a few seconds, she knew it. She hoped the merlons would surface on the other side, give her a chance to breathe. If Orpheon and the aquatic creatures simply wished to kill the five friends, this was a very complicated way to accomplish it.

But once they were all through the breakwater, instead of taking their captives up for air, the merlons followed the ocean floor as it dropped sharply away to shadowy depths. Gwen's lungs were about to explode, and the merlons were going deeper and deeper!

The water grew cooler, darker, or maybe her vision was fading. Oddly enough, the pain from the claw wounds in her throat had subsided. Now they itched rather than burned.

Her head pounded, but she couldn't let herself pass out. It wouldn't just be fainting, it would be *dying*.

She struggled for a few last moments of life while her merlon captor squeezed harder, digging vicious claws into her arm. But how much more harm could they do to her now? She wished she'd had a chance to say goodbye to Uncle Cap.

Finally, when she could bear it no longer, Gwen drew in a huge breath, knowing that it would be heavy, liquid death and not blessed air. At least she would foil whatever plans Orpheon and the evil merlons had for them.

But as she drew in a gulp, instead of choking she felt the cool water rush through the slash wounds in her throat. It was like breathing! Water flowed in, filled her lungs. It was the strangest sensation, like a dense bubble inside her. The slashes in her throat were . . . gill slits! Orpheon had worked some kind of spell, and she was drawing oxygen from the seawater.

Gwen coughed, jerked, spasmed, and took in another gulp. Her vision began to clear. She blinked in amazement. Water circulated through her windpipe and lungs just like air. Because of the thickness of the seawater, she had to work harder to breathe — but she *was* breathing! Breathing water.

She turned to see Tiaret thrashing, amber eyes bulging as she desperately tried to hold her breath. Vic had already succumbed and was now sucking deep breaths of water through his gill slits, an expression of comical surprise on his face. He looked at Gwen and pointed to his throat. She nodded. Sharif was also breathing through gills, as was Lyssandra. When Tiaret finally began to draw in water, she fought with a greater determination, struggling until a second merlon seized her other arm.

Their captors continued dragging them downward, far out to the depths of the sea. Once the five friends grew too weary to struggle any more, their merlon captors paused to fit them each with a heavy belt made of seashells to reduce buoyancy, like the weights scuba divers used. Uncle Cap had kept something like that with his gear on the purple speedboat.

Then the merlons took hold of the sharks' fins, as if the deadly creatures were pet dolphins, and let the predators pull them and their captives swiftly along. The journey seemed interminable.

Gwen's eyes gradually adjusted to the dimness. Knowing they had no chance of escaping, she grew dismayed. Only an hour ago, their future had looked bright and optimistic. Uncle Cap had just arrived, the repairs to the city's harbor were almost complete, Rubicas was re-creating his shield spell, and all Elantyans were preparing to stand together against the merlons.

But they had been caught off-guard yet again.

Their undersea captors towed them over anemone-strewn coral reef cliffs and dropped down into a waving forest of golden and green fronds that looked like the doolya stalks they had used for filling Rubicas's tank. The sharks guided the group through the seaweed forest, knowing their way.

Because of her interest in marine biology, Gwen couldn't help being intrigued by her environment. Although being held captive by merlons dampened a bit of her natural scientific curiosity, she looked around her, identifying species of fish, mollusks, and undersea plants — some of them, that is. There were plenty of creatures here she had never seen before. She wondered if even the most famous undersea explorers had ever seen such marvels.

On the silty sea bottom, giant purple clams gaped open, showing what looked like large gray tongues inside. The shadows of the passing sharks triggered a reflex in the clams, and the big shells slammed shut like warehouse doors being locked for the night.

As they were all dragged along, Vic showed wary interest, and Lyssandra appeared withdrawn. Sharif looked stunned and outraged while, from the mesh sack dangling on his chest, Piri throbbed through a series of angry reds and oranges. Tiaret's entire body seemed to project righteous fury, but she had ceased her overt struggles, for now.

Waving to get everyone's attention, Vic pointed ahead, and Gwen turned to see something she had never expected to encounter again: the *Golden Walrus.* The broad cargo ship that had served the students on their training voyage now lay tilted to one side on the ocean floor, displaying the gaping holes in its hull. Tatters of the rigging chewed by the flying piranhas now rippled in the water currents as if blown by a ghostly breeze. When they passed over a rocky ridge, the shipwreck disappeared from view.

Finally, up ahead, Gwen saw their destination — an enormous merlon city at the bottom of the ocean. Buoyed by water, the architecture relied on sweeping organic shapes integrated into the tall rocks on the sea floor. The multihued towers, frilly balconies, cupolas, and spires looked as if they were made from coral and mother-of-pearl. Some smaller buildings were obviously created out of immense shells, and Gwen guessed that the merlons must kill giant undersea creatures to use the shells for individual dwellings, like hermit crabs did. The city had no streets, because swimming merlons needed none. Seaweed and anemone gardens floated up in stair-step paths.

At the outskirts of the merlon city, ferocious-looking eels patrolled the gates, like guard dogs. The creatures crackled with a barely contained glow, and Gwen was sure they were a species of electric eel. Pearls larger than Piri's eggsphere lay scattered on the ground near the buildings. Undersea lawn ornaments?

Gelatinous glowing fish tethered to the ground drove back the undersea dimness; though they strained against their thin chains to escape, the poor luminescent creatures would bob and drift as living streetlights to glow until they died. Then, no doubt, the merlons would cut the creatures loose and tether other glowfish in the same positions.

More merlons, wearing full seashell armor and carrying sea-urchin clubs and long mother-of-pearl scimitars, came out of the strange buildings to intercept them. The new group of merlons held iridescent black shells in their webbed hands; about the length of Gwen's index finger, each shell was oddly cupped and whorled, like an ear turned inside out.

When Orpheon spoke aloud to Lyssandra, Gwen heard only a bubbling humming through the water; she could understand none of it. Orpheon took the black shells from the merlons, pointed to the apprentices, and explained something. Lyssandra's cobalt-blue eyes were defiant, and she shook her head but made no sound. The red gill cuts in her neck pumped furiously.

Orpheon insistently put a black shell to Lyssandra's ear and shouted something. When she continued to resist, Orpheon threatened Sharif with the teaching staff he had stolen from Tiaret. He pressed the sharp tip against the prince's bare ribs so hard that blood oozed out. Nearby, the restless sharks reacted to the scent of blood with obvious hunger. The implication of the threat was clear.

Finally Lyssandra relented. Pulling free from her merlon captors, she took one of the black shells and swam over to Vic. The petite girl's ponytail had come undone, and copper hair drifted around her head. She made a reassuring gesture and placed the black seashell to their friend's ear. The curved shell fit inside as if it belonged there.

Vic blinked in surprise. He opened his mouth and sounds came out — the same strange, vibrating, bubbly tones as Gwen had heard from Orpheon. Then Lyssandra went to Tiaret with a second black earshell. Orpheon angrily gestured toward Gwen, insisting that she be next, but Lyssandra ignored him. Merlon guards took a black shell to Gwen and then to Sharif. Vic, who seemed excited and impatient, made strange incomprehensible gestures.

Wondering if she would hear the sound of rushing waves, Gwen took the shell, looked at it suspiciously, then touched it to her ear. All of the underwater sounds became sharp and clear. Vic yelped, "Hey, Doc, can you hear me now?" His voice came directly into her ear.

Lyssandra said to the traitorous assistant, "There, I have done as you asked. Just because my friends can hear you, however, does not mean they will cooperate."

"Lyssandra's right. We won't cooperate with you!"

Orpheon gave Gwen another sneering smile. "We can be quite persuasive, but I hope you do not surrender too easily. I am looking forward to this."

He called in a loud voice, speaking to the merlons in their own language; Gwen realized that through some magic in the communication shells, she could understand. "They can now hear and comprehend the orders they are given. They no longer have the excuse." Orpheon stroked in the water, pointing toward the highest underwater building. "Now, take them into the hall of the merlon king. Barak is waiting for them."

The merlon escorts led them into the many-towered structure. The fortress gate was threatening, made of the forbidding rib bones of enormous dead fish and studded with jagged teeth from giant sharks. The archways were draped with rippling algae curtains.

Colorful fish flitted everywhere, as Gwen might have expected birds or butterflies to do in a garden. Inside the great undersea palace was an open courtyard, a huge throne hall that looked out upon an undersea cliff that dropped off to regions of the sea that were deeper yet. Merlon servants used clubs to beat on large, round drums, sending rich vibrations through the water.

Orpheon spoke in a loud voice. "My Lord, I have brought the prisoners you requested."

The answering voice came from a throne surrounded by feathery seaweed. "I asked for two — only two. But three is better than two. Five is better than three. You brought me five. That is better than the two I demanded — and what I demand, I get."

"Yes, King Barak," Orpheon said with a bow.

Pushing away seaweed, a lanky merlon covered with ornate shell garments stood up from the throne. Taller than the other merlons, his skin was iridescent, and the pupils of his overlarge eyes were slitted. The scalloped ruffle across his brow and down the back of his skull was larger than any other merlon's; rust-red fins ran down his spine in a spiky frill. "Welcome to Oo'regl, capital of the Ocean Realm of Szishh. I am King Barak. I am your King. I am your master." He came forward, stroking more than walking, to glare at them. "I am so glad to have new strangers. I get bored easily."

His voice held a snarling hiss. "We will eat. I command a banquet. I summon food for all of us." Then he turned. "Well? What are you waiting for?" The merlon guards darted away like startled fish in a pond.

Then from behind the tall throne emerged another figure. A human living among the merlons, like Orpheon. Straight, jet hair framed a handsome face made all the more mesmerizing by the man's unusual eyes — one green, one blue. It was almost impossible to look away from him. Slightly taller than Vic, the man was dressed in shimmering robes made of a silken fiber that sparkled as if it were woven from spun jewels.

Beside Gwen, Sharif spat out a violent curse in a language

she didn't recognize. Straining against one of the few merlon guards that had remained in the hall, Sharif cried out in the underwater language, "You killed my brother."

Gwen had recognized the man, too. She had seen him before in the stands at the Ocean Kingdoms Learning Center and Amusement Park. He had worn jeans back then, and his brow had been furrowed in an expression of intense anticipation. This mysterious man had somehow driven Shoru the killer whale into a frenzy, endangering Gwen's life.

Her heart turned to ice. She also realized that this man — directly or indirectly — had murdered her parents.

Azric.

9

VIC HAD NEVER EATEN underwater before. After being surrounded by sharks, having his throat slashed, nearly being drowned, being taken to the hall of the merlon king, and coming face to face with the evil man who had killed Gwen's parents and made his own mother flee to save his life, Vic couldn't say he was particularly hungry.

King Barak seemed completely manic, excited by the slightest stray thought, consumed with his own plans. After watching for only a few minutes, Vic could see that Azric had corrupted the merlon king by manipulating him and playing on his emotions. Azric knew exactly how to get what he wanted, while making Barak think the desires were his own.

At the moment, the merlon king apparently believed that Vic, Gwen, and their friends were actually guests, rather than victims who had been dragged underwater against their will.

Given his obviously tempestuous personality, Barak could change his mind at any moment.

Male and female merlons, servants in the undersea court, swam in and set up a long table in front of the king's throne. Heavy dishes were set on the table and rounded stone seats placed around it. Officious merlon servants directed everyone, including the five captive apprentices and dozens of merlons, to take their places by the table. Everyone waited for the king to sit, but he floated around fidgeting, impatient with everything. Azric waited nearby looking completely in control, his loose garments drifting in the currents.

With an indignant scowl that turned his scaly face into an even more hideous mask, the king pointed to Tiaret's teaching staff, which Orpheon still held. "That is a scepter for a leader, not a minion. Give it to me." Reluctantly, Orpheon handed it over, and Barak shooed him away. "You may withdraw now. I have one shape-shifting human sage here. That is quite enough!" He held Tiaret's staff, rapped its pointed end on the table, and finally took his seat.

Orpheon swam away in a huff, self-consciously flickering his body to assume the form of a merlon again, though no one was convinced.

As if sharing a secret with Vic and Gwen, Barak leaned toward them. "Azric and Orpheon are certainly ugly, but they have the redeeming quality of being able to alter their appearance to look as beautiful as merlons." He moved his fishlike face closer to Vic's. "Do you have that ability, or are you trapped with those hideous features?"

"This is who I am," Vic said. "Why would I want to look like anything else?"

"Why, indeed?" Azric said, his voice drawn out and far too sweet. "A face only a mother could love — and I'm sure his mother does love him. We're counting on that. When was the last time you saw your mother, Vic?" Azric did not call Vic by his Elantyan name. And his dialect sounded much less formal than Elantyan speech.

"I saw her right before she disappeared — to keep us all safe from you!"

"Hmm, I wonder where she went," Azric said with a taunting smile.

King Barak sat on his throne and made an impatient gesture. Guards forced the five friends to sit. Swimming attendants reverently placed what appeared to be a potted plant in a polished stone urn next to Barak. The large urn contained a waving tentacled thing that was more than a plant but not quite an animal, either. Whiplike fronds swayed in the currents. Half of the tentacle fronds were topped with what looked like eyeballs, gazing in all directions.

The tiny colorful fish that flitted in and out of the throne room seemed to be fair game for the writhing plant-thing. Any fish that swam close enough to the creature was in danger of being lassoed by the thready appendages and dragged struggling down into the potted creature's crunching jaws while its numerous tentacle eyes peered down, watching the meal.

"My pet obviously prefers the blue fish." King Barak made the pronouncement without any clear basis in fact. "I decree that more blue fish shall swim into my throne chamber. And no more red ones."

Watching the potted creature eat, Vic wondered if the merlon king sampled his pet's food for himself. "One fish, two fish," he muttered to Gwen. "Red fish, blue fish?" Trying to be discreet, she kicked his leg under the table.

"What is that nonsense?" Barak roared. "Do you dare challenge me?"

"N-no," Vic stammered. "It's from a, uh, children's rhyme, and I —"

Azric smoothly changed the subject. "Speaking of rhymes, did you know that there are prophecies about you two? I doubt you are even aware of your potential powers. Your mothers kept them secret from you, you know. They didn't share very much information with their own children, which is really quite a pity. But I've studied the prophecies. I can help. There is so much you could accomplish."

"In other words, you want us to do something for you," Gwen said. "What makes you think we'd ever agree to that?"

"Oh, you will," Azric said. "In fact, there is someone who —"

"Is it not rude to carry on a private conversation when I have so many guests?" the merlon king said.

"Ah, but Majesty, this business regards an important prophecy about the two children, information that —" Azric began.

The frills on the merlon king's head flared a brighter red, standing out like the spines on the back of an angry dragon. "The only prophecies I care for are the ones about merlons.

Like the one that goes: Merlons, merlons, unite. And so forth. All other prophecies are unbearably tedious!"

"Of course they are." Azric remained unruffled, as if experienced at placating Barak's capricious moods. The look the evil wizard sent Vic and Gwen warned them that the discussion would continue later. He gave the king a brief bow. "Leave this to me. I can take care of everything, and you need never be bored with the details — just as when the cities of Oo'nisl and Oo'beebl were late in sending you their tribute, hmm? Did I not convince them in only a day to pay you twice as much as they owed?"

The king looked somewhat mollified. "Insolent chieftains. It was high time they showed the proper respect. Fools!"

"Exactly. And fools cannot be allowed to wield power, can they?" Azric gave him a slight smile. "Now, perhaps a banquet will cheer you up, and afterward you can choose any entertainment you like."

"Yes. Food! I want to be served now," Barak shouted. "Where is the food? Bring the feast!"

More guards and servants swam in, carrying individual platters loaded with round, rubbery steaks, held in place by a thick spike at the center of each dish.

"Ah, delicious!" The merlon king's eyes lit up like lamps. "Not many have ever tasted battle kraken."

"Battle kraken?" Gwen said, gulping.

"Certainly. We had to do something with the creature. Why not eat it?" King Barak waved his webbed hand. "The beast was quite a nuisance."

"Is this the same battle kraken that attacked the Elantyan harbor?" Tiaret scowled down at the meat on her plate. Sharif poked at it with a pearly carved-shell utensil, but he didn't take a bite.

"The same one," Barak said. He stroked a frond of the plant creature in the urn beside him, then devoured a large chunk of kraken steak. "Tentacled things are never as intelligent as you expect them to be."

"Huh. You'd think that the task of manipulating all those appendages would require a certain amount of brainpower," Vic said.

Azric drifted forward. "Sadly, the battle kraken's attack against Elantya turned out to be less effective than we had hoped, and the creature was injured."

"Yup. In fact, I had a front-row seat. Sage Polup and I shot Grogyptian Fire into its face from a cannon," Vic said. "Lyssandra was there, too."

"*You* killed my battle kraken?" King Barak roared.

Gwen pushed away her plate and fisted her hands in her lap. "We defended our island. What did you expect us to do?"

"I expected you to be defeated. How very irritating," Barak said. "The injured battle kraken went mad with the pain. It came thrashing back here to Oo'regl, the capital itself, and caused enormous damage, simply enormous! That beast destroyed many of our buildings, killed merlon soldiers who were trying to defend our city. They were very useful soldiers, too. I make another decree: No more soldiers shall be killed by a kraken. Write that down!"

"Sheesh, I feel so guilty about all the trouble we put you

through," Vic said with even heavier irony. "Poor old Squidzilla."

The king took another bite, which seemed very satisfying to him. "No matter. We succeeded in killing the creature and making this lovely feast." He stabbed another chunk of the meat. "And we do have enough slaves to rebuild the city. So, not such a nuisance after all."

"I'm afraid our captives have little appetite, King Barak," Azric pointed out, smiling. "Children get queasy about the strangest things."

"You mean like getting kidnapped?" Gwen muttered to Vic.

King Barak finished his meal and frowned at Sharif, who had not even tasted his kraken steak. Abruptly, the king reached over, grabbed Sharif's plate, and tossed the hunk of squid to his potted plant-creature. The tentacles grabbed the meat and stuffed it down into its crunching jaws. Then the king snatched Lyssandra's meal and took it for his own, eating even more of the grayish meat. "My two best generals were riding the battle kraken," he grumbled. "They were killed in that attack, too."

Tiaret addressed the merlon king. "If those were your best fighters, then their training was inadequate." Her tone was matter-of-fact, as if she were simply offering an observation.

"They were my commanders, my strongest fighters!" Barak pounded his webbed fist on the banquet table. "But strong is not enough. I need great, imaginative, and undefeated generals to lead my armies. How else can I complete the destruction of Elantya? Now that those two are slain, I must replace them with the best my merlons have to offer."

Azric leaned over and whispered something in the king's ear. Barak nodded vigorously. He made a snort, and swirls of water curled up from his fishy mouth. "I may care nothing for ancient tales about seal-breakers and crystal doors, but ancient customs are another matter. You make a good suggestion, Azric. A traditional merlon competition to choose new generals would be just the thing to lift my spirits."

"Yes, King Barak." Azric sounded pointedly patient. "And I will see that we use the talents of these children to free my immortal armies that have been locked away for centuries by the Great Closure. Only then can we bring back the golden days you've been longing for. You know the prophecy."

Shimmers, shimmers of light,
    Fallen to disgrace,
Glimmers, glimmers ignite,
    Evil ones displace.
Swimmers, swimmers, unite,
    Take your rightful place!

Churning, churning the wave,
    All around the Key,
Turning, turning to save,
    Freedom in the sea.
Yearning, yearning we crave,
    Merlon victory!

Olden, olden the rage,
    Higher yet it towers,

Bolden, bolden the Sage,
In the darkest hours.
Golden, golden the age,
That shall then be ours!

"You see, Barak, *I* am that sage who will lead you to victory and usher in the Golden Age of the Merlons."

The king looked unconvinced. "Your hordes of immortal soldiers will bring thousands more land dwellers to our world. My first aim is to remove the blot of Elantya from my world. Stupid island! We must sink it and return Szishh to its pristine ocean environment. No dry land! The interlopers never asked our permission. They simply decided to create an island we did not need. *That* is the priority, Azric. We continue our plans. After we deal with Elantya, then we can play with *your* prophecy." He stood, raising his clawed hand. "But before we start, I require new generals!"

Azric bowed. "Of course, King Barak. Choose your generals." He nodded to Vic and Gwen and their friends. "And then I have other things to do with our new guests."

"Naturally, one does not simply choose powerful generals at random," the merlon king said to the captive apprentices as if he were teaching small children. "It must be done properly, in a magnificent combat. Yes, a combat! I demand it right now. Send word to any of my fighters who wish to be considered." He addressed his potted plant creature, patting the eyeball tentacles. "You shall watch with me." Then he bellowed for merlon servants. "Take away the table and the rest of this banquet. I have had my fill."

Vic had just been getting up his nerve to taste the battle kraken when swimming servants yanked the platters away and disassembled the table.

"I will enjoy this very much." Barak beamed at his new captives. "It is not often we have a death-joust with sea serpents. The perfect way to finish a meal!"

10

THE DEEP TRENCH IN front of the expansive underwater throne room served as the merlon king's combat arena. With flashing light signals from luminescent pearls and pounding vibrations transmitted through the salt water, the merlon combatants were summoned to prove their military skills. Electric eels darted by, as if looking for something to shock.

King Barak leaned forward, his potted tentacled plant by his side. His slit-pupilled eyes were as round as saucers, and his fishy lips parted in an eager grin, showing needle teeth. Waiting in silence, Azric gave the capricious merlon king an indulgent smile.

"What's going to happen?" Gwen wondered aloud.

Tiaret studied the preparations darkly. "I believe we are about to witness a trial by combat."

"Cool," Vic said. "All-star wrestling for monster mermaids."

In the open water above the deep trench, they could see movement through the shimmering curtains of water, a long sinuous flicker and a splash of color. Six ferocious-looking sea serpents plunged toward the amazing underwater city.

"Look, they're wearing combat armor," Gwen said.

Each of the sea serpents wore a harness and metal spikes in addition to its already pointy fins and frills. Brass horns had been strapped onto their heads, and overlapping seashell armor plates and hammered silver shields were attached to vulnerable spots near the gills. Long feelers protruded from around the serpents' mouths like the whiskers of a catfish.

Each great serpent carried a merlon rider who sat in a sturdy saddle strapped to its scaly back. Several of the merlon candidates carried iron-hard spears tipped with wicked-looking points made of narwhal tusks. Vic decided he wouldn't have wanted to fight against even the weakest of these champions.

The six candidates wrestled their sea serpents into some semblance of order and presented themselves before King Barak. One combatant was a muscular male with a black frill that glistened like obsidian smeared with oil; he carried a jagged spear, and at his side hung a barbed hook connected to a braided silken rope. Across his chest, like war medals, he wore five calcified starfish whose arms had been sharpened to menacing points.

Another burly merlon had a square chest with plated scales like the belly of a crocodile. He wore the shell of a sea turtle on his back. Swimming in among them, a golden-skinned female merlon rode a coppery sea serpent, which reared like a hard-to-control stallion. Goldskin ducked and bobbed on the back of her mount like a flexible seaweed frond curling in a current. The other three merlon candidates had their own quirks and weapons; all of them bore scars that gave evidence of the many other vicious duels they had been in.

Near the edge of the open fighting space, a corral made of lumpy coral bars held hungry-looking sharks, each with a prominent symbol branded onto its dorsal fin.

Viewing the challengers, Barak stood up from his seat, unfolding his long arms and legs. He waved his webbed hands and bellowed with vibrating words through the water. "I, Barak, king of all merlons, require the best fighters so that we can destroy the humans and erase the island of Elantya from our world. I have already lost my two best generals — hmm, that means they must not have been my best. They were weak! I cannot afford to have weaklings. Are any of you strong enough to command?"

All six responded with bubbling, defiant cheers.

"Then show me which two of you are the strongest," the king commanded, waving Tiaret's teaching staff. "Let the battles commence!"

A school of dazzling scarlet fish was released from one of the tall towers, and the flurry of bright color, like spurting blood, served as a signal banner. The six merlon combatants pulled on the reins of their sea serpents and circled, buying time to prepare their weapons and choose their opponents.

The brawl began.

Blackfrill lowered his long spear and drove his sea serpent headlong toward a merlon with spotted skin. Spotskin responded in kind, deadly points aimed toward vulnerable areas.

"It's like a jousting match." Vic could hear and understand everything through the strange seashell mounted in his ear.

"If the merlons wish to fight and kill each other, then let them do so," Tiaret grumbled.

Sharif stole a sidelong glance at the silent dark sage, who sat looking confident and patient. "Maybe there will be an accident. One of the merlons could mistakenly kill Azric." Sharif sounded hopeful.

"Little chance of that," Tiaret said. "These warriors handle their weapons well."

Blackfrill and Spotskin collided with a vibrating crash that sent thrumming ripples through the water. The sharp lance point struck the seashell armor on the spotted merlon's serpent. Blackfrill wrenched his spear forward and trailed a long gash on the ribs of the other serpent. While Spotskin struggled to control his frenzied mount, Blackfrill snatched one of the pointed starfish medals from his chest and with a cruel snap of his wrist, spun it like a throwing star. The sharp weapon swished through the water, and two of the points sank into Spotskin's throat. He jerked, clawed at his neck, then drifted free from his saddle, dead.

The wounded sea serpent, lost without a rider or master, swam away, looking confused. Merlon handlers swiftly corralled it.

After the death of one of the six fighters, the thin coral bars on the underwater pen opened, and several branded sharks swam out. Ravenously hungry, they tore at the body of the dead merlon fighter, filling the water with drifting clouds of blood and making the view murky.

The other merlons did not pause in their dueling.

Vic found the joust absolutely riveting, but part of his mind told him that he should look away, that the practice was repulsive and decadent and immoral, like gladiator fights in ancient Rome. Yet there was another part of his mind that disagreed.

He and his friends were in a unique situation. As far as he knew, merlon civilization was unexplored, undocumented, a riddle waiting to be solved. And the sages could use this kind of knowledge to understand their enemy. Plus, there was that whole it-was-like-a-train-wreck-and-he-couldn't-look-away thing. The five friends owed it to Elantya and the other worlds to learn as much as they could and then escape. Why had the merlons lived at peace for thousands of years and then, a mere century ago, taken action against all land-dwellers? Could it have been the influence of Azric and Orpheon? Azric certainly seemed to be calling the shots down here.

Goldskin goaded her sea serpent, which like the others had long brass horns strapped to its head. On a rampage, her serpent rammed her sharp-fanged opponent, knocking the fighter off of his mount. In each hand, the unseated Sharpfang held a scalloped scimitar with flow holes cut through the blades. He swung and slashed, but could not dodge the horns of Goldskin's monster. The sea serpent gored him as he tried to defend himself with both curved swords.

Now two of the merlons were out of the fight.

No matter how many science fiction and fantasy books, TV

shows, and movies Vic had read or watched, he wasn't prepared for what he saw. This was real — as real as the attacks on Elantya and the *Golden Walrus.*

While square-chested Turtleshell fought his opponent, Blackfrill and Goldskin swam close to each other, having already bested their rivals. Vic expected them to attack each other, but instead of fighting, the pair quickly conferred.

As soon as Turtleshell dispatched his enemy, Blackfrill and Goldskin turned on him. Vic thought the tactic made perfect sense, since two merlons ganging up against another in the free-for-all had a far better chance of winning. Vic was no stranger to fighting and strategy. His mother, so paradoxically gentle, had taught him the art of *zy'oah* since he first began to toddle. He had memories of them practicing on the lawn in their backyard when he was young. Kyara would teach him a move, then "attack" him in various ways to allow him to practice the technique. Although as an instructor his mother was serious about her subject, many was the practice session that had ended with the two of them tumbling onto the grass laughing, using their quick *zy'oah* moves to tickle one another.

Blackfrill and Goldskin drove their sea serpents toward Turtleshell. Blackfrill removed his barbed hook and swung it on its silken cord like a grappling hook. He latched the back of the sea turtle shell, hooking the burly merlon, then reared his serpent back. The powerful undersea creature tore Turtleshell from his own mount.

Doing her part, Goldskin streaked upward. Their mutual enemy struggled, using a scalloped dagger to slash the cord connected to Blackfrill's grappling hook. Goldskin found a vulnerable spot and thrust her long pointed trident deep into it. Seconds later Turtleshell was dead.

King Barak was both surprised and delighted by their unexpected cooperation. "Excellent, excellent! I want to do that again."

"As delightful as this competition was," Azric said in a silky voice, "you will need all of your warriors to fight the Elantyans."

"The joust is a merlon tradition!" the king snapped. "It is how such decisions are made. Merlon generals must be prepared to give their lives to fight for their people. That is why the joust is to the death."

"Hey, we'd like to see a few more combats," Vic said, hoping to egg on the merlon king. "In fact, have all of your warriors kill each other."

Gwen jabbed him and spoke in a rushed whisper. "Quiet, Taz! What if he decides to throw *us* into the gladiator arena to fight the sharks or sea serpents?"

"Oh, I hadn't thought of that." He glanced over at Tiaret, Sharif, and Lyssandra, all of whom wore stoic looks, as if they had seen worse before and steeled themselves against this. Lyssandra's face, however, had paled by several shades, and Vic was starting to learn to read her face for emotional responses as surely as Piri indicated hers by glowing in various colors.

Vic reached out and put a hand on Lyssandra's and saw the color gradually seep back into her face. He was glad that they could draw strength from each other. As long as the five friends stayed together, he was sure that they could survive and find a way to escape. Now that there were new merlon generals, however, it brought the next attack on Elantya that much closer.

Blackfrill and Goldskin swam up before the king, giving Vic a better view of the yawning pink mouths of the sea serpents than he had ever wanted. The blood in the water seemed to have made them hungry for more fighting.

"Congratulations, my two new generals." Barak seemed smug. He presented Blackfrill with Tiaret's teaching staff and gave Goldskin an ornate seashell dagger that looked wickedly sharp. "You will train our other soldiers. Arm yourselves with the best weapons and armor." The merlon king turned his eyes toward Azric. "And you, Azric — use your powers of persuasion to encourage those anemonites to work harder. I have never seen jellyfish brains move so slowly! We need more weapons! We need breakthroughs. I command it. Torture a few more of them if they do not cooperate. Better yet, send Orpheon to do it."

"Do not forget, King Barak, that we now have two seal-breakers," Azric pointed to Vic and Gwen. "They can give us access to my armies — a stronger weapon than any other we possess."

"We're not giving you access to anything," Vic said.

Azric's eyes shone with a look Vic could not interpret. "We shall see. You will change your minds soon enough."

11

WHEN THE DEBRIS FROM the joust was cleaned up, the merlon king left his open throne hall and retired to his chambers.

Now that Barak would no longer scold him, Orpheon returned to the hall, swimming in like one of the small fish that darted around the arches. Azric, who had summoned him, looked at their intimidated captives. "It's time for us to get to work, Orpheon. I am only interested in the two seal-breakers." He gave Vic and Gwen an avid smile that Vic did not find at all comforting. "You can take the other three and do whatever you wish — so long as you remember they may still be useful to me."

Orpheon ran an assessing gaze over them with a smug expression that held an edge of cruelty. "I cannot tell you how long I have anticipated this." He leveled an index finger at Sharif, Tiaret, and Lyssandra. "You — come with me. Now."

Vic gulped. He wasn't sure what would be worse, being stuck with Azric, or with his traitorous assistant. As his three friends reluctantly moved to join Orpheon, prodded by merlon guards, Vic noticed that Tiaret's amber eyes glinted with defiant challenge, Lyssandra looked wrung-out, and Sharif shielded himself with a look of haughty disdain. Orpheon knew that he had the upper hand. "Forget all thoughts of that weakling Rubicas. I will show you what a real sage can do. *I* am your master now."

Merlon warriors accompanied by electric eels administered brief shocks of "encouragement," driving the three out to where guardian sharks circled them. Orpheon ordered each human to hold on to the dorsal fin of a shark, which pulled them along at great speeds through the water. As they were whisked away, Lyssandra, Tiaret, and Sharif turned to exchange anxious looks with the cousins. None of them could stop what was happening.

After their companions were gone from the hall of the merlon king, Vic swallowed again. "He wouldn't kill them, would he?"

"I don't think so," Gwen said. "He's too in love with the idea of being their master. On the other hand, I doubt he'd hesitate to *hurt* them."

"Perhaps you should be more concerned for yourselves." Azric now floated before the cousins, fixing them with the discomfiting green-and-blue stare of his mismatched eyes.

"We have so much to learn together. No one else can teach you the skills that I offer."

"What do you want with us?" Gwen asked.

Azric wore a look of wide-eyed innocence. "Right now, all I want is your *cooperation.*"

Vic snorted, water swirls streaming from his nose. "Now why does 'cooperation' sound like such a bad word coming from you?"

Azric made a burbling, *tsk*ing sound. "Such harsh judgment coming from someone I barely know."

"First of all, we've heard enough stories about you to have an opinion," Gwen said. "Second, you killed my parents. That's all I need to know."

Azric spread his hands as if to say it was only natural. "I never intended to harm them. I merely needed your mother's assistance in a matter of great importance to me. She would have come to no harm had she merely complied with my request. But they resisted me, she and your father. They chose to sacrifice themselves battling against forces they couldn't possibly defeat, rather than just do me a very small favor." The dark sage gave what appeared to be a sincerely helpless shrug. "So I had no alternative, you see. I didn't really have anything against them."

Though her neck gills still drew in water, Gwen found herself breathless and speechless at this casual description of her parents' death.

"And what about Gwen?" Vic's angry words lashed out like a whip. "Dad told us you're the one who made that killer whale attack her at Ocean Kingdoms. She could have died!"

Floating in a relaxed position with his legs crossed, Azric pressed his fingertips together. "To be sure, to be sure, but that was hardly my intent. It was really more of a test, you see. I knew, of course, that your mothers were Kyara and Fyera. I had done my homework. You know —

Born beneath the selfsame moon,
Only they may bind the rune,
And create the Ring of Might,
Right the wrongs, reverse the rite.
Sharing blood, yet not the womb,
Two shall seal the tyrant's doom.
Darkest Sage, in darkest day,
With his blood the price shall pay.

"I could not be certain that you were the children of the prophecy. One of the problems with such flowery predictions is that they never mean quite what you think they do. Why, you're not even brother and sister, and I was searching for twins! I needed to find out if the two of you had inherited any of your mothers' powers, or if you were merely normal children."

"We're not children," Vic growled.

Gwen crossed her arms over her chest as if to protect herself from his ruthlessness. "And what if I had turned out to be just a normal girl?"

Azric shrugged, as if the answer was obvious. "Why, then you would have died. However, you would have been of no use to me, so it would not have mattered." He seemed almost surprised at her question. “But why worry about what might have been? You reacted exactly as I had hoped — and you lived.” He gave a watery, dismissive wave. “So, other than that, what have I done to earn your mistrust?”

“Besides kidnapping us all, you mean?” Vic quipped.

“According to the stories, you murdered your own parents, too, so that you could have all the power for yourself,” Gwen said.

Azric did not take offense. “If you have read the legends, then you know my parents were evil. True tyrants.”

“And you’re not?” Vic replied.

“No, I don’t believe so.”

“Trust me, you’re not the most objective judge. Sharif says you killed his brother —”

Again, Azric used that maddening come-come-now-let’s-be-reasonable tone. “Why dwell in the past? We’ve all made a few missteps along the way.”

“Yup. I skipped a class at school once,” Vic said. “Not exactly the same ballpark as murder.”

“Perhaps, but neither have you spent thousands of years dwelling in many other worlds and amassing great wisdom. My hard-earned knowledge assures me now that you are the children of the prophecy. Therefore, I require your help.”

“The question is, what makes you think we’d go along with anything you want?” Gwen said. “I don’t see any reason to help you.”

The dark sage gave them a kindly smile. “Why, I thought you would grasp the most obvious reason right away: if you don’t cooperate, I will be forced to kill your three friends.”

12

WHEN SHARIF, LYSSANDRA, AND Tiaret were separated from their other two friends, they had a terrible uneasy feeling. Four merlon guards stroked along beside them, always ready to deliver a painful shock with their accompanying electric eels. Sharif wanted to comfort Piri, to stroke her eggsphere and somehow communicate with her that they would find a way out of this.

He couldn't believe the merlons had not snatched his beautiful djinni from him. She hung on his chest inside her mesh sack. Everyone could see her, especially when she glowed her wonderful colors. The merlon king had taken Tiaret's teaching staff from Orpheon, but somehow Piri hadn't intrigued him enough. And as for Orpheon and Azric, they hadn't given the eggsphere a second glance. Maybe they did not think it was of any use. Still, Sharif felt very vulnerable with her. Someone could snatch his precious djinni at any moment.

Beside them, leading the group away from the merlon city, Orpheon swam like an eel. With his shape-shifting powers, he had transformed his hands into wide webbed scoops like a merlon's, and his body moved with rubbery undulations as he twirled through the water.

Sharif could tell by Tiaret's body language that she very much wanted to fight and make a good accounting of herself, but he didn't see that they had any chance of escaping. Neither he nor his friends could ever outswim the sharks or merlons. If they could, it would have meant leaving Gwen and Vic behind. On the other hand, if even one of them managed to get away, they could warn the Elantyans of the situation, and the sages could figure out a way to rescue them.

And, Sharif told himself, *one of us escaping is better than none of us escaping.* But no opportunity presented itself.

"Where are we going?" Lyssandra asked after the sharks had borne them beyond view of the ethereal undersea city.

Orpheon's eyes were dark and hungry. "We can always use new workers at Lavaja Canyon." His laughter made a bubbling sound beneath the water. "It will be marvelous even for the merlon slaves to watch you do all the work. I wonder how long you pampered children will last."

Tiaret did not rise to the bait. "Time will tell."

Orpheon turned his evil smile toward Sharif. "The thing I most look forward to is breaking this spoiled prince. He needs to learn that his social position is an illusion. We will teach him that lesson in a way he will never forget."

Sharif decided that it would be unworthy of him to answer. Instead, he took comfort from Piri's presence in the mesh pouch around his neck.

Their merlon escorts led them swiftly through warm currents and down a slope, skimming not far above the ocean floor. Ahead, a hot, shimmering light rose from the seabed, as if the sandy floor were on fire. Orpheon extended a webbed hand. "Even from this distance, you can see the power boiling out of Lavaja Canyon. The power of the magic there can easily bring about the end of Elantya, if it is channeled properly." The fanatical merlon guards seemed very pleased at the prospect.

Lyssandra looked deeply troubled. "This is not natural — a wound in the world. I dreamed about this. The waves of energy make me feel sick inside, as if something is wrong with the magic."

Sharif noticed the strange sensation, too. The water felt tainted somehow from the volatilized crystal.

Orpheon smiled. "Yes, a fascinating effect, isn't it?"

Soon they came close enough to see down to the yawning fissures in the canyon floor. Jagged fractures in the crust reminded Sharif of a hatching egg. Bubbling silvery orange magma oozed along the cracks. The landscape seemed to be in flux, with splits zigzagging and opening up, while others sealed back together again.

The water had grown extremely warm and tingly, as if it were effervescent. Amazement replaced Lyssandra's anxiety. "Is that lavaja, from fire aja crystals?"

The furious glow bronzed the traitor's face. "Compared to

this, fire aja is a mere spark beside a bonfire. Lavaja bubbles up like the blood of the world itself. The heat, the incandescence, and the magic come from the spirit of fire. We have tapped into a substance more pure and powerful than anything an Elantyan sage has ever dared use. This raw essence of power will help us defeat your weak island."

As Sharif's eyes adjusted to the bright glare, he saw many plain-looking merlons, definitely members of a lower class, probably slaves. Some of them rode giant sea turtles whose bodies were protected by leathery armor, their reptilian heads covered with horned plates. Metal blinders shielded the turtles' eyes while the merlon slaves prodded them with sharp goads, making the lumbering creatures plod closer to the edge where lavaja bubbled up. Like pets on leashes, other slaves were tethered by thin cords of woven doolya to boulders embedded in the mud.

Wrestling with long poles, the merlon slaves maneuvered large heat-resistant buckets into the seething molten magic to scoop out lavaja. As soon as they were removed from the intensity of the cracks, the full crucibles were placed on the backs of turtles who plodded away with their dangerous deliveries.

As Sharif and his friends watched, the slaves and the turtles began to scramble back from the edge of the lavaja cracks in alarm. The workers moved as far as their ankle tethers allowed them. A vibration jolted through the water, the main fissures split farther, and, like a crack shooting through glass, a new jagged line widened the burgeoning lavaja outlet.

"You cannot hope to control such power," Lyssandra said.

"Do the merlons not have magic to seal the fissures? If you do not stop the damage, you put the whole world in jeopardy."

The merlon guards laughed, and Orpheon sneered. "Stop it? Why, we encourage it! Each crack brings forth the freshest, most potent lavaja, crude and undiluted. That is what we tap."

One merlon slave writhed as a ribbon of scalding lavaja plumed too close. His scales flaked off in a long line of rippling blisters. He made a strange gargling sound of pain. Guards dragged him away, though they didn't seem concerned about rushing to get him medical attention.

Orpheon continued, "The most potent lavaja is out in the heart of the devastated regions, where the sea floor is constantly churned. Too dangerous to harvest there, unfortunately. We've lost dozens of workers already — and always need more . . . volunteers — which is why I brought you out here. It will be my special pleasure to make the spoiled prince do work befitting his true station in life!"

Sharif struggled to keep his anger in check. "I am a prince because my father is a great sultan. He was powerful enough to banish Azric, once we discovered his evil."

"Ah, but not before Azric killed your poor brother. Your plan to catch the dark sage at his wrongdoing must have been complicated indeed!"

"You need not remind me that Azric must still pay for his crime."

"Just as you and your friends will pay for the crime of being land dwellers in Szishh."

"You will attempt to coerce us into extracting this lavaja for you," Tiaret said. She didn't have to add that she meant to resist in every way possible.

Lyssandra seemed most distressed. "But what purpose does it serve?"

"I will show you that next," Orpheon said. "I'm sure you will find your work much more rewarding once you are aware of how it will contribute to our noble goal." He turned and stroked away. The sharks carried the three friends and the contingent of merlon guards after him. "Tomorrow you will become intimately familiar with the lavaja cracks."

As the three companions followed Orpheon, Sharif realized that being towed by sharks, suspended above the ocean floor, reminded him of flying on his carpet. That gave him an idea for escaping.

With the summoning spell from the Pentumvirate, he could still call his flying carpet to him. Sharif had not attempted it since being dragged under the sea. But was there any reason the carpet could not plunge into the ocean and fly underwater? With the magic carpet, Sharif and his friends might be able to streak away faster than the merlons could swim. Wasting no time, he spoke the words to activate the rune woven into his carpet.

Orpheon, the merlons, and the sharks continued swimming with the captives to their next destination. Sharif's heart sank as minute after minute passed. Somehow he'd expected the carpet to appear instantly, although even at its best speed, the magic rug could not have come all the way from Elantya yet. He had no idea how long it would take. Sharif kept glancing nervously up toward the ripple of reflected sunlight on the surface, but he saw no sign of the flying carpet. Eventually he began to give up hope that the summoning spell would work. Had the water blocked the spell somehow? Or what if the carpet could not move under water after all? He was comforted, at least, that Piri was still with him.

When Orpheon led them to the merlon equivalent of a research laboratory, Lyssandra cried out immediately, her words echoing in the black communication shells. "The anemonites!"

In a cleared area of a knobby coral reef, bounded by a thick and forbidding doolya forest, fifty of the brainlike jellyfish creatures were held captive. "This is where they use science and magic to convert the lavaja into powerful weapons against Elantya." Orpheon scowled. "At least they *pretend* to work. Progress, so far, has been disappointing."

Two marked sharks and three electric eels circled the area ominously, and a pair of merlon guards watched over the anemonites with sharp tridents and scalloped swords. "The guards are not really necessary, except for intimidation purposes," Orpheon added. "Since we clipped the frills of those anemonites, they could not swim far even if they tried to escape."

"Such cruelty." Anger bubbled in Tiaret's voice. "No wonder the anemonites do not wish to help you."

"And yet they do help. They are our brain trust, and with their designs, we will use lavaja to sink Elantya — a festering sore in this beautiful ocean." The merlon guards grumbled in agreement with Orpheon's grand words. "They have already produced many small, simple bombs, but with that new installation" — he indicated a strange construction assembled from shipwreck components and raw undersea materials — "they will intensify the reaction enough to rip through the foundations of the island itself." The half-completed tower construction, with stiltlike legs and a large reservoir on the top, would apparently store the molten lavaja and dispense it down troughs.

"We already know the anemonites are geniuses. You remember, of course, how Sage Polup developed his Grogyptian fire cannon," Lyssandra said innocently. "That is what drove away the battle kraken and defeated the first merlon attack." It was just the right jab for her to use. The aquatic warriors looked very annoyed with her.

"That was a fluke," Orpheon said.

"Not a fluke," Sharif said, rubbing it in. "Sage Polup has helped Elantya a great deal — as you well know."

Orpheon turned the tables on them. "Then imagine — just imagine — if *one* anemonite brain can produce such wonders for Elantya, how much more fifty geniuses can aid the merlon empire. These anemonites will provide us with all the weapons we need."

"Why do they help you?" Lyssandra said.

"Because they are tortured, of course," Tiaret said. Sharif surreptitiously looked around for his flying carpet, but still saw nothing.

"Yes, we do offer some slight encouragement. There used to be a great many more than fifty anemonites. It's a pity, but we've had to use scores of them as examples." Orpheon didn't need to explain further.

Closely watched by guards, two of the anemonites rode large armored kraegas. The thick-shelled crustacean steeds had long bodies with six pairs of jointed legs beneath strong swimmerets, and a broad flippered tail. By temporarily retracting their legs, the lobsterlike kraegas could propel themselves forward in low, powerful leaps along the ocean floor, while anemonites rode on their backs.

With their frills clipped, anemonites could only putter from place to place over the sand and mud, but when mounted on kraegas, they moved with much greater agility. The jellyfish-brains could use the kraegas' antennae as writing instruments, guiding them with their pseudopods to scribe equations, spell fragments, and patterns of power into the thick coating of mud scraped across flat stones.

Over by the edge of the waving doolya forest, the apprentices spotted more of the kraegas being kept behind bars. Sharif remembered that Sage Polup had talked about the symbiotic relationship between anemonites and their kraega steeds. Anemonites helped to cultivate and capture food for the kraegas, while the lobsterlike creatures made the jellyfish-brains much more mobile.

"Why do you keep the rest of them caged?" Lyssandra asked. "Couldn't the anemonites do more work if you allowed them more kraegas to move about?"

Orpheon said, "Any more, and they might try to escape. We value the anemonites for their intelligence, not for their mobility. They can think right where they are."

"In that case, it is a tactical error to keep so many kraegas so close to the anemonites," Tiaret observed.

The traitor answered with a cold smile. "I prefer to leave the kraegas in full view of our anemonite scientists — as a constant reminder of what they have lost and how much more we can take from them if they do not cooperate."

"Your cruelty will be your undoing, Orpheon," Sharif said. "As my people say: Those who feast on cruelty will someday choke on it."

Suddenly alert, the guardian sharks whirled and darted away. Sharif stroked with his hands to turn around and saw one of the horned sea serpents swimming toward them through the seaweed forest that fringed the reef. The serpent carried two merlon passengers: the merlon king and the new general, Blackfrill. King Barak looked overwrought, while the dark-finned general simply seemed threatening.

The sea serpent spooked the anemonites, who scuttled and scattered, ruining much of their work, smearing scrawled spells and equations. Their panic seemed exaggerated, and Sharif wondered if the jellyfish-brains were using the situation as an excuse to stall their progress.

Blackfrill jabbed the serpent with Tiaret's teaching staff, bringing it to a halt. Seeing the merlon general wield her special weapon, Tiaret glared at him. King Barak remained mounted high on the creature's back, holding the reins. He lorded it over the captive anemonites, while Blackfrill dismounted and swam down to stand next to Orpheon.

"Listen to me so that you may hear my disappointment," said King Barak, his voice high-pitched with fury. "You anemonites have a job to do. I gave you my command when we first captured you. And though we have given you all the spell scrolls you need and unlimited lavaja as raw material, you have achieved far less than I expect of you. If you really are the greatest minds, you should want to show off your genius! Up in Elantya, one traitorous escaped anemonite has done great things for our enemies. So I know that the rest of you can do better."

The sea serpent thrashed, and the merlon king held on, glowering at the cowed jellyfish creatures. Even the kraegas behind their cage bars seemed frightened.

"I asked myself the reason for these delays. Why so many accidents? Why so many mistakes? Finally, the obvious answer occurred to me: You are stalling intentionally! Anemonites are making mistakes to hinder our war effort. For what reason do you not wish the merlons to retake this world? Maybe you are not as intelligent as you claim."

Through the black seashell in his ear Sharif heard one of the anemonites squeak, "That is not true, Your Majesty."

"Oh, but it is!" The merlon king jerked his head from side to side. "I commanded Azric to study your many mistakes. He is very intelligent, too. He found where values were intentionally changed, words from spell scrolls were transcribed incorrectly, and designs were drawn with careful errors. Were these simple mistakes? No. These were deliberate sabotage!" Barak was livid. "In fact, can it be called a mistake if it was done on purpose? I wish there were a better word." He pondered, distracted, for a long moment, then whirled back to the cowering jellyfish-brains.

"You must be punished, and you must work harder. I decree it! Time grows short. Our first tests for the destruction of

Elantya have begun, and some of the bombs are already planted, but we need you to finish your work." He pointed to the half-built lavaja tower structure. "Now! Therefore, I have assigned one of my new generals to be your slave master and overseer. I give him my permission to do anything he believes necessary, so long as he produces results."

Blackfrill drifted forward, holding his weapons, as the merlon king continued, "Orpheon, you will assist him. Azric thinks you are worth something, so prove it! Get me results. I do not care what you do to these creatures in order to achieve my goals."

In a huff, the merlon king wheeled the sea serpent about and darted away, leaving a frothy wake behind him. Next to the captive anemonites, Blackfrill and Orpheon looked at each other, then smiled at the new opportunity they had just been given.

13

THE OCEAN CURRENTS SEEMED to grow cold all of a sudden. Sharif watched the merlon general, puffed with new authority, swim in among the anemonite researchers like a bully, gripping Tiaret's unbreakable teaching staff like a club.

The two scientists riding kraega steeds were so shaken and cowed by King Barak's tirade that they could not control the precise scribing of the crustaceans' antennae. Their spells and equations became all scrambled on their mud-streaked writing tablet. Leaving the three companions by the guards, Orpheon swam beside Blackfrill, eager to see what his new partner intended to do.

Tiaret was a simmering mass of anger. "It is easy to intimidate a small floating creature. You should threaten someone who can stand against you." She clenched her fists, and Sharif could tell she wanted to grab her teaching staff and fight

Blackfrill. Despite her brashness, though, it was obvious the merlon general would best her in underwater combat.

In spite of their clipped frills, the anemonites scurried to get out of the way of their intimidating new slave master. The two riding kraegas quickly scribbled a complicated spell design with the creatures' antennae to demonstrate their earnestness.

"We will work harder," cried one anemonite. "Together we will accomplish what the merlon king demands." The other jellyfish-brains all chimed in.

"You have said that before," Orpheon said. "I am certain Azric could complete much of your work himself, but he has other priorities. We require your best efforts — without any more mistakes."

With a clawed hand, Blackfrill snatched one of the anemonite scientists at random. "You have all sabotaged your work and stalled our plans. King Barak showed me his proof." The jellyfish creature squirmed in the general's clawed hand.

"You will not be disappointed," the anemonite squeaked. "I, Gedup, will see to it."

"I am already disappointed. Fifty of you have done unacceptable work, but I am willing to wager that after this demonstration, *forty-nine* of you will be perfectly sufficient." He lifted Tiaret's teaching staff, ready to skewer the poor anemonite with the sharp point.

"Do not kill him!" Lyssandra cried. "You might be destroying the greatest genius among them."

"They are all geniuses," Orpheon sneered. "Interchangeable. But an unmotivated genius does us no good."

In complete dread, Sharif knew Blackfrill intended to murder Gedup while they all watched, to set a gory, shocking example. The hapless anemonite scientist reminded him of Sage Polup, who had done so much for Elantya, and for the five friends. Sharif remembered the anemonite sage's tale of longing for the day when his people could be free.

The doomed anemonite squirmed in vain to pull itself out of Blackfrill's clawed grasp. The general prodded with the sharp tip of the staff, tormenting the creature. Sharif desperately looked around again, hoping for some flicker of movement, a shadow of his flying carpet coming in like the cavalry.

But the waters remained calm and still. Too calm. High overhead, the reflected sunlight beckoned him. Maybe his carpet was above the waves, just circling. If only he could get up to the open air again, he was sure the beautiful rug would be there waiting for him. . . .

Piri's sphere weighed heavily in her pouch at his chest. He could sense her agitation and knew the nymph djinni was aware of their danger. Sharif remembered how he had once used Piri's dazzling glow to drive back the light-sensitive merlons who tried to invade Elantya by coming up through undersea tunnels.

Orpheon leered with delight as Blackfrill held Gedup in one hand and drew back his other hand, ready to thrust with the sharp staff—

Sharif could think of no other way to prevent this, and he had no time for second thoughts. He yanked out Piri's egg-sphere and shouted to his comrades, purposely using the

Elantyan language. "Friends, cover your eyes!" He hoped the merlons near him couldn't understand as he raised the crystal sphere toward Blackfrill. "Shine, Piri! *Shine!*"

He squeezed his eyes shut as the nymph djinni went nova in his hand. A blaze of blinding white light dazzled like a thousand fireworks. The surging burst was enough to make Blackfrill recoil, dropping both the teaching staff and the hapless anemonite.

The flash caused even Orpheon to cry out and back away. The merlon warriors scattered, momentarily reeling and disoriented. Seizing his chance, Sharif stuffed Piri into her pouch, grabbed Gedup, and stroked with all his might toward the surface. "Tiaret, Lyssandra — follow me!"

Holding the scientist under his arm, he unclasped his heavy seashell belt, dropped it, and swam with all of his strength. The new gill slits in his neck pumped water through his neck into his lungs. He had not planned this very well, but he had no other choice. He'd needed to act instantly or watch the innocent anemonite be slaughtered. Below him, though surprised by the unexpected move, Tiaret and Lyssandra opened their eyes, took off their belts, and began to stroke after him. Piri's sphere dimmed and grew faint as they rushed upward. The little djinni was obviously exhausted.

Knowing he had to abandon the other anemonites, and leave Vic and Gwen behind in the merlon city, Sharif silently vowed to come back and bring help from Elantya. Kicking and stroking, he thought of his flying city of Irrakesh, the great uprooted metropolis that drifted along with the winds and clouds above his desert world. This was like taking a glider up into high drafts, but much more than that — this was life or death!

Beneath them, Sharif caught a glimpse of dark shapes, flashing torpedolike shadows that raced upward in pursuit. Sharks! The merlon guards were also coming after them, furious but still half-blinded.

Sharif tried to swim faster with the anemonite under his arm. Tiaret was a strong young woman, but Lyssandra was a better swimmer. The two caught up with Sharif, stroking frantically.

But it wasn't enough. Not even halfway to the surface and blessed sunlight and open air, he could already see that they would never make it.

The first shark shot past him like a torpedo, then circled and came back, flashing its rows of sharp teeth. A second shark rammed Sharif aside with its rough sandpapery nose. Sharif nearly lost his grip on Gedup. Tiaret and Lyssandra clustered close to him and turned back to back for mutual defense, facing outward, ready for their last stand. Inside her sphere, Piri remained weak and drained; the blast of light had used most of her energy.

Blackfrill was the first merlon to reach them, brandishing Tiaret's staff. Sharif saw that the scales on the merlon general's face and chest were now slightly discolored, possibly a consequence of the brilliant djinni flash. Sharif was sure that now the enraged merlon would use the sharp teaching staff to impale him instead of the anemonite.

"It was a brave attempt," Tiaret said.

He turned to give his two companions a sad look. "I had to try."

Orpheon finally caught up with the escapees. He gave the three companions a twisted smile that frightened Sharif even more than Blackfrill's obvious anger. "That was very foolish." He drew a glistening, curved knife from a sheath at his waist. "But in a way, I am pleased. We no longer need to sacrifice one of the anemonite geniuses to make our point. You have given me an idea."

The knife slashed toward Sharif's chest. Orpheon slit open Piri's mesh bag, snatched the glowing crystal sphere, and said, "A much better idea."

THEY WERE ALL DRAGGED back to the cracked landscape of Lavaja Canyon. Blackfrill, the sharks, and the merlon guards had also herded all of the anemonites close to the lavaja cracks so that they could watch.

Sharif knew that whatever was about to happen would be far worse than a day of harsh slave labor in and around the glowing fissures. Gedup was safely back with the other anemonites, but Orpheon still gripped the crystal djinni sphere. Sharif wished he could hold the ball to comfort Piri. She had indeed given her all, expended more power in the single escape attempt than he had ever seen her use. Piri was just a nymph, very young for a djinni, and he couldn't protect her. He had failed them all.

Three merlons put the seashell belts back on the apprentices, while several guards held weapons at the ready, as if daring the three companions to try something so that they would have reason to retaliate with force.

"I should have confiscated this from you, spoiled prince, when we first took you and your companions under water," Orpheon said. "I remember how often in Elantya you flaunted your noble breeding, showed off your fancy flying carpet, and boasted that no one else had a young djinni like this one. And now it seems that *I* have her."

"Piri will not follow your commands!"

"I know. But she can serve a higher purpose."

Sharif remembered all the times Ven Rubicas's surly assistant had been annoyed with them, but neither Sharif nor the others had ever guessed how deep the man's hatred went.

The armored sea turtles and the weak-looking merlon workers had been rounded up from the blazing fissures. Molten lavaja bubbled up, heating the water as the underwater landscape continued to churn and reshape itself. Lavaja flowed to the surface, like blood oozing from a cracked scab.

"Your nymph djinni possesses an unusual magic." Orpheon frowned down at the glowing red sphere, inside of which Piri shook her tiny fist at him in anger. "It is insignificant, of course, compared to the powerful magic of the lavaja. Together they might create an interesting synergy. I think it far more likely, however, that the searing magical fire will utterly destroy her."

Without another word, Orpheon tossed the crystal djinni sphere at the nearest blazing fissure. Piri dropped toward the bubbling cauldron of incandescent melted crystal.

Sharif's heart lurched. "No!" He lunged, but the merlon

guards held him back. One jabbed him with his spear, making a shallow cut along Sharif's side, but he didn't feel the pain. "Piri!"

The eggsphere seemed to fall in slow motion. Sharif tried to reach out to her. The crystal walls of her tiny ball would never protect her from the magical inferno. The dazzling, silvery orange glow of the lavaja reflected off the crystal ball, making it flash like a tiny sun.

He caught one last glimpse of the djinni pounding the walls of her sphere before plunging into the furious heat. Piri sank into the dazzling lavaja that quickly engulfed her eggsphere.

Had Sharif been on dry ground he would have collapsed. As it was, here in the hot, foul-tasting water, he went limp and drifted like a dead man. "Oh, Piri," he kept saying. "Oh, Piri."

The ocean water washed away his tears. He stared at the fiery cracks until his eyes burned. Tiaret and Lyssandra held him up, trying to give him strength. For what seemed like an eternity, he watched the bubbling surface of molten magic, but his beloved nymph djinni did not reappear.

14

FOR THE REST OF the day, long after their three friends had been taken away by Orpheon, Vic seethed over Azric's nonchalance. The dark sage didn't seem to think Gwen should be bothered by his part in the death of her parents, or how Vic's mother had fled in hopes of protecting her family from Azric. Vic had already decided to hate him, whether or not he and Gwen were the supposed "children of prophecy" who could break open the long-sealed crystal doors to the worlds where Azric's immortal armies had been trapped.

The ageless wizard left the implied threat to Sharif, Lyssandra, and Tiaret hanging as he guided the cousins to a tall structure, where the immortal tyrant intended to "enlighten" them.

"This is just plain creepy," Vic said, swimming beside Gwen.

"There's plenty of creepy stuff to choose from," she shot

back. "One, there's a whole barbarian civilization down here. Two, at this depth and temperature, we should all be getting hypothermia. Three, we're *breathing* water. Water has less oxygen in it than air, you know, so in theory human lungs shouldn't be able to absorb enough oxygen from the water to —"

Vic was exasperated. "It's magic, Doc. Live with it. Anyway, I'm not talking about getting cold or breathing under water." He glanced back at the merlon guards following them, making sure they went where Azric commanded. "It's the *prophecy* stuff. You've been trying to brush it off ever since we got here, pretending it applied to somebody else. These people really think you and I have some spectacular destiny."

Swimming ahead of them, Azric led the way into the highest tower in the spectacular merlon city. He glided through a scalloped window-doorway, or "windoor," as Vic instantly dubbed it, into the uppermost room, as broad and high as Rubicas's main experimental chamber. The tower's exterior was made of ornate coral and the interior was lined with glossy mother-of-pearl. Strategically placed windoors made it seem as if the ocean outside, teeming with fish and merlons, might be some sort of vast never-ending aquarium. At several points along the iridescent walls, tapestries rippled upward from the floor, woven from several colors of living seaweed, as well as nova starfish, bits of shell, and baby sea anemones.

Vic and Gwen looked around in wonder. "Wait here. I must make preparations," Azric said. He stationed merlon guards at each scalloped windoor and left.

When they were alone again, however briefly, Vic leaned toward his cousin and spoke in a quiet voice. "Let me lay it out for you, Doc. Right from the beginning you tried to convince yourself that our being in Elantya was some sort of colossal stroke of bad luck and that we didn't belong here. Then, when we talked to Dad through that crystal window thing we opened up, we learned that he was actually *trying* to take us to Elantya in the first place, that our moms thought we'd be safer here. Admit it, we both always knew there was something . . . unearthly about them. Our mothers weren't just really smart housewives who happened to teach us kids some advanced form of martial arts that nobody on Earth had ever heard of before."

Gwen's violet eyes dodged his earnest gaze. "I never thought our moms were just housewives."

Vic gave a burbling sigh. Leave it to his cousin to pick one thing in his explanation that she disagreed with and focus on that. Couldn't she see what was right in front of her face?

"Snap out of it, Doc! Even after we found out that we were both Keys and that we have a synergy with Sharif, Lyssandra, and Tiaret like nothing that's been seen in Elantya for thousands of years — even then you refused to believe the prophecies have anything to do with us. But Dad told us what was in Mom's letter, and there's no doubt she thought the two of us were special, and in danger. Your parents *died* trying to keep us safe from this guy." He pulled out his trump card now. "Face it, if Azric — a powerful, ancient sage — went to all this trouble to kidnap *us* and believes we're the children of the prophecy, then it's probably true."

"But he tried to kill me at Ocean Kingdoms."

Vic nudged aside one of the billowy colorful tapestries rising in front of the chamber wall. "I don't think so. He said it was a test. And by the time he kidnapped us, he knew full well who we were. Remember, Azric's had five thousand years to study the prophecies — he didn't come after us because of some clerical error. He knew what he was doing."

"Prophecies can't be understood with logic. They're more like dreams or fairy tales — only more confusing." Gwen seemed to be grasping at straws. "Anyway, none of this makes sense. You and I are completely normal. Don't you think if we were supposed to fulfill some sort of ancient prophecy we'd *know* somehow, we'd feel it?"

"We're both smart," Vic pointed out, "and we're really good swimmers and problem solvers."

Gwen shook her head. "But that doesn't make us legends. We're still just normal teenagers. We fight, we make mistakes, we bleed. . . ." The last few words came out in a strangled voice.

"I don't *want* to be special," Gwen continued in a choking hiccup. "I don't want to fulfill prophecies. I don't want to believe my parents had to die to save me from an evil wizard." Her face worked strangely, and Vic could tell she was crying, even though no tears could flow down her face underwater. Gwen buried her face in her hands.

Vic put an awkward arm around her and felt his own throat constrict with emotion. He took a deep breath of water. In a husky voice, he said, "I'm sorry, Doc, but I've always hoped for more wonder in my life. In a weird way we each got what we wanted. You, uh, always wanted to be an oceanographer or marine biologist. Me? I always wished for mystery and strangeness and adventures. Still, I never expected anything like this."

"In other words, be careful what you wish for?"

"Yup. I know you wish we were born ordinary," Vic went on. "Maybe our parents even wished *they* were just ordinary, but they weren't."

Gwen's violet eyes flashed with denial. "Our fathers weren't unusual."

Vic sighed. "I'm not so sure anymore. Some of the things Dad has said and some of the stuff in my mom's letter make me wonder now." He swam over to nearest windoor and poked his head out. He wondered where Azric had gone but was not anxious to have the dark sage return. Two of the merlon warriors swimming guard outside turned toward Vic and thrust intimidating undersea weapons at him, encouraging him to stay inside the chamber. He obliged.

Gwen nibbled at the corner of her lower lip, and her eyes became unfocused as she reviewed everything he had said. "I guess sometimes people who seem perfectly normal find themselves in unusual situations and end up doing extraordinary things because they have to. And that's why there are legends about them."

"Or prophecies," Vic added.

"Or prophecies. All right, I surrender. Let's proceed on the assumption that you and I are stuck doing extraordinary things, even though I feel normal and want to be ordinary. We can't just sit around waiting for other people."

"To rescue us?" Vic asked.

"For starters, yes. We can't assume anybody will be able to find us. And it's not just us, but Sharif, Lyssandra, and Tiaret. I don't trust Orpheon."

"Join the club," Vic said. "So we start looking for a way to escape?"

The two of them drifted away from the scalloped windoor and the merlon guards outside. They hovered next to another slimy tapestry, speaking in hushed voices. "We've got to be smart about this, Taz. Our only advantage is that Azric thinks you and I are valuable to him. If we're ever going to get a chance to escape, we have to let him think we're so scared that we'll go along with whatever he tells us to do."

Vic gave a grim smile. "Well, that scared part shouldn't be too hard."

"That means we've got to pay attention to everything. No more Dr. Distracto —"

Just then, something in the water changed, a slight temperature fluctuation or current on their skin. Gwen cut off her words quickly and looked around. Was there a different smell perhaps? Vic wondered if he could even smell underwater at all. Yes, sort of. His sense of smell seemed linked to the taste of the water passing through his new gills, but he wasn't quite sure how to interpret the data that came in. In any case, he sensed the guards snap to attention, and he knew that Azric had returned.

Gwen and Vic turned to face the dark sage as he entered. Azric swam back through the windoor, dragging an amazing creature behind him by a thick chain.

The closest Vic had ever come to seeing anything like the thing was in one of his Japanese anime cartoons, though Gwen was probably trying to identify the genus and species. It had a conical body core and six slender tentacles, each about as big around as Vic's index finger. Attached to the top of the body core by a sort of fleshy collar was a glowing green eye that could rotate to see in every direction. Light and heat radiated from the strange squidlike creature as it rippled through colors ranging from deep red to orange to pale yellow.

Vic's stomach clenched, and his natural inclination was to hide his fear behind a cocky mask of bravado, but he had to remind himself to *look* frightened, as he and Gwen had just decided. It wasn't hard to allow himself a shudder. "What is it with these people and tentacles?"

Merlon warriors swam in through the scalloped windoors. One of them carried a bloated round sack made of a leathery material. The warrior wrestled the heavy bag open to reveal a massive spiny sea urchin. In ominous silence, Azric nodded to the guards, who lunged toward the cousins, grabbing them by the shoulders and arms.

"You could just tell us what you want us to do," Gwen said in her let's-be-reasonable tone. "We don't really need all these guards, do we?"

Azric plucked a foot-long spine from the coral-colored sea urchin, which cringed. Concentrating deeply and not explaining a thing, the dark sage pressed the raw end of the thorn against the belly of the squid-thing, which released a squirt of deep purple liquid that filled the hollow spine. A cloud of residual inky color drifted in the water around it. Then, with a smile of anticipation, Azric approached the twin cousins.

Before they could squirm away or ask questions, the dark sage snatched Gwen's hand, twisting it to expose the pale underside of her forearm. She tried to yank her arm free, but the merlon warriors held her in place.

Vic yelled, "Leave her alone! What are you doing?"

Azric paid no heed. With the quill, he punctured the skin on Gwen's wrist. Vic had no need to fake his terror, and neither did Gwen. Her eyes went wide and her body stiffened, making Vic wonder what was in the squid ink. Acid? Poison? Gwen bit her lower lip until her teeth drew blood.

"This might hurt a little bit," Azric said. "Or a lot."

He raised the sea-urchin spine again and made another puncture beside the first one. This time Gwen couldn't help herself. She cried out. Azric repeated the process again and again. Ribbons of blood fluttered from Gwen's wrist, mingling with ink from the urchin's spine. She tried to thrash away from her tormentor.

In the grip of uncontrollable fury, Vic shouted at Azric and the merlons while his cousin screamed. When the pain was too much for Gwen, she went limp, floating in the merlons' grasp. The ink left a stain on her wrist in a curious pattern. It took a while, but Vic finally saw what Azric had done. "A tattoo?"

Putting the finishing touches on it, Azric gave a satisfied nod. "Yes, and quite painful, I assure you. The fire squid feeds in Lavaja Canyon around the volcanic vents. The ink burns with a magical heat all its own. Sadly, I have no choice but to use force, since I cannot be certain of your cooperation."

Next, Azric reached for Vic's arm.

Vic's attempts to break free were no more successful than Gwen's had been. The wizard hummed to himself as he pressed the urchin spine to Vic's wrist. It was a long, long time before the young man passed out.

15

PIRI WAS DEAD.

Gone.

Forever.

In the mind of Ali el Sharif, in his heart and at the core of his physical being, anger warred with sorrow and loneliness. His grief threatened to bring him to his knees, though Lyssandra and Tiaret were by his side. Fury, however, could keep him on his feet and give him strength to fight. He couldn't tear his eyes from the hot, oozing fissure where the djinni sphere had vanished. Heat. Blazing magical heat. Consciously, Sharif used the vision to add fuel to the bonfire of his anger.

Worst of all was Orpheon's expression of cruel pleasure as he watched the effect of his actions on the prince from Irrakesh.

The anemonites quivered as if they'd been beaten. Gedup,

the jellyfish-brain who would have been killed in Piri's stead, was dismayed and docile.

"I hope that gave you all the encouragement you need," Orpheon announced, "as well as a bit of entertainment." He and Blackfrill laughed together.

Merlon warriors rounded up the anemonites and prepared to drive them back to the reefs where they would return to their work with greater fear and, presumably, better results. Still tethered by their ankles, the other aquatic slaves at the edges of the blazing fissures blinked solemn eyes and said nothing.

Sharif still floated, stunned but reaching a boiling point of madness. Sensing the danger that Sharif might do something violent and foolish, without regard for his own safety or the lives of his friends, Orpheon ordered merlon warriors to bind the young man's wrists and ankles with strips of tough doolya seaweed.

Azric's henchman seemed to want nothing less than to leave Sharif completely broken. "Today, Prince, you have learned that any mistake you make will bring punishment for others." He made a mock sad face. "Alas, your father learned the lesson too late to save your brother. Perhaps the loss of your dear little nymph djinni will teach you your place."

Though he was tied, Sharif lunged at Orpheon. He knew it was a futile gesture, but he didn't care. He felt a fierce satisfaction when his head connected with Orpheon's belly, and he heard the man grunt. Blackfrill moved swiftly, grabbing Sharif by the hair and yanking him away.

Orpheon glowered as he tried to recover his composure.

"Have a care, Prince — or I will give you stronger demonstration. You and your two friends here are completely expendable. Azric has already said so."

These words lashed Sharif like a whip across the face. Poor Piri had not deserved to be incinerated just because of Sharif's ill-considered escape attempt. What if Orpheon decided to hurt Tiaret or Lyssandra next?

Before Sharif could concede, or the traitorous assistant could make good on his threat, Blackfrill pointed toward a large shape moving in the open water beyond the lavaja cracks. Everyone turned to look at the graceful flying shape, large and flat, that glided through the water with gentle undulating movements.

Sharif's heart leapt, sure that it must be his flying carpet, responding to his summons after all! He struggled against his bindings. Both Lyssandra and Tiaret also saw it and couldn't believe their eyes.

"A great jhanta!" Blackfrill said. "Very rare — and very useful. I command you to capture it." He nodded to six of his merlon warriors, all of whom carried spears, hooks, nets, and other weapons they used on slaves. "Go! I want the creature alive . . . though a few injuries may be acceptable."

As the merlons streaked off, Sharif saw to his dismay that his imagination had shown him only what he wanted to see. This was not a flying carpet at all, but a flat creature with broad wing-fins, large enough to carry riders or heavy cargo.

The mantalike creature reacted to the oncoming merlons, only by fluttering its wing-fins. It didn't seem to realize its danger. Sharif wanted to shout a warning, but the jhanta would not understand. The merlon warriors spread out, flanking it, readying their hooks and tridents and nets.

The jhanta stroked and picked up speed. It was completely unprepared for the barbed hook that sailed through the water and snagged on one of its tough wings. The creature thrashed and yanked backward, setting the hook deeper as a merlon pulled on the cord. More warriors closed in, throwing a net in front of the jhanta's snub head.

In its violent struggle, a merlon was knocked loose to twirl through the water. The rest of the aquatic warriors piled on, weighing down the jhanta. A second wicked barb was set in the other wing-fin, and the captors quickly immobilized the creature. Pulling on the lines and hooks, they dragged it down to the sea floor, where they anchored the ropes to heavy rocks.

Sharif, torn by the failure of his flying carpet and devastated by the loss of Piri, felt a startling connection to the graceful yet helpless creature.

Orpheon was jubilant. "This bodes well for our success. We now have several new workers to help us in our mission to destroy Elantya."

16

WHEN GWEN GROGGILY AWAKENED from the painful tattooing process, she found that Azric was no longer with them. In fact, she was no longer in the tower chamber, but being towed along by a cord tied to her wrists and hooked through a heavy ring in a shark's dorsal fin.

Her arms and shoulders ached from being pulled through the water, but it was not enough to dull the fierce throbbing from her marked — poisoned? — wrist. She turned her head, disoriented and queasy, unable to get her bearings.

Her stomach gave a strange lurch when she realized she couldn't see the ocean floor, the buildings of the merlon city, any reefs or upcroppings, the surface of the water, seaweed. Without any landmarks, she had no way of telling which direction was up or down. Even the merlon guards around her faced every which direction, making it impossible for Gwen to get her bearings. Her stomach heaved and churned as her mind rebelled, and Gwen wished that she had a bit of shinqroot to chew on to calm her queasiness.

Finally, beside her she saw Vic also being towed along by a shark. He stirred, still regaining consciousness from the ordeal in the tower. She wondered what the marks on her wrist meant — were they symbols of ownership, a method of controlling captives, or some sort of runes?

When Vic woke up and looked around, he groaned. The sharks swam swiftly, and they must already have covered a great distance from the merlon city. "Sheesh, now I know what a balloon feels like on the end of a string," he said. Gwen could have sworn that if the two of them hadn't been in great pain and held captive by evil merlons and a sinister dark sage, her cousin would have been enjoying this.

"How's your wrist?" he asked. "Mine feels like it's been through a meat grinder."

Gwen gave him a faint smile. "I think someone poured acid on mine."

Their journey continued for what seemed like hours, past swirling schools of fish, distant merlon settlements, and colorful coral reefs that went by like blurry pictures taken through the window of a speeding car.

More than once, Vic demanded, "Where are you taking us?" but the merlon guards ignored him. When at last they reached an underwater seaweed forest, Azric was there already, waiting.

The merlon guards unclipped the rings from the sharks' fins and let the predators swim away. Gripping the seaweed ropes, the warriors allowed the cousins enough play that they could move a little, but not enough to reach Azric.

The immortal wizard's mismatched eyes gave the two cousins a sad, apologetic look. "I wish I could release you, I really do. From your bonds, I mean. But there are certain things one simply cannot leave to chance. Your new tattoos, for example, and the lesson I am about to teach." He folded his hands, with his index fingers extended and pressed together in a steeple. "If I find you to be obedient, we may be able to dispense with the restraints in future lessons."

Gwen and Vic exchanged a meaningful look. Both knew that if they hoped to escape, they needed to play along and convince the dark sage that he had their full cooperation, without actually helping Azric with any of his plans.

Azric seemed both eager and pleased. "Now, then, you two do know that you are Keys, don't you?"

Gwen said, "All students at the Citadel get tested."

"Yup, and we sure lit up the crystals," Vic added. "But you knew that already, or you wouldn't have been so keen to kidnap us."

"True, true," Azric went on. "But I believe that you both inherited a rare ability from your mothers, an ability possessed by only one in ten thousand Keys.

"You two are Master Keys, able to open *any* crystal door to *any* world that was not sealed in the Great Closure," Azric continued, as if he were revealing a great secret. Curious in spite of themselves, the twin cousins listened intently. Vic cocked an eyebrow at Gwen with a look that said, *Now* this *is interesting.*

"Impressive enough, certainly, but there's more." Azric smiled at them like a benevolent teacher. "If the prophesy is correct, you two are greater than Keys, greater even than Master Keys. Like your mothers, you can be *seal breakers.* They wore xyridium medallions exactly like yours — though alas, the charms are useless in the hands of anyone who doesn't have the potential."

Fingering the medallions that hung around their necks — the only things they wore, aside from their brevis — Gwen and Vic exchanged a curious glance.

"There's a prophecy that goes,

Brothers twin and sisters twain,
  Ancient lines of blood entwine,
To begin the new campaign,
  Sundered worlds to realign.

"I now believe that the 'entwined blood' refers to the two of you. And that realigning sundered — or sealed off — worlds is your true purpose." The twin cousins exchanged uneasy glances as Azric continued. "You have the power, Vic and Gwen, to reopen the crystal doors to a universe of worlds that were foolishly closed off ages ago."

"In other words, you think we can force open the doors so that your evil armies can come swarming through," Gwen said.

Azric seemed infinitely patient. "I mean, you could help *rescue* entire worlds, entire civilizations that have been quarantined for far too long. Think of all those poor worlds isolated in the Great Closure and never able to visit other places, like Elantya. Surely they don't deserve to be locked away from all the benefits of knowledge and culture that other worlds share through the crystal doors? Earth was one of the worlds sealed off in the Great Closure, you know. Think of how much your own people could have benefited. There aren't any 'evil armies' waiting there to swarm through."

"All right, I'll concede the point . . . for now," Gwen said, careful not to lay it on too thick.

"So if Earth was blocked off, then our mothers must have forced open the crystal door because they're seal breakers?" Vic mused. "But how did *you* get there, unless you're a seal breaker yourself?"

"Ah, such intelligence and curiosity! I can see I wasn't wrong about you two." He smiled warmly again. "I was not far from your mothers when they broke the seal to Earth's door, hoping I would not think to search for them in a sealed world. I had planned to slip through the door behind them before it closed, but I was too late. Fortunately for me, once the seal was broken any Master Key could open the door to Earth again. So, I found a Master Key and used all of my . . . persuasive skills to convince her to open it. By the time she did, why, the poor woman was of little use to me anymore, so after we passed through to Earth I left her in the water by the crystal door. It was a place on Earth you call the Yucatan. Very wild and mysterious."

Gwen felt outrage building in her. "You left a Master Key to drown out in the middle of nowhere?"

Azric gave an elegant shrug as if he hadn't bothered to consider the question. "I suppose so. Or perhaps she managed to summon help in some way or swim to shore, or reopen the door, go through it, and flag down a ship. We'll never know, will we? Not worth losing sleep over." Dismissing the thought as if it were irrelevant, he continued. "By the time I got through that door, your mothers were long gone, but I knew they were stuck on Earth. Breaking open a seal in such a way saps all of a seal-breaker's energy for several years. Therefore, I knew your mothers would be vulnerable to my persuasive abilities, if only I could find them. I had quite a time locating your mothers again. It took years of research and — well, you know the rest of the story."

"How did you get back here to Elantya?" Gwen interrupted. "Did you find another Key?"

"Well, naturally I had to find another Key. I, alas, am not a Key of any sort. But as you've surely guessed by now, any major city in any world is teeming with them. There could be dozens, even if they don't know it. And the one I found was far more easily persuaded than the Master Key who let me in."

"Do you know if my mother is alive?" Vic blurted. "Do you know where she is?"

Azric looked surprised, then pleased. "I do indeed have that information. If you want to learn those things from me, however, you will have to earn my trust. Which brings us again to the topic of our lesson. I need you to open a door or two for me, just simple ones at first."

"I think you're getting ahead of yourself, Azric," Vic said. "We don't know how to open *any* crystal doors."

"That is what I intend to teach you today. The first thing." He motioned to the merlon warriors to follow him and swam straight upward through the shadowy tangles of doolya toward the light high above. Vic's and Gwen's guards followed, dragging the cousins along by the ropes tied to their aching arms.

When they broke the surface, Gwen tried to breathe air, but the water in her lungs would not allow it, so she and Vic were forced to bob with their heads barely above the water and continue to breathe through the gills in their necks. The guards removed Gwen and Vic's seaweed chains, so that they could move freely.

Using his magic, Azric rose to hover just above the gentle waves, as if he were standing on the water. He threw his head back and swept a hand in an intricate gesture through the air, leaving behind a glowing vapor trail that formed curious symbols. Looking directly into the airborne rune, the dark sage spoke a series of harsh, guttural syllables that made Gwen want to cringe in fear and disgust. She and Vic found themselves miraculously rising from the waves to hover above the water, as Azric himself had.

Vic went into a fit of coughing. Gwen desperately wanted a deep breath of water through her gill slits, but she was in the air now. Spewing water from her lungs, she coughed several times and willed herself to draw a deep breath of insubstantial-feeling air.

Vic finally cleared his lungs of water and croaked, "So, uh, what brings us out here on the open water?" Gwen could tell he was trying to sound reasonable and cooperative, but his voice shook slightly. "Are we planning to blow something up?"

Azric shook his head in amazement. "Can you not feel it? Where we are?"

Gwen closed her eyes for a moment and concentrated, surprised that she could indeed sense something, a faint tingle that started between her shoulder blades and ran down both arms to the wrists.

Vic squirmed in the air. "Sheesh, the hair on the back of my neck and my arms is starting to stand up. You aren't going to strike us with lightning or anything, are you?"

Azric gave a knowing smile. "That tingle means that you are close to the crystal door that leads to your homeworld, and today you will open that door. Merely as practice, mind you. I have no need to go back to Earth." He paused to let the implications sink in. "There's no question you'd be reluctant to assist me. I know your reservations. But this crystal door leads back to your home — wouldn't it be valuable to know how to open it?"

Though they had already decided to pretend to cooperate, Gwen could not keep the excitement from her face. She couldn't deny the value in having that kind of knowledge, even if it did come from Azric.

"I see you agree. Now then, look at the underside of your wrists, at the symbol closest to your hand." Hanging in the air, she and Vic did as they were told. "Now look away from the symbol and repeat after me." Azric intoned a series of strange syllables in an unfamiliar language. His words sounded for all the world to Gwen like "take butter off Queequeg's unctuous duckling" — that was as close as her mind could come to grasping the sounds, many of which didn't even exist in the English or Elantyan languages.

Gwen hesitated and glanced at Vic. They had agreed to

cooperate — up to a point — in order to gain Azric's trust, but uncertainty flooded her mind. In the space of a few heartbeats, she weighed the pros and cons. First, what if this was a trick, a destructive spell rather than just opening a door to Earth? Second, since his ultimate intentions were evil, did they dare do what he asked, no matter what? Third, Lyssandra, Tiaret, and Sharif were being held hostage; would Azric follow through on his threat to kill them if Vic and Gwen resisted? Fourth, pretending to cooperate might give them their only chance to get away, and Elantya could be destroyed if the friends didn't manage to warn them. Fifth, she and Vic needed to learn how to open crystal doors, even if they never intended to break a seal.

Instinct told her that, at least in this instance, Azric was telling the truth: This was the door to Earth, and he wanted them to open it simply for the practice. So, they both did their best to repeat the syllables Azric had spoken.

The dark sage was obviously not impressed. He took a deep breath and started again at the beginning, this time speaking only one syllable at a time. He made them repeat the first sounds again and again until he was completely satisfied with their pronunciation and intonation. He did the same thing with the next syllables, and when they had mastered those, strung the sounds together. Then a third batch of syllables, and so on.

How strange, Gwen thought, that in those few syllables it seemed like there was more to remember than there had been when she had memorized Lady Macbeth's soliloquy for Mr. Doherty's English class last year.

Gwen and Vic concentrated fiercely and did as Azric told

them. To their surprise, the dark sage seemed to have a great deal of patience. Maybe it came from having five thousand years of perspective, Gwen thought.

When one of them bumbled in learning a syllable, or when Vic intentionally pronounced something incorrectly, Azric simply flicked his finger, which dropped the cousins into the water. There, they would choke and sputter, trying to breathe either water or air. Another finger flick from Azric hauled them back out of the water, where they would drip and cough and retch — and start all over. It was a slow and painful process, but eventually the twin cousins learned the entire phrase, perfectly.

"Now you, Vic — look only at that first symbol on your wrist and recite what I have taught you."

Vic obviously knew better than to argue, and he recited the spell with admirable enunciation and inflection. The effect was instantaneous, eliciting a gasp from both Gwen and Vic as a huge bright backdrop appeared behind Azric in the shape of a half-arch. Glittering, vaguely geometric shapes swirled in transparent designs within the semicircle. It looked as if someone were throwing handfuls of confetti made of glass shards.

Vic shook his head in amazement. "I think somebody spilled glitter in the Stargate."

Breathless, Gwen said, "It's so . . . is that —"

"— the crystal door to Earth?" Azric asked. "Yes. Fitting, isn't it? I trust you can now see how useful this skill could be. Your own mothers broke the seal. Now Vic has opened it. And you, Gwen, will be the next."

17

THAT EVENING, THE FIVE apprentices were reunited in the tower room where Gwen and Vic had received their tattoos. All but one of the windoors had been blocked with a heavy mesh of woven doolya strands. The merlon guards carried the exhausted cousins through the only open windoor — then stationed themselves outside it to swim guard.

They were glad to see their three companions unharmed, but before Gwen or Vic could express their joy, they sensed that something terrible had happened. Sharif floated in place, staring at the floor in abject misery.

Vic looked back and forth. "What is it? What's wrong?"

"We bring sad news," Lyssandra said.

Sharif looked up, and his voice was heavy. "Orpheon murdered Piri. It was my fault." The prince turned his face away and hunched over in silent agony. It seemed to Vic as if he had barely had time to blink before Lyssandra, Gwen, and Tiaret were all gathered around the grieving young man, putting their arms around him and murmuring words of comfort.

Wanting to know the answers, but not willing to press his grieving friend, Vic joined the circle. "Whatever happened, Sharif, you can't blame yourself for Orpheon's evil." Scanning the faces around him, he noticed that Tiaret appeared grim and somber, and Lyssandra's cobalt blue eyes looked as if they might be crying.

"Can you tell us what happened?" Gwen asked.

Sharif's throat worked with emotion, and then, in a halting voice, he told his story. As he relived the experience, the boy from Irrakesh grew more and more agitated. Vic found his own outrage building just to hear what had happened, and he questioned his decision to cooperate with Azric. He had every reason to hate both of the dark sages.

Cutting off the discussions, merlon servants brought in a meal of cooked fish and seaweed, perhaps roasted over a thermal vent, along with shell cups filled with a viscous fluid the color of eel skin. To everyone's surprise, the thick silvery liquid did not mix with the ocean water, but stayed in the cups until they tilted them up to drink. Whatever it was, it had a pleasant sweet-sour taste. When the merlons left again, the friends ate and drank, and resumed their conversation. Though Sharif couldn't have had much of an appetite, he forced himself to eat.

"We must escape and find a way to destroy these murderers before they destroy Elantya," Sharif concluded. "Piri's death must be avenged."

The cousins briefly filled the others in on what they had learned. Even though everyone knew that the cousins had been the object of the merlons' kidnapping scheme, Vic was uncomfortable explaining why, and that Azric had threatened their friends to ensure Vic's and Gwen's compliance.

Gwen said in an intentionally loud voice, in case the guards were eavesdropping, "It's been a painful day. We should all get some sleep." Then she whispered directly to her friends, "If we pretend to sleep, maybe they'll leave us alone."

Outside, glowfish lights were covered, so that the sea became as dark as the night sky. In order to sleep, the friends found that they could tether themselves to rings on the floor with thin doolya cords, as they had seen other merlons do to keep themselves from being moved about by currents.

Slowly and quietly, Tiaret went to the main scalloped windoor, and looked out. She pointed at the opening, pantomimed guards and sleep, and stationed herself by the windoor to keep watch. The companions clustered close together, speaking in hushed, conspiratorial voices.

"It might take us a while to observe our surroundings and plan a way to escape. Did we learn anything today that might help us?" Gwen asked.

"You two discovered that we can breathe both in the water and out of it," Tiaret said in a low voice. "That might be valuable information."

Lyssandra pursed her lips. "And we learned that Orpheon and the merlons are pitiless and cruel."

"Yup," Vic said, "Azric too. In a way, he's even scarier

because he talks about murder like it's just *unfortunate*—you know, like stubbing your toe or something."

"Whereas Orpheon enjoys his cruelty," Sharif said.

Vic nodded. What could he say to console a friend who had experienced such brutality and loss? "I'm sorry." It sounded so weak and unhelpful. He was no good at this sort of thing. How could he say anything comforting to Sharif, when he was still in shock himself? If Orpheon could so easily dispose of Piri, he wouldn't balk at killing Sharif or Lyssandra or Tiaret, if Gwen and Vic disappointed Azric.

"Piri's light was beautiful," Tiaret said with a surprising catch in her voice. "I will honor her memory in the Great Epic."

Lyssandra gave Sharif a little smile. "Yes, watching her always cheered me up, even after I had bad dreams."

"We're all going to miss Piri," Gwen said softly.

Vic tried hard to sound optimistic. "We'll make sure Orpheon pays for what he did. Vengeance first, escape later. Or the other way around, maybe. We need to use any advantage we find."

"Okay," Gwen said. "One advantage is that we're all together, and they took off our restraints. If we can keep them from tying us up again, we'll have a better chance when the time is right."

"Maybe Aquaman will show up to rescue us." Vic rubbed at the raw place on his right wrist where the seaweed rope had chafed. "On the other hand, we can't outswim a bunch of merlons or their pet sharks."

"Perhaps we could find a helpful spell scroll?" Lyssandra suggested.

"I don't think they use spell scrolls down here," Gwen said.

"The merlons use molten aja to work strong magic," Tiaret pointed out. "We have never seen a scroll in this place."

"Yes, merlon magic works differently from Elantyan magic," Lyssandra agreed.

Vic scratched his nose; his loose dark hair floated around his face. "We'll just have to make our plan based on what we know and on our skills. Each day, we've got to learn what we can and incorporate it into our strategy as we go."

"And we must remain alert for opportunities," Tiaret said. "Any opportunities."

18

THE NEXT MORNING AFTER the glowfish were uncovered, Vic noticed that the merlons began to treat the five friends differently. They were no longer just captives, but slaves and playthings, as well. After spending a restless night in the submerged tower prison, Vic was separated from his companions, including Gwen.

The new female merlon general, Goldskin, seized Tiaret and Gwen for what she called a "fighting practice." A pair of merlon guards dragged Lyssandra away, saying that she was needed to attend to the anemonite scientists. Blackfrill, brandishing the teaching staff stolen from Tiaret, took Sharif to labor at the lavaja cracks.

Which left Vic alone with Azric. Cringing at the smile on the dark sage's youthful face, Vic crossed his arms over his chest as the others were taken in separate directions. "If you hurt my friends, I'll never help you."

"Dear boy," Azric answered mildly, "who said anything about hurting them? We intend to expand their horizons, make them more well-rounded."

"Yup. I've heard that sort of speech before. But the strategy to separate us is obvious — divide now, conquer later."

"Why, we only separate you for your own protection. I fear that if you are all together you might be tempted to . . . do something unwise. Bear in mind that I really need only one seal-breaker, whether it be Gwen or *you.* The two of you together are more useful, of course, but it would be unwise to try my patience. Now come with me. I have much to show you about the wonders of the undersea world."

Vic refrained from commenting that Gwen was the one more interested in studying the ocean realm.

As if in response to a silent command, two sharks swam up to the tower openings. Azric held onto the sharp dorsal fin of one and motioned for Vic to do the same. Soon the aquatic predators streaked away, carrying them along.

The dark sage spoke in a friendly, conversational tone. "You know, *you* could learn to control these sharks."

"I'd rather control a sea serpent," Vic said.

"That's possible. It's only a matter of degree."

Vic gave the wizard a false smile. "Then I could have it bite your head off."

Azric actually chuckled. "Now, that would be a waste of your talents. You have so much to offer. Not only could you help me control the entire merlon kingdom, but once I open the sealed doors and unleash my armies, you could rule any world you chose. Imagine what you could do with an entire population at your beck and call."

"Sheesh, the bad guy tempting me with promises of power, while trying to turn me to the dark side. Do you have any idea what a cliché that is?"

"It's a valid offer, Vic," Azric said, unruffled. "You did well yesterday in repeating the spells, but I didn't sense your wholehearted participation. I do not reward insubordination. If you don't cooperate, then perhaps your cousin will. If you both defy me, your friends will begin to die. First Lyssandra, perhaps. Or should it be Tiaret? Or that poor grieving prince of Irrakesh?"

The sharks had carried them over a rugged seabed where four giant armored turtles plodded along, each footstep sending up a puff of silt. The sea turtles, with merlon brands burned into their leathery shells, moved along like slow pack animals hauling baskets of ore that merlon smelters would use to make more weapons. Two of the turtles carried sealed containers that glowed with warmth and light, apparently full of fresh lavaja taken from the cracks in the seabed.

Azric said, "Do you like turtles, Vic? You could control those creatures as well. Everything here in the undersea realm is interconnected, like a large web. You could place yourself at the center."

"I've never liked spiders much," Vic said.

"Would you rather be a spider or a fly?" Azric said. "You will have to choose."

"Why? I have no interest in either option."

"It seems you require a fresh perspective." The sharks dove down toward the plodding turtles. "For the next several days, I will assign not only your friends to work with the other slaves, but you and Gwen as well, hauling cargo with the sea turtles, laboring at the edge of the lavaja cracks. Once you understand what it feels like to be a fly, I think you'll change your mind."

Armed merlon warriors swam up from the sea turtle convoy to intercept Vic and Azric. They grasped the young man's arms. "Don't damage him too much," Azric said. "At least do no irreparable harm."

The merlons pulled Vic away.

GWEN AND TIARET FACED their own ordeal in the watery arena by the hall of the merlon king.

"The most effective method for teaching merlons to fight humans is to let them practice against real surface dwellers," Goldskin said, looking at the young women with strangely hungry eyes. "Therefore, you two will be instrumental today in training merlons to slaughter humans more efficiently."

The female merlon general drifted in the huge empty space in front of the undersea palace — a three-dimensional fighting arena. Silvery fish flitting around like tiny spectators left the area when she swam forward. Two large eels, one scarlet, the other obsidian, curled around her legs like pets begging for a snack.

The female general was armed with a wickedly sharp seashell

dagger and a long club topped with a spiny sea urchin; a grappling hook on a finely braided cord dangled at her scaly waist. She grinned, showing the needle-sharp teeth in her fishy mouth. "Come — both of you fight me at the same time."

With a quick glance at Gwen, Tiaret growled, "Your skills will be insufficient to defeat both of us. Are you prepared to sustain injuries?"

Goldskin laughed. "I can triumph over a pair of weak hatchlings. Choose your weapons." She pointed to a display of deadly undersea implements on a rack formed of coral extrusions.

"I fought in the Grassland Wars," Tiaret said. "I am no stranger to adorning my weapons with the blood of an enemy. I plan to refamiliarize myself with that sensation today."

Nibbling the edge of her lower lip, Gwen looked uneasily at the spiked clubs, long scimitars, pronged tridents, and jagged spears. "I'm not sure how well I can fight with any of those, Tiaret. My reflexes are good, but I'm not the seasoned warrior you are."

"Nevertheless, your instincts will protect you. Your reactions are swift and you often employ unexpected maneuvers."

Gwen and Vic had received a fair amount of specialized training from their mothers in the ancient discipline of *zy'oah.* At the time, never suspecting the existence of hundreds of strange worlds connected by crystal doors — or that their mothers might *come* from one of those worlds — the cousins had thought they were learning an obscure martial arts technique. After Gwen's parents died and Kyara left, Cap had encouraged Vic and Gwen to keep up their *zy'oah* practice sessions.

"I'll do my best. What other choice is there?" Then, taking a deep breath of water through her gills, she muttered to herself, "Suck it up, Pierce. Let's see what you've got."

The two young women swam to the weapons while Goldskin and her eels waited impatiently. Merlons gathered to watch the contest, along with Orpheon, who seemed quite intrigued at the possibility of violence. Gwen sensed a ripple in the water, a murmur of excitement, and saw that the merlon king himself had arrived.

King Barak was attended by colorful fish and a pair of guardian sharks, as if they were royal retainers. His large reptilian eyes were wide and curious, and he looked thirsty for blood — Tiaret's blood, Gwen was sure. Because of Azric's claims about the cousins' powerful potential, she doubted Orpheon or the king would allow either of them to be slain. But they might let her get hurt, and Gwen was uncomfortably aware that the evil wizard considered her lean, dark-skinned friend to be expendable.

Tiaret studied the selection of weapons and chose a heavy spear tipped with a sharp narwhal tusk. A barbed hook attached to the side of the spear appeared to have been cut and sharpened from the fallen anchor of a ship. Tiaret experimentally jabbed and swung the spear in the water, then nodded with satisfaction. "This is similar to my teaching staff."

Gwen chose the longest sword she could find and a broad golden shield made from the discarded scale of a sea serpent.

Flow holes perforated the wide sword blade so that it swept sideways more easily through the water. She swished the sword several times, trying to accustom herself to its movement. Each time, she seemed to be battling in slow motion, unless she turned the sword precisely edge-on to the direction of her movement, or when she thrust forward. Either way, she decided she could cause some damage.

The female merlon general snarled, "Those are fighting weapons, not playthings!"

From where he observed, Orpheon chuckled. "Some might consider fighting to be play, Goldskin."

The merlon king shouted, "I grow tired of this! Begin your exercises immediately. But try not to spill too much blood in the water. It may be difficult to control the sharks."

Gwen and Tiaret floated side by side, prepared to face their opponent. Holding up her shield, Gwen raised her sword to defend herself. Tiaret drifted, kicking her feet, on guard.

Goldskin sprang at them. As if they had rehearsed and coordinated their attack, she and her two eels struck from different directions.

"Careful, Gwenya!" Tiaret lunged forward with her horn-tipped spear. The crimson and black eels easily darted aside. Goldskin seemed to ignore Gwen, seeing Tiaret as the primary threat. She pulled out her weighted grappling hook, swung it in the water, and hurled it toward the girl from Afirik.

Tiaret spun out of the way, and the hook sailed past her. Goldskin yanked the cord to an abrupt stop and pulled it back, like a fly fisherman reeling in her cast. Tiaret whirled and held up her spear in defense. The grappling hook caught on the spear. Goldskin tugged, but Tiaret's grip was strong. They wrestled. Tiaret would not let go.

Switching tactics, Goldskin drew her razor-sharp seashell knife and slashed the cord, severing the connection to the grappling hook. At the unexpected release, Tiaret tumbled backward in the water. The female general snatched her chance and swung furiously with her ornate seashell dagger.

Meanwhile, both eels came at Gwen, flashing jagged teeth and preventing her from helping her friend. Instinctively, she raised the golden scale shield, and the black eel chomped on its edge. Its jaws were strong enough to dent even the sea serpent armor. Like an alligator with its prey, the eel tried to shake the shield free, but Gwen ripped the scale away, then turned it and smashed its edge down on the black eel's head.

She didn't have time to think. The crimson eel came at her from below. Gwen realized another primary difference between fighting on land and battling here under the sea: During their exercises in Elantya, she only practiced fighting opponents coming at her from various directions at ground-level. Here, though, she had to worry about up and down as well, fighting in three dimensions instead of two.

Gwen yanked her feet up, did a half-somersault in the water, and began churning back down straight toward the oncoming eel. Surprised by her aggressive move, the red serpentine thing darted sideways to rejoin its black counterpart, which had recovered from the stunning blow from her shield. Gwen turned to face the two eels, shield in one hand and perforated sword in the other, waiting for their attack.

Nearby, Goldskin drove in, dodging the jabs and thrusts of Tiaret's spear. The black shell in Gwen's ear amplified the vibrations of the weapons clashing in the water. The merlon king cheered and applauded, while Orpheon seemed to be waiting for someone to get hurt.

The female general swam close enough to grab Tiaret's spear by the shaft and pull herself forward to grapple with the girl. Her dagger slashed, and Tiaret squirmed away, but the blade's edge sliced her arm, releasing a splash of red into the water. Tiaret didn't even wince as she grabbed the merlon general's wrist to prevent Goldskin from stabbing with the tip of her dagger. They wrestled, whirling in the water.

While Gwen was distracted for just an instant, both the red and black eels streaked toward her like fanged javelins. Her body was attuned now, her reactions set on a hair trigger — just as her mother had taught. The deadly eels considered Gwen's hesitation to fight a mark of weakness. They came in low, mouths wide, clearly intending to bite off a foot or rip a great mouthful of meat from her thigh.

As the creatures flashed in, Gwen tucked her feet close to her body and twirled the sword, turning the blade exactly edge-on as she slashed through the water. She sliced down just as the black eel lunged up. Feeling barely any impact at all, she chopped cleanly through it.

The two halves of the black eel twitched and wriggled, as if trying to reassemble themselves.

The crimson eel recoiled in shock upon seeing its partner sliced in half. Gwen swung her sword sideways, water flowing easily through the holes in the blade. Then, with a flick of her wrist she stabbed upward, gutting the second eel. Its innards spilled out. Still writhing, the two dead creatures drifted away.

Seeing both of her eels dispatched, Goldskin let out a strange cry. She yanked away from Tiaret and plunged murderously toward Gwen, who stared in momentary surprise at her own success.

Tiaret, though, would not let her friend be attacked from behind. She spun her narwhal spear and used its barbed hook to snag the back of Goldskin's armor. The hook jerked the female general backward, thrashing and snarling, so that she accidentally dropped her shell dagger. Goldskin tore off her armorplate and extended her curved claws, ready to tear both Tiaret and Gwen to shreds.

"Enough!" King Barak shouted.

Tiaret yanked back on her spear, releasing Goldskin's heavy armorplate, which sank slowly toward the sea floor.

"You need more practice, Goldskin," the king said in an annoyed tone. "Your two opponents seemed to be competent fighters, but one of my own generals overestimates her skills."

"Maybe these two girls should lead your armies, King Barak," Orpheon taunted the merlon leader. As he laughed at his own joke, Tiaret acted on impulse. She hurled her narwhal-tusk spear with all of her strength. Even before knowing what the man had done to Piri, she hadn't needed more reason than his betrayal of Ven Rubicas to kill Orpheon. Her long pointed shaft flashed like a bullet through the water on a precise course.

Orpheon only had time to look up in surprise. He raised his hands and recoiled, but not quickly enough. The sharp spear plunged into the center of his chest, through his heart, and emerged bloody-tipped from his back.

Shocked to see the spear protruding from their enemy's chest, Gwen stayed on guard next to her friend, holding her shield. She swallowed. They waited for the attack to come, certain the merlons would respond violently.

All of the apprentices despised Orpheon, Gwen as much as anyone. Like the merlons, Azric's henchman wanted to destroy all of Elantya and every person who lived on it. He had committed enough atrocities to warrant a death sentence ten times over. Even so, she felt nauseated to see him skewered by the harpoon.

Orpheon did not cry out in pain, however. Nor did he die as Gwen had expected.

With a mystified and annoyed expression on his face, he looked down at the shaft protruding from his chest, and reached behind him, clumsily trying to grasp the sharp end that stuck out from his spine. Looking aggrieved, he grasped the spear and pulled it out one inch at a time.

When he finally succeeded and let the loose spear drift away from him, the gaping wound in his chest quickly sealed itself. Hardly any blood had wafted into the water. "That hurts," Orpheon said angrily. "Surely you knew that Azric and I are both immortals. A simple spear or sword can't harm either of us."

Tiaret recovered from her shock and disappointment. She glared at her nemesis. "Nevertheless, I am glad to have tried."

After what she had just witnessed, Gwen shuddered at the implications. Until now, she hadn't quite believed the stories about the dark sages' immortality. If Azric did force her and Vic to break open the sealed crystal doors, entire armies of such immortal warriors would be unleashed. Even if Elantya could collect all the bright sages from all the worlds, how could they stand against such a powerful threat?

With a glare of disappointment at her two dead eels, Goldskin swam away in angry defeat. Merlon guards came forward to take away Gwen's shield and sword. Then the sharks, always hungry, were allowed to gobble the remains of the eels.

19

FOR THE NEXT SEVERAL days, working at the edge of the lavaja cracks was like hell underwater — a constant reminder to Sharif of how Piri had been destroyed. Although the young man from Irrakesh hardly noticed the miserable conditions, he could not forget how he had watched Orpheon hurl the djinni sphere into the fissure of molten crystal. He also felt acute disappointment that the summoning rune had not worked on his flying carpet. He simply existed from second to second.

Droplets of lavaja continued to erupt sporadically from the cracks, splattering and burning Sharif's skin. The instability of the oozing hot crystal and the landscape made him wonder if Piri's death had caused an underground storm. Poor Piri. . . .

After her training duel against the female merlon general,

Tiaret had been assigned to labor beside him and the broken merlon slaves at Lavaja Canyon, while Vic and Gwen guided the plodding sea turtles off to where Lyssandra worked with the anemonite scientists. Sharif saw his other friends only in the evenings, when they were all thrown together again in the tower room. There, they could commiserate, compare notes, and secretly refine their developing plan for escape.

Sharif, though, felt empty inside. The challenges seemed insurmountable. Even if he had still possessed Piri and his flying carpet, how could the five friends have hoped to defeat the entire merlon kingdom, overthrow two immortal wizards, and save Elantya? It did not seem possible.

Searingly bright molten crystal bubbled up at the edge of the ever-expanding cracks in the sea floor, and the downtrodden slaves were forced to use heavy crucibles, insulated scoops, and reinforced barrels to harvest the lavaja. Tiaret, with her easy strength, lifted scoops to fill thick-walled barrels that the sea turtles plodded away with, taking the precious magical substance to the anemonites, who worked on their experiments under the hostile and watchful gaze of Blackfrill.

Working beside Sharif now, her ankle tied to a seaweed tether just like his, Tiaret seemed to focus all of her thoughts on anger, striving to find a way to fight back or to escape.

"Interesting, is it not," she commented, "that any merlon can aspire to leadership and attain it merely by proving fierceness in battle and an ability to survive?" By now, the five companions had observed merlons enough to understand that theirs was a laddered society based on personal merit and physical skill, demonstrated in combat and leadership.

As a born prince himself, Sharif *had* found it unusual. Servants could become slave drivers, slave drivers became guards, guards became warriors, warriors became generals, and generals could become kings or queens. Beneath the servants were only the useful animals and the slaves. He labored with his scoop in silent contemplation.

Since first arriving in the merlon city, Sharif had frequently found himself wondering what he was — a thought that had rarely occurred to him in Elantya, where Virs and fisherfolk, sages and apprentices, and individuals from every craft and trade shared nearly identical privileges. As with any group, there were leaders and followers, of course, though Elantyans took care not to lord it over one another, even when they were endowed with greater authority, technical skill, or magical powers.

Around the ragged, blazing ocean bed, merlon guards kept close watch on their workers, moving the excavation teams, sending off the transport animals. The lavaja was capricious. Cracks opened, spewed hot crystal, then sealed up again like healed wounds.

Parts of the canyon floor resembled marshes of bubbling lavaja. In these wide expanses, unfortunately, the most potent molten crystal surged up. But as the work leaders dispatched slaves to retrieve it, the danger became painfully apparent. In the past two days of working here, Sharif had watched five of the merlon slaves die in mishaps, venturing too far forward on the hot, unstable ground and into the boiling water above it. What a waste of life.

Naturally, Sharif himself had always known that he was

better than most others, simply by birthright. As the son of a powerful Sultan, he automatically inherited great wealth, as well as the right to receive the best education and to demand the respect and loyalty of the people he was destined one day to rule.

After his brother's death, though, Sharif had changed. He turned his back on the Air Spirits of Irrakesh, refusing to acknowledge their authority in any way, since they had failed his brother. He rebelled against his father's expectations and the strictures of court life. He flouted traditions. That had made it all the easier for Sharif not to mention who he was when his father had sent him to study in Elantya.

Maybe he was a bit flashy, speeding here and there on his magic carpet and showing off his nymph djinni, but he had left everything else behind and felt he deserved at least those small pleasures. No one on the island treated him with the slightest bit of deference, and that was just fine with him. Perhaps he had shown off a bit too much, though, thought himself more important than the others. . . .

But here in the merlon capital, everything was stripped away from him — not just Piri, but hope, as well. Only now did he understand what he truly was: a slave, one step below the sea creatures that the merlons valued or found useful. Idiot that he was, Sharif had considered even Piri to be a kind of possession, not fully comprehending how good a friend she was.

Now he realized that he had never even seen his carpet for the privilege and treasure it truly was. He had, at least unconsciously, considered it his due. His very ownership of the flying carpet had served as a silent demonstration of Sharif's superiority. What a fool he had been! The lessons Sharif was learning from his own mistakes were more compelling than any he had learned in a class.

What had he actually *earned* in his life? He had done nothing to deserve the friendship of Vic, Gwen, Tiaret, and Lyssandra, who had accepted him without reservation. Neither had he considered whether he had merit as an apprentice for Ven Rubicas, who arguably had the most brilliant mind and kind heart in all of Elantya.

Sharif had merely assumed himself worthy. How much more vain could he have been? Inside the Citadel, it was the highest form of insult to flaunt your talents in front of someone less skilled, therefore implying that you were a better person. Arrogance was one reason that Orpheon had always rubbed Sharif the wrong way. There had been undeniable friction between them. What was it his people said about pride? "Self-pride is the enemy of wisdom." The sages of Irrakesh were wise, indeed.

He swung the scoop, pouring more dazzling lavaja into a thick-walled barrel, which another slave capped off. The slave looked up with concern as a commotion occurred beyond the outskirts of the lavaja mining area. Sharif turned, only dully interested.

Hauling on ropes made of braided doolya strands, several angry merlons wrestled with the huge gray jhanta they had captured a few days earlier. Obviously, the aquatic warriors were trying to force the creature to work, but it had not yet been branded with a merlon symbol and the underwater guards did not have the magical ability to control the jhanta.

The majestic creature thrashed, beating its wide and sinuous wings, yanking four merlons along with it even though they swam backward, struggling to anchor the jhanta in place. Furious merlons holding tridents and narwhal-tipped spears poked and jabbed at the sleek great jhanta, cutting into its hide, driving it into a wild frenzy. The merlons barked to each other, joking, taunting the thing. It was clear they meant to kill it, since it was so unruly.

In his mind, Sharif felt anger flaring as brightly as when Piri had shed her blinding flash of light. Not caring for his own safety, entirely fed up with the violence he had watched his underwater captors inflict, he pulled the tether on his ankle taut. Looking down, he poured lavaja from his nearly empty scoop onto the seaweed rope, burning through it and breaking him free. Sharif dropped his scoop and plunged toward the fray.

The nearest merlon guard at the lavaja cracks bellowed for him to come back, snarling threats. Tiaret snapped a word of caution, but Sharif kept swimming, not caring. He had never moved so swiftly through the water, but he seemed to be part fish now. All he could think of was losing Piri and his flying carpet. Somehow this beautiful jhanta symbolized both for him.

He swam in among the raucous merlon guards, knocking one aside, snatching the trident from another, and bashing the warrior on the side of his scaly head. He knew he couldn't kill all of the undersea warriors and didn't even try. He just meant to distract them from the great jhanta.

For the briefest instant, he thought about freeing the creature and facing the undersea people, attacking as many merlons as he could before they brought him down. He didn't think they had orders to kill him, but their anger might make them forget. And King Barak could easily change his mind at a moment's notice.

"Sharifas, do not throw your life away!" He heard Tiaret's anxious words thrumming through the black seashell in his ear, and he realized that he could not only get himself killed, but his friends as well — not to mention the jhanta.

He acted on a last desperate hope. Sharif did not know anything about the behavior of the great jhantas, only that they were beautiful, like a flying carpet under the sea. The jhanta had seemed gentle, intelligent, loving its freedom. With two of the twined seaweed cords now loose, the jhanta flapped its great fin-wings to get away. Sharif approached. The two remaining merlon guards clung to their ropes, yanking backward. The hooks in the jhanta's tough hide dug deeper.

Sharif flung himself onto the creature's back, holding its wings the way he remembered holding the fringe of his flying carpet. "Stop," he said in a soothing voice. "I'll protect you, but you have to stop. Calm down. Calm . . . calm." He tried to be comforting. With his hands moving automatically, he traced patterns on the smooth, gray back of the undersea creature, as he would have traced the runes embroidered into his magic carpet. Those spells wouldn't work here, but the effect of his gentle touch provided the control that he needed.

Having severed her own tether, Tiaret swam up, looking ready to fight to the death beside her friend. The merlon guards had gathered their weapons, and more than a dozen of them now converged on the huge jhanta and its human rider. The graceful creature circled, struggling to maintain a guarded calm.

The merlons roared, brandishing their weapons, but Sharif shouted at them. "Leave it alone! You're provoking it. You caused this yourselves."

Attracted by the disturbance, General Blackfrill finally swam up, turning his wide, slit-pupilled eyes to gaze upon the scene. "So the human prince has found a new friend. Maybe we should just slaughter the jhanta and let him learn the consequences of his —"

"That would be stupid," Sharif cut him off, using the cold iron-hard voice he had heard his father use when pronouncing a harsh sentence. "This creature can be an asset to you. It can make your work here much more efficient."

"It is untamed and violent," Blackfrill said. "Useless to us."

"Useless only when mistreated." Sharif still worked to calm the creature. It felt very natural to be on its back. "For example, I could take this jhanta into the dangerous zone — where you keep losing slaves. I could use a crucible in a xyridium harness to scoop up the most intense lavaja. Is that not what Azric would want?"

"I do not care what Azric wants."

"Then what about your king? Would he not be displeased to hear that you threw away such an opportunity?" He nudged the jhanta and it responded, moving one way and then another. “See? I can control it.” He stroked the back of its snub head with the palm of his right hand. “Let me show you what we can do. Just do not harm it any further.”

The dark general considered, then his wide lips spread in a grin that exposed needle-sharp teeth. “You can be as unruly as that creature, human. Let this be a test for both of you. Prove yourselves — or you will suffer the consequences.”

The work parties reassembled, and merlon guards drove the slaves back to their places. Sharif felt weak with relief on the back of the graceful creature. Although Tiaret gave him an admiring glance, the boy from Irrakesh wasn’t sure what he had just gotten himself into.

20

ANOTHER TWO DAYS TRAPPED under water.

The plodding armored sea turtle carried its heavy burden in addition to Vic and Gwen, who rode the turtle, guiding it to its destination. Warm, tainted water swirled around the cousins as the creature lumbered forward with sealed containers of fresh lavaja. They would deliver yet more heavy barrels to where the captive anemonites were held — where Lyssandra should be prepared to do her part in the dangerous escape plan.

Watched by guardian merlons, the jellyfish-brains created weapons from the hot magical substance. Weapons to use against Elantya. No longer able to stall, they produced dazzling capsules of energy that could be planted and then released with explosive, destructive consequences. Day after day, the five apprentices had also been forced to cooperate, all the while keeping their eyes open and planning. . . .

Now that they worked closely with the lavaja in the tasks Azric had assigned them, Vic knew that the thick barrels were made from the empty pots of a stony sea plant. Because the senses of smell and taste were inextricably linked in the water, the lavaja "fumes" that escaped from the lidded barrels tasted very bitter.

"You know, I used to like sea turtles," Gwen said, her voice somber. She looked at the prominent rune branded into the lumbering creature's armored shell. "I guess it's not really fair to blame them, though, since they serve the merlons as unwillingly as the other undersea creatures do."

"At least we got one of the easier jobs," Vic said, riding beside her. "Azric could have given us more dangerous work."

"He wants us to see that he can control every part of our lives. But he won't let us be killed if he thinks we're some sort of rare seal-breakers. How else would he set his immortal armies free?"

Vic swallowed hard. "Maybe if he found my mom . . ."

When starting their delivery route more than an hour earlier, the cousins had left a despondent Sharif and a defiant Tiaret back at the fiery cracks in Lavaja Canyon. They were all prepared to play their parts in the careful plans they had made, whispering to each other in the darkness at night after they had learned their routines well enough. Each of the five had a vital role, and timing was going to be crucial.

Now, as the sea turtle slowly crawled forward, Gwen and Vic steadied the heavy containers of still-simmering lavaja.

Sharks and occasional merlon warriors swam past, making sure the cousins didn't try anything, but after several uneventful days they had let their guard down somewhat. They were certainly going to be in for a surprise, Vic thought.

When their big turtle approached the coral reef where the anemonites continued their enforced cogitation, he looked at Gwen. The time was drawing near, and he felt a knot in his stomach. The wheels had already been set in motion. "You ready for this, Doc?"

"I'm just hoping that the merlons *aren't* ready for it."

BECAUSE OF HER TELEPATHIC powers of understanding, Lyssandra had been assigned to the anemonites. Both Orpheon and the merlon king had warned her that they would be perfectly happy to slaughter one or more of the jellyfish-brains, if the anemonites did not perform to the best of their abilities. They placed the burden of all fifty lives on the young girl's shoulders. Orpheon, who had seen Lyssandra work with Rubicas and knew her talents, had suggested this assignment for her. Azric had agreed that keeping the five companions separated, playing them against each other as mutual threats, was probably the best way to control them.

In fact, it gave the apprentices a broader range of opportunities to strike against the undersea kingdom.

While spending her days with the diligent jellyfish-brains, Lyssandra did indeed communicate with them. As far as the anemonites were concerned, their comrade Polup had disappeared; none of them were sure what had become of him, although some of them had guessed that he was the one that King Barak had mentioned a few days earlier. She took great pleasure in telling them in detail about how Polup had escaped, and survived, and used his mental powers to help the island of Elantya. The downtrodden anemonite captives took heart from what Lyssandra said, and were overjoyed when she explained the complex escape plan to them. They were part of the plan, as well.

Since the anemonites' frills had been clipped, they would never be majestic, swift swimmers again. The jellyfish-brains dealt with their limited mobility, though, and Lyssandra knew how to overcome the handicap. In their tiny burbling voices they chattered in the anemonite language, which Lyssandra could understand, but the merlon guards and General Blackfrill could not.

While waiting for the crucial moment to arrive, the anemonites discussed their anxiety over whether they could actually find freedom from persecution again. Since their attempts to stall and to sabotage their work had earned them the wrath of the merlon king, they had few choices. The small lavaja bombs they had been making had not satisfied Barak. They would have to produce some powerful weapons soon, or be killed. Or escape, as Lyssandra suggested.

Lyssandra listened to their discussions and reminded them, "I will be here to help you. I will not leave until I am certain you are all well on your way."

The anemonites voted to escape.

When Azric and King Barak had begun hounding the

anemonites and harassing them to work faster, the scientists had focused on an extravagant, towering structure to intensify the energy output from the lavaja ore. Large vats and a skeletal cistern and pumping chamber had been erected near their coral reef laboratory and testing area.

The two lead anemonites on their lobsterlike kraega steeds, pretended to make intricate calculations with the crustaceans' pointed antennae, but they were recopying old, harmless spells and waiting for a signal. While seeming to cooperate with the slave master's threats, they had prepared the large experimental apparatus, but the merlons did not suspect the results they would get — as soon as the two cousins arrived with their sea turtle.

Lyssandra saw the armored sea creature plodding toward the reef, carrying another load of lavaja containers. She felt a flutter of relief and a thrill of anticipation as she watched Vic and Gwen coming closer. Ready to play her role, she casually sidled over to where the numerous restless kraegas had been imprisoned in a coral cage.

AT THE CRACKS, THE lavaja glow burned upward into the water, filling the currents with impurities that made it difficult for Sharif's and Tiaret's gills to breathe. The acrid taste of molten aja infused the water, and the acid glow — so different from the warm illumination of Piri's crystal eggsphere — pierced Sharif's heart. Somewhere down there in the blazing liquid magic, his lovely nymph djinni had dissolved. Maybe in a last gesture of defiance she had blazed some of her own beautiful light into this furious glow that bubbled up from beneath the surface. . . .

Because he had shown an affinity for the great flying jhanta, Blackfrill let Sharif ride the mantalike creature, as long as he proved himself by harvesting more potent lavaja than anyone else. Riding its back, nudging it with his knees and tugging its wing-fins, he was able to guide the jhanta close to the hot cracks and scoop up crucibles of the most intense bubbling lavaja faster than any other workers could. Orpheon foolishly believed that by throwing Piri into the molten crack, he had crushed Sharif's will to resist. The young man from Irrakesh intended to show him his folly.

Tethered closer to the gaping, ever-widening cracks of shifting lavaja, Tiaret labored hard. The muscles on her brown arms flexed as she swung a long pole, dipping a heat-treated scoop into the churning molten crystal and dumping it into the wide mouth of the insulated crucible. Seeing how hard she worked, her lips drawn back, her teeth clenched, Sharif thought Tiaret must surely be sweating even underwater. Though he resented the labors forced on him by the merlons, it seemed that Tiaret had discovered an important thing: The harder the humans worked, the less attentive the merlon guards became.

After delivering a crucible of particularly potent lavaja, Sharif took the jhanta back out. But instead of heading toward the dangerous zone, they stayed close to Tiaret now. Gracefully flapping its winglike fins, the large jhanta dropped lower. The hook hanging beneath the harness dangled just above the large crucible. As Tiaret added a last scoop of lavaja, the jhanta moved forward to hook the handle of the crucible. Then, straining against the hot currents, the creature rose up and carried its shimmering cargo away. Tiaret looked over her shoulder toward the laboratory area where the anemonites worked. Sharif also watched.

Gwen and Vic had departed more than an hour ago. Both he and Tiaret knew the cousins would act soon, triggering a sequence of events that, if all went as planned, could not be stopped. The signal would be unmistakable. Moment by moment, Sharif and Tiaret waited for their dangerous freedom.

A FEW MERLON SLAVES came forward to assist with the heavy delivery as Vic and Gwen directed their lavaja-laden turtle toward the jellyfish-brains near their tall experimental apparatus. Blackfrill watched, looming over them with his pointed trident in one hand and Tiaret's teaching staff in the other. Working from anemonite diagrams, merlon constructors had finished building the reinforced lavaja tower with its troughs and a wide reservoir on top. It reminded Gwen of the unusual water clock in Elantya's central square.

As soon as the tank at the top of the experimental tower was completely filled with a large volume of the magical substance, the anemonites would be expected to work their new spell to intensify the already powerful lavaja. At least, that was what the merlon king expected. Gwen knew, though, that the merlons could never be allowed to possess a super-potent form of lavaja. All of Elantya was at stake.

General Blackfrill swam forward, though certainly not to help. Noting that Lyssandra had surreptitiously gone over to the kraega cage to stand ready, Gwen made her way to the tall structure and prepared to open the lavaja reservoir, as the merlons expected.

Vic grinned as he brought the turtle to a halt among the merlon workers. The anemonites clustered together as if working on a difficult technical problem. Everything was ready. Gwen gave a slight nod to her cousin, who turned to Blackfrill. "Hey, General! Here's the big delivery you've been waiting for."

Instead of carefully lifting the large container of lavaja to the waiting merlon slaves, as he had done so many times before, he tore off the lid and, using both feet, gave the barrel a hard shove. The container teetered, tipped, then dumped its blazing cargo out among the merlons, who scattered. The sea turtle jerked and backed up in alarm. Vic knocked over the second container of lavaja, dumping superheated magical ooze across the ground. Blinding light flooded upward like a signal flare.

As soon as her cousin began to move, so did Gwen. She ripped at the pulleys and chains in the experimental tower, releasing the emergency latch beneath the mostly-full reservoir, and large quantities of lavaja gushed out like boiling oil, eating into the supports so that the whole construction began to topple.

The blaze grew brighter. Lavaja spilled and exploded. She and Vic swam away from the dazzling blasts as furiously as they could.

Then the real mayhem began.

* * *

IN THE DISTANCE THE bright glow from the anemonites' reef acted as a signal flare. Though he had been expecting it, Sharif was startled by the brilliance of the blaze and the erupting flash. He should have known not to underestimate the power of the lavaja. Their merlon work masters at the canyons also saw the distant flaring light and must have assumed something had gone wrong with the dangerous anemonite experiments.

While the guards were distracted for just a moment, Sharif went into action.

He nudged with his knees, and the great jhanta rose, carrying a heavy crucible on its hook toward the unsuspecting merlon guards. Sharif fumbled with the harness on the creature's back, tilted the crucible, then released it. The whole crucible tipped and tumbled, pouring lavaja through the water onto the frantically scrambling merlons.

Straining her muscles, Tiaret pulled on the pole, swung her scoop around, and upended it to splatter hot lavaja on the nearest merlon guard, who had already begun to swim toward her, anticipating an escape attempt. She seized one of the guard's daggers and slashed the seaweed tether on her ankle.

The merlons went wild. Many were gravely burned, others blinded, all of them bewildered. Guiding the great jhanta with his ankles and knees, Sharif swooped downward. Tiaret extended her hand, and Sharif reached down, grasped her, and pulled her up beside him onto the sea creature's back. Together, before the merlon guards could stop them, the two raced off to help their friends.

* * *

WHEN THE REEF LABORATORY burst into a display of light and magic, Lyssandra grabbed at the bars of the kraega pen, working the latch. The eruption of molten crystal threw the merlons into crazed confusion. The cage's latch bolt had been designed to prevent the weak jellyfish-brains from freeing their symbiotic partners, but Lyssandra had no difficulty opening the rough gate.

"Now!" she shouted. "Anemonites! It is time."

Though they did not understand what was happening, the kraega steeds knew enough to lunge for their freedom. Dozens of them boiled out of the pen and scrambled to find their anemonite partners.

Puttering as best they could with their clipped frills, the anemonites raced toward their beloved kraegas, which could carry them away at far greater speed than they could hope to swim. Finding their steeds, anemonites began to flit off a few at a time in different directions.

"Go!" Lyssandra cried. "Now is your chance. Get away!"

As the lavaja began to cool, dwindling to an orange and then a red glow, she saw Vic and Gwen near the dense seaweed forest. Lyssandra concentrated on shepherding the anemonites in their escape.

21

EVERYONE AND EVERYTHING SCATTERED.

Just like in one of those prison break movies Vic loved to watch. Even before the blazing spilled lavaja began to cool down, anemonites on their large lobsterlike steeds flashed off into the depths.

Vic's heart pounded. This was even better than he had imagined! His strange gills pumped water as if he were panting from running a marathon. He and Gwen had to get to safety now that they had set all their plans in motion. They couldn't just huddle by the seaweed and watch. Their chaotic diversion was bold and unexpected, and might just buy them enough time to break free. "Lyssandra, come with us!" Vic shouted.

The petite girl gestured with her hands, rushing more anemonites away from the wreckage of the test tower. "I must get them to safety! I will join you if I can. If not, I will make my own way to Elantya."

Gwen grabbed Vic's arm. "Sharif and Tiaret must be coming by now. Let's get to our meeting place."

"But Lyssandra —" he began.

The coppery-haired girl gestured him away. "Do not worry about me. We all know what to do."

"Come on, Taz, we've got to take advantage of the confusion," Gwen said, tugging on his arm. "Lyssandra can take care of herself. She knows to meet us at the wreck of the *Walrus* if she can. We all saw where it was."

Even with the blazing sparks and mayhem swirling all around them, Vic knew they didn't have much time. "All right. Be careful, Lyssandra!" He and his cousin plunged into the waving forest of thick doolya at the edge of the anemonite holding area.

Blackfrill had been singed by the first flash of unleashed lavaja magic. His scales were discolored, his eyes milky and temporarily blinded. Even so, the new merlon general bellowed for his guards, most of whom were disoriented and injured. Blackfrill thrashed wildly around the reef laboratory zone in search of something he could tear to shreds with his clawed hands.

Sharks torpedoed in toward the now-empty kraega enclosure, prowling around for anemonites. Trying to regain control of his forces, the merlon general waved his trident and ordered the sharks to find the escaped scientists. But three sharks could not round up fifty escaped anemonites, not to mention Vic, Gwen, and Lyssandra. Most of them would escape.

Weaving their way through the shadowy seaweed, the frantic cousins made a break for it, cutting far from Lavaja Canyon and the holding reef of the anemonites. Vic swam vigorously, and Gwen kept pace with every stroke.

Oddly, he remembered the story about the background for Guise Night, when Sage Therya, on the run from evil pursuers, had been hidden by helpful strangers, who kept her alive. He wasn't sure how many helpful strangers they would find here under the sea. . . .

Instinctively following the directions they had memorized, Vic and Gwen darted over the uneven ocean floor. Far in the distance, the lavaja cracks still cast a ruddy glow into the water. Out there, Vic was sure that Sharif and Tiaret had arranged for as much chaos as he and his cousin had caused when releasing the anemonites.

Far ahead, Vic at last spotted the slumped hulk of the sunken ship. The *Golden Walrus!* The keel and ribs forming its hull remained intact. Planks enclosed a cavernous protective structure where many types of fish, mollusks, and sea plants now made their homes.

Still fleeing, Gwen stroked harder, pulling ahead. Vic had mixed feelings at the sight of the broken hull. It hadn't been so long ago when he and Gwen, still new to Elantya, had sailed with their friends on that beautiful cargo ship to learn both practical and magical nautical skills. One terrifying night a swarm of flying piranhas had stripped the *Golden Walrus* almost bare, shredding the sails and rigging. After Gwen and Sharif had left on the flying carpet to get help, the merlons returned with a full-fledged attack. Vic, Tiaret, and Lyssandra had fought back furiously, using spells as well as makeshift weapons to drive back the enemy. By the time the Elantyan navy arrived to rescue them, the *Golden Walrus* was mortally wounded, doomed and sinking.

"I never thought I'd see the *Walrus* again," Vic said. "Let's hope it keeps us safer than it did when we were students on board."

The once majestic vessel had come to rest in the muck on the ocean floor. Several huge holes marked where planks had been shattered. Strewn about the sandy sea floor around the sunken wreck, Vic spotted a few human skeletons, picked clean by carnivorous fish — most likely crewmembers who had died in the struggle against the merlons or the flying piranhas. Vic hoped they were resting in peace.

He and Gwen swam through one of the gaping holes into the cargo hold of the wrecked ship, to hide and wait for their friends. Now their pursuers could not see them, unless one of the merlons thought to look here specifically. The two cousins drifted deeper into the murk, catching their liquid breath and waiting.

Not much useful remained in the vessel. They found no possessions abandoned by the students or crew, no packaged food in the storehouse lockers, only scraps of rope, rusty metal chains with a patina of algae, and slimy wood.

Vic grasped a cross-beam, recalling the *Walrus* as it had

been when it was a learning vessel — solid and comfortable and dry. *Dry* seemed to be a very strange concept right now.

Drifting and resting, Gwen peered out through a ragged hole in the hull, keeping watch. Before long, she said, "I see something moving out there, and it's coming straight toward us."

"Is it Blackfrill? I bet he sent out sea serpents and sharks to hunt for us." Vic pushed closer to see.

"No, the shape is different — oh, it's the great jhanta!"

The graceful swimming creature stroked closer, wafting along, and Vic could make out the figures of Sharif and Tiaret on its back. "Lyssandra's probably on her way," he said.

"Unless she's escaping on her own." Gwen nodded soberly. "By freeing the anemonites from the merlons, Lyssandra has probably done more to protect Elantya than any of us."

When the huge jhanta approached the sunken wreck, Gwen and Vic emerged from a wide hole in the hull. Sharif and Tiaret waved. The jhanta circled, bringing its passengers close, and the two finally dismounted, letting go and swimming for themselves.

Sharif hovered in front of the giant manta creature, stroking its snub-smooth head. The prince from Irrakesh said, "You have done all we could ask of you. And you do not belong in captivity. Go now. Be free. We will get the rest of the way home by ourselves."

"If we can elude capture." Tiaret swam warily, keeping watch.

"Yup, that's an important part of the plan," Vic agreed.

Giving the creature one last caress, Sharif urged the great

jhanta on its way. The graceful beast nudged him in the chest, languorously circled the *Golden Walrus,* then struck off toward deeper water and freedom. After the large jhanta had dwindled into the dim distance, the four friends ducked inside the hulk of the sunken ship to prepare for their final escape.

Together, the apprentices kept watch through cracks in the waterlogged hull. They were dismayed to see torpedo-shaped shadows cross the water. Prowling sharks circled the wreck as if sniffing, hunting for prey. Their prominent brand marks told Vic that these weren't wild sharks.

After a minute, the gray predators swam away, only to be replaced moments later by two large sea serpents.

So far, the merlons hadn't guessed where the companions had fled, and Vic wanted to keep it that way.

"So now how do we get out of here?" he said in a quiet voice. "Lyssandra'll never make it through that blockade of searchers."

Tiaret watched the open water. Beside her, Sharif was clearly forlorn after having sent the "flying" jhanta away. Another friend gone, just like Piri, just like his brother.

"When the time is right," Tiaret said, "we must make our escape."

22

CONSIDERING THE EXPLOSIONS AND the blazing spilled lavaja, it was no wonder the merlons went into a frenzy chasing after the instigators. When Vic and Gwen bolted after their outrageous sabotage, and Sharif and Tiaret wrecked operations at the fiery fissures, the merlons raced after them all.

They had not expected Lyssandra and the freed anemonites to stay so close to their former prison. Quiet and watchful, she waited for the right moment.

With their intense mental powers and their detailed planning abilities, the jellyfish-brains had envisioned several scenarios for the grand escape. Most had ended in utter failure — the anemonites were practical, after all — but when they spotted the opportunity, they immediately launched their "Plan B."

The jellyfish-brains had communicated with Lyssandra

what they planned to do. They knew that with or without swim frills, the anemonites who did not have kraega steeds could never move faster than hunting merlons. They needed some sort of advantage. Because their vast intellect was a terrible weapon that Azric and the merlon king had abused, they were determined to disperse and take themselves out of King Barak's control.

For a long time, the anemonites had intentionally corrupted their work and delayed their experiments. Lyssandra admired them for their brave deception, but that had not been good enough. Now, however, Azric monitored their work closely, and General Blackfrill had demonstrated that he was willing to kill some of them to force the others to cooperate.

Despite the difficulties and danger, escape was their best option.

Now, as Lyssandra helped them, she understood — as did all of the fleeing creatures — that they had made their minds up to die before they could be captured and used again by the merlon king or the dark sage Azric.

So some of the scuttling jellyfish-brains had taken the freed kraega steeds and, using their pseudopods to grasp the creatures' exoskeletons, jetted away in various directions with remarkable speed. But there weren't enough kraegas to carry even half of them.

Two dozen of the remaining anemonites floated down the currents, out past the segregated reef outcropping where they had been forced to perform calculations and spells. Lyssandra saw them puttering along, squeezing water through their membranes, flailing their clipped frills, moving faster than merlons probably thought they could go. Throughout their captivity, the anemonites had made themselves appear weak, confused, unable to complete their work. Therefore, the merlons underestimated them, just as they had underestimated the five human apprentices.

The dozens of swimming anemonites did not try to go far. Familiar with the area, the anemonites hid in cracks, crannies, and holes in the rocks along the reef and the ocean bed. A few settled down on the silty bottom of the ocean and quickly squirmed and twitched until they burrowed themselves into the soft sea bottom. Within seconds they vanished entirely. While the merlons hunted far and wide for their jellyfish scientists, these would creep away at their leisure.

Lyssandra ducked into a small patch of waving seaweed to hide. Several anemonites on kraega steeds clustered around her. This was the riskiest group, the ones following her. "We will send scouts," said one of the anemonite scientists. "We will watch over you."

Lyssandra tried to take reassurance. "I need to meet my friends at the wreck of the *Golden Walrus.*"

"Too dangerous," said a few of the anemonites in unison. "Too far to go. Too many chances to be captured."

Though it pained her, Lyssandra knew the jellyfish-brains were right. "Then I need to get back to Elantya. We freed you from the merlons, but it is vital that we reach the island, where we can work to help defend the people."

"Not just the people," one anemonite said, "but this whole world. The merlons and Azric have wrought great destruction already, and that is only the beginning."

From the underwater city of Oo'regl, many scouts, sharks, and sea serpents had been dispatched for the widespread pursuit. Lyssandra hoped that the other kraegas with their anemonite riders had gotten away. She and her small group of jellyfish scientists clung to their lobster steeds and gradually moved from hiding place to hiding place. First they ducked among rocks, then rested for nearly an hour in a marvelous array of dense fan coral. The water around them slowly became dark and inky with the fall of night far above.

Lyssandra was amazed that they had managed to make it so far. Though she was constantly worried about the safety of her friends, she could think of no spell, no telepathic potential that was great enough to let her sense what was happening to Vic, Gwen, Sharif, and Tiaret.

Peering through the murky water, Lyssandra could see the glow of the underwater capital in the distance, and flickers of light like elongated sparks, as merlons attached glowing eels to long poles and continued to search for the escaped anemonites and humans. She and her unusual companions hid and waited. Lyssandra leaned against the nearest large kraega, stroking its long antennae.

"Have no fear," one of the anemonites said. "We will see you safely to Elantya."

23

HUDDLING INSIDE THE OLD wreck, the friends waited for hours in the shadows, hoping Lyssandra would make her way to the waterlogged ship. They watched merlons pass time and again as they continued to hunt for the escaped humans. Eventually, the apprentices knew they couldn't wait any longer. Though her companions had made it this far, Gwen knew they were not yet safe.

"What is taking Lyssandra so long?" Vic asked for the tenth time in five minutes. "She knows to come here, if she can."

"Maybe the plan with the anemonites changed," Gwen said. "I hope she's not hurt."

"I would not underestimate her," Tiaret said.

"Oh, I'd never do that," Vic said. "Worry, maybe — underestimate, never."

"Nevertheless, we must make our move soon," Sharif pointed out. With so many sharks, merlons, eels, and sea serpents passing by, their hiding place could not remain secret for long. "We can be cornered here too easily — and at least one of us must reach Elantya."

Tiaret strained at one of the broken planks of the *Walrus*'s interior, ripping loose a spear-sized splinter. "We should arm ourselves. Sooner or later, we will have to fight. I intend to be prepared."

Scavenging among the tilted decks of the *Golden Walrus*, they stripped out some debris that could be used to defend against their underwater enemies. Gwen found a sharp metal pin as long as her arm that had been used to keep a winch from unwinding. Vic used long iron nails embedded in a plank to create a makeshift spiked club. Tiaret took a jagged shard of crystal from a broken porthole and used strands of doolya seaweed to lash it to the end of her wooden spear.

Vic nodded his approval. "Nice MacGyvering."

Gwen tried not to count the minutes. She peered out, scanning carefully in all directions, but saw no prowling sea creatures, no enemy merlons. High above them, closer to the surface, she could see a wilderness of waving wild seaweed that would give them shelter. A perfect place to hide. Gwen remembered the broad thickets of doolya not too far from the island realm.

"It's going to be night soon, and the water will grow dark. I think we should risk it."

"Yes, I am tired of hiding," Tiaret said.

"Well, that's it then." Vic rushed toward the hull opening.

"We make a dash for the seaweed forest, then make our way back home, step by step."

Gwen kept watching for their lost friend, very worried about her. "Lyssandra said she'd get to Elantya alone, if she couldn't meet us here."

"Now that she has freed the anemonites," Sharif said, grimly changed by what he had been through, "I would not be surprised if they saved her in return."

"I will go first." Tiaret clutched her crystal-tipped spear and darted out of the sunken ship. She stroked powerfully upward, kicking with her feet. The girl from Afirik no longer had any difficulty swimming. Impulsively, Vic bolted after her.

Sharif looked at Gwen, then glanced longingly up into the water. "I used my summoning spell days ago to call my flying carpet, but it never arrived. The special rune did not work. I have lost Piri, and my carpet, and now my friend the jhanta."

"But you haven't lost *us.*" Gwen put a hand on his arm to reassure him. "And the best thing we can do right now is get back to Elantya and warn them what the merlons intend to do. Think of how many lives we can save."

Sharif nodded and the two swam out after their friends under slanted beams of late-afternoon sunlight.

Once they left the shipwreck, Gwen felt very exposed in the open water. At least they wouldn't leave any footprints or telltale signs of their passage. She wondered if the branded sharks might be able to detect a faint scent of their prey in the water. So far, they hadn't seemed to, but the thought was enough to make her kick and stroke harder toward the dubious shelter of the doolya forest. They had to get away!

She looked all around, uneasy that a group of aquatic predators might be after them even now. As they continued to swim higher and higher, she saw sleek gray shapes far below, skimming the ocean floor like a wolf pack, and then a much larger sinuous form, a golden sea serpent. She could just make out the figure of a merlon — Blackfrill — driving it along in pursuit. The merlon general shouted, gesturing upward.

"They've spotted us!" They all knew they couldn't fight Blackfrill, not to mention the sea serpent or the group of sharks.

With their targets in sight, the sharks shot upward as if fired from cannons. Vic looked down in a panic. "Anybody have other ideas?"

"Into the seaweed forest," Tiaret called. "Hurry!"

Gwen wasted no more energy looking back at her pursuers, while she and Sharif struggled to catch up with their two companions.

The snaking strands of leathery weed formed a sort of camouflage net. Colorful fish darted in and out of the doolya, nibbling on the variegated green vegetation.

Gwen was surprised by how fast they plunged in and got lost among the waving stalks. A long, slimy leaf slapped against her cheek like the tongue of an amorous cow. She pushed the strands aside, holding onto some of the softball-sized bladders that kept the doolya afloat. Within a few seconds, they were swallowed up by the maze.

Gwen had a hard time following even Sharif, who was right in front of her, scrambling after Tiaret and Vic. The four of them spread out, thrashing deeper into the dense thicket of undulating weed. She didn't know how Blackfrill or the sharks could give chase in here, but she didn't believe for a moment that they were safe. It was still a long way to Elantya, and freedom.

The taste-smell of the water around her was strange, full of iodine and vegetation. Maybe the doolya itself would muddle the sharks' keen sense of smell and blur any faint lingering scent the humans left in the water.

The glittering gold-orange light streaming down from the surface grew dimmer, and she realized it must be sunset up above. Soon they would be winding through the sea forest in complete darkness. Unfortunately, the deep purple shadows would probably hinder the four friends more than their aquatic pursuers.

Far beneath her feet, Gwen saw a flicker of gray skin and a triangular fin cruising after them, searching. The four friends continued to climb toward the air, pulling themselves through the tangled, waving fronds. Another shark passed through the seaweed to Gwen's left. She thought she had read in her marine biology studies that sharks weren't able to see very well. That was one consolation, at least.

Someone grabbed her arm and yanked her down. Gwen jerked back and almost screamed, but saw it was Vic desperately trying to pull her into a dense knot of doolya. Like a giant golden dragon, a sea serpent cut through the thick weed, its large arrow-shaped head nudging the heavy doolya aside. Gwen hid next to her cousin and watched the thick golden scales pass by. The two drifted backward, among the thickest stalks, no longer able to see either of their friends.

The sea serpent continued to prowl. Riding its back, Blackfrill shoved wafting seaweed away with Tiaret's staff. He looked very upset. Gwen used the long metal pin clutched in her hand to move aside a slimy clump so they could slip behind it for cover.

The movement must have caught Blackfrill's attention. The merlon general turned and focused his round, fishy eyes on the spot from which Gwen had just disappeared.

"I think he saw me," she said quietly to Vic.

Goading his serpent, Blackfrill turned the creature's armored head and plunged toward them, ripping tangled fronds aside. A vibrating underwater bellow from the serpent rumbled like sea thunder.

Suddenly, Tiaret darted in front of Blackfrill, slashing with her crystal-tipped spear. The jagged edge caught one of the extravagant frills around his head, slicing through the webbing of his crest. The merlon general recoiled and nearly lost his grip on the serpent's harness.

Startled, the sinuous monster opened its jaws and roared again. Tiaret jabbed inside the glistening pink mouth, piercing tender tissue. The sea serpent went into an agonized frenzy, and Blackfrill had all he could do to hold on as he struggled to reassert control over the monster. Tiaret darted away, having accomplished what she needed to for the moment.

Gwen and Vic swam furiously, putting more and more distance between themselves and their pursuers. "Sheesh, talk about exciting," Vic said. "But I've had enough excitement for today — in fact, maybe for a whole year."

When the cousins came together with Tiaret and Sharif again, all four of them were grim. "Now that they know we are here," Sharif said, "the merlons will concentrate their efforts on this doolya forest. They can call more sharks, serpents, hunters. . . ."

"We will have a difficult time escaping," Tiaret said.

"On the bright side, if they think we're here, maybe Lyssandra has a better chance of getting away," Vic said. "The merlons will assume we're all together."

"We have to keep moving," Gwen said. "I'm not ready to make our last stand yet."

Defiantly she swam onward, picking her way through the doolya forest, always looking out for the merlons. Darkness was falling overhead, and she found it harder to see around them.

Something gray-green darted in front of her, like a serpentine ribbon surrounded by a lambent glow. Two glittering eyes stared at them, and crackles of static raced along its hide. Gwen recognized the blunt nose, the mouth full of tiny, sharp fangs. An electric eel! She didn't need to see the brand mark on its side to know that this creature was a spy for the merlons.

"Yow, look out!" Vic cried, swirling backward with an instinctive move that his mother had taught him.

"Do not let the eel get away," Tiaret said. "It will report where we are."

The sparking eel turned to dart off. Without thinking, Gwen moved with the coiled swiftness of *zy'oah* that her mother and Aunt Kyara had taught the cousins. She took

Tiaret's spear, jabbed, and skewered the creature on the first try. The eel thrashed, trying to bite at the spear. Its teeth fastened on the shaft, but without effect. It writhed before finally dying.

"Way to go, Doc!" Vic said as she gave the spear back to Tiaret. "You've got a real talent for harpooning."

"Just how many undersea creatures did the merlons actually enslave?" Gwen looked at the familiar merlon symbol sizzled into the scaly hide. The very idea of such scars angered her, even on an electric eel. She studied books on oceanography and loved to visit aquariums, marveling at the wonders of sea life. It offended her that the merlons would turn eels, sharks, and fish into their slaves.

As she simmered with anger at the merlons, Gwen noticed a doll-sized creature like a tiny mermaid hiding among the shadowy leaves. "Not all sea creatures serve the merlons."

Vic spotted the creature, too. "An aquit!"

Gwen bit her lower lip. Aquits were messengers of the seas, loyal to Elantya. "At least we can send a warning." She coaxed the creature out of its hiding place. "It's okay. We're your friends. We won't hurt you."

"We're from Elantya," Vic added. "You know — the good guys."

The aquit swam out of its hiding place, looking warily around for sharks or eels.

"Please swim to Elantya. Take this message to Ven Rubicas," Gwen said.

"And to my dad," Vic added. "Dr. Carlton Pierce. Sage Pierce."

Gwen spoke quickly. "The merlons captured us and were

holding us in an undersea city. They worked some kind of magic on all of us so we can breathe under the water." She pointed to the gill slashes on her neck.

Vic blurted, "Orpheon is here, and so is Azric!"

Gwen concentrated on the attentive aquit, choosing her words. "We're trying to escape — but in case we don't get away, we have to let you know. The merlons are preparing to attack Elantya. They're planting lavaja bombs under the island. They want to sink it!"

"We don't know all his plans yet, but Azric's up to some major bad stuff," Vic added. "Please send a rescue team for us — if you can figure out how."

The aquit suddenly darted away and vanished into the tangled seaweed. Gwen turned to see Sharif and Tiaret looking alarmed. The warrior girl whirled, jabbed at something behind her with her crystal-tipped spear, then continued to swim.

Knowing their pursuers were close again, Gwen bolted upward. Near the surface, she could see a glow from the full moon shining down. It was dark outside now. She stroked harder, still holding her sharp iron bar.

Sharks circled closer. Blackfrill had returned on his golden sea serpent, and now two other ferocious-looking serpents had joined the hunt, guided by more merlon warriors. Gwen realized with a sinking heart that she and her friends had no place to go. No way to escape. They were discovered!

The sharks drove in like wolves, bumping the escapees, not using their sawblade teeth but herding the four friends together. Gwen imagined that the predators wanted the four apprentices to fight back, which would give them an excuse to attack. Blackfrill and his merlon fighters closed in. Two of them swung barbed grappling hooks on silken cords; four held weighted nets.

"There's only about two merlons for each of us," Vic said, "uh, not including all the sharks and sea serpents. You think we can fight our way out of this?" He swished his nail-spiked club through the water in a threatening gesture.

Tiaret seemed perfectly willing to fight to the death, and a resigned Sharif was right beside her. The muscles in Gwen's chest contracted. What should they do? The aquit had gotten away with the message, and Lyssandra might have, as well. Maybe there was a chance, somehow. . . .

A large, graceful shape flashed in front of them, like a black hang glider with broad fleshy wings. It dove among the merlons, scattering the sharks.

"My jhanta!" Sharif cried. The intelligent ray came in like a jet fighter, swooping around, butting the sharks, slapping them with its tail, driving directly toward the nearest fanged sea serpent. It flapped its wide fin-wings in the sea serpent's face like a matador taunting a maddened bull with his red cape. The enraged serpent lunged, snapping uncontrollably with its jaws even though the merlon riding it yanked at the reins, trying to hold it back. The jhanta circled out of the way, luring the merlons farther from the friends.

Gwen couldn't tell if the helpful creature wanted them all to grab onto its back and fly away, or if they should try to escape back into the doolya forest. Even the large jhanta could not carry all four of them away fast enough.

Blackfrill raised Tiaret's stolen teaching staff and angrily snarled orders. The jhanta careened in again, and Sharif shouted a warning, but too late. Several merlons threw their nets. The heavy meshes spread out like spiderwebs, and the plunging jhanta unwittingly dove right into the trap. The nets tangled its flapping fin-wings, weighing it down.

With no concern for his own safety, Sharif swam toward the creature, swinging his makeshift weapon at the warriors. Gwen, Vic, and Tiaret gave up caution and joined the wild fight.

This time the merlons were ready for them. The sharks drove in, forcefully separating the four companions. When the jhanta was captured, Vic let out a groan and wasn't even looking when a merlon guard yanked the spiked club out of his hand.

"Way to focus, Dr. Distracto," Gwen muttered as she parried spear thrusts with her sharp iron pin. A merlon came up behind her, as well, and grabbed both of her elbows while a second wrested her weapon away.

Tiaret and Sharif continued to inflict minor injuries, but a pair of nets snared them, pinning their arms and legs. Blackfrill caught the nets with his curved hook and pulled them tight. Gwen and Vic struggled against their captors. The jhanta flailed helplessly in its restraints.

But it was clear to everyone that their escape attempt was finished. Their plan had failed, and they were once again prisoners of the merlons.

24

LYSSANDRA'S UNDERWATER JOURNEY WAS long and dangerous. Curtains of daylight and then murky night shimmered down through the depths. She counted four days as they progressed warily from one hiding place to the next — tall coral trees, dense and shadowy doolya thickets, knobby boulders.

The situation reminded her of Warrior Sage Therya fleeing from the dark sages. And, like Therya, Lyssandra and her band had help. Krill, crabs, and other creatures friendly to anemonites and kraegas kept watch for prowling sharks and sea serpents. They saw several of the merlon-branded creatures along the way, but each time, Lyssandra and her friends managed to hide. Although Lyssandra felt an urgent need to race back to Elantya to warn everyone, she knew her recapture wouldn't help anyone but the merlons, so she remained cautious.

She hoped that her other four friends had succeeded in their plan, met at the wreck of the *Golden Walrus,* and then moved on without her. But Lyssandra knew she *might* be the only person to have escaped the merlons. Somebody had to get back to the sages — especially the anemonites, who could help in the defense of the island.

After a seemingly interminable journey, led by the fastest kraega steeds, who would not abandon their anemonite partners, she finally saw the land rising ahead. The sea floor tilted upward with steep rocky slopes, like a singular mountain towering up out of the deep ocean.

Elantya!

She had been born on the island, and since their escape, Elantya had drawn her as steadily as a magnet drew iron filings. Even if the anemonites, with their knowledge of the sea and the world's geography, had not been with her, Lyssandra would probably still have found her way home.

Relief, guilt, and anxiety mingled in her brain, swirling from her head to her stomach and back again: relief that she could finally see the solid mass of Elantya ahead of her, within reach; guilt at possibly being the only person who escaped from Azric and Orpheon and the deluded merlons they led; and the urgent need to share the news of what was happening. Once she got back to Ven Sage Rubicas and the Pentumvirate, she could help them mount a rescue if her friends hadn't made it back. She and the anemonites could provide vital information about the merlon cities and their underwater projects.

Yet the danger was only just beginning. Murky memories

of dark, prophetic dreams echoed in her mind, dreams of a possible future in which things did not go well for her friends. Was it possible that the merlons had already recaptured and killed them as punishment for trying to escape? No, she could not allow herself to think that way. She had to assume they were all alive and needed her help. She had to hope they had gotten away, too.

She now understood some of her earlier nightmare visions — the earthquakes, a xyridium medallion like the ones Vic and Gwen wore sinking to the bottom of the ocean, the flashes of sharks and menacing tridents, the feeling of drowning. Other dreams, still unclear, had shown her spectacular battles against undersea armies with the fate of Elantya at stake, poor Piri blazing brightly at the center of a colossal whirlwind, massive waves crashing into the island and leaving the sea foam red with blood, the faces of Vic and Gwen as still and white as death, Azric looming as tall as fifty men above the Citadel. . . .

Worry spurred her to greater speed.

As the island rose steeply in front of her, she felt like a mountain climber, moving from ledge to ledge, pushing herself upward, swimming when she had to, using her feet on the sloped seabed when she could. Clumps of dark green seaweed poked out of crevices; sea anemones fluttered their colorful tentacles at her as she passed.

The anemonites and their kraegas moved along with her, spreading out, alert for any signs of merlon pursuit. At last, Lyssandra removed her weighted shell belt so she had more buoyancy and rose swiftly and easily. She didn't know what section of the island they were approaching, whether they would arrive in the harbor or up against the cliffs. She had to find some place where she and the rescued anemonites could get help.

Finally, she and the anemonite scientists reached the last ledge before the surface, where sunlight shone down, stippling the choppy waves. Surprised to find her way blocked by an even rock wall that curved along the surface like the battlements of a castle, Lyssandra suddenly realized what it was: the breakwater that sheltered the calm cove where the five friends had gone swimming on the fateful day of their capture.

Swimming along, she found the neat circular tunnel made by the merlon magic, through which the merlons and Orpheon had breached the wall. Now the passage provided easy access for Lyssandra and the jellyfish-scientists to the cove. And the shore. And safety!

Once inside the breakwater, Lyssandra propelled herself upward with all the force she could muster. Her head burst above water in the calm cove.

Vic and Gwen had warned her that it would be difficult, but she knew she could breathe the air again. A current pushed her from behind as she moved forward, treading water, letting her nose and mouth drain, spilling water from her gill slits. Although it was a strange sensation, she contracted her chest to force seawater out of her lungs. She gagged as it gurgled up and out of her throat and poured from her mouth. Her half-empty lungs screamed for something to fill them.

She swam toward the lonely shore until the water was only

waist-deep. She stood and tried to take a deep breath. Her gills worked to draw in water, but there was none. A sense of panic nearly overwhelmed her. There was nothing to breathe! She couldn't feel a thing. She could draw no more oxygen from the water in her lungs, and her body was rejecting the very weightlessness of the air around her as unbreathable.

Behind her, the anemonites and their kraegas breached the surface, and puttered around the cove.

Lyssandra sloshed and staggered toward the beach. Sparkles of darkness and light clouded her vision, but she pushed herself forward, now only ankle-deep in the water. She coughed, forcing more water from her lungs. Her attempts to breathe drew the water back into her throat, which made her cough again. The spangles of darkness and light in front of her eyes became more pronounced.

As she dropped onto her hands and knees on the gritty beach, the bright spangles faded entirely from her vision. She fell forward, unconscious on the sand.

25

THE WASTELAND AROUND LAVAJA Canyon shimmered an angry red, as if reflecting the mood of Orpheon and General Blackfrill. Although the four apprentices were captives once again, Sharif was not ready to bow his head in defeat. He was glad to see that Vic was openly defiant, Gwen appeared aloof, and Tiaret was not bothering to hide her disdain for the merlons and Orpheon.

The last time Sharif had tried to get away, Orpheon had destroyed Piri. The ache and grief still burned like an ember in Sharif's heart. While he floated beside his companions near the edge of the lavaja operations, Sharif felt a sudden apprehension at the thought of what their captors might do this time. Would his own life, or Tiaret's, be forfeited now? Although Orpheon clearly had orders not to kill the two seal-breakers,

Sharif knew that he and the girl from Afirik were not similarly protected.

Orpheon sneered at the recaptured apprentices. "We thought you had learned your lesson. Azric will be greatly disappointed."

"I have no interest in pleasing Azric," Sharif growled, unable to stop thinking of how the disguised dark sage had killed his brother in the flying city. "Or you."

"What did he expect from us?" Vic asked. "A handwritten thank-you note for all the wonderful things he's done? A parade?"

"He murdered my parents and kidnapped us," Gwen said in a brittle voice. "That's not exactly a good way to earn loyalty." When they were all hiding in the *Golden Walrus,* Gwen and Vic had decided not to pretend any further cooperation with the dark sage, no matter what. It would do no good.

The traitorous former apprentice scoffed back at them. "You should be grateful for your lives, at least. Just accept the fact that you will never escape."

Now that their escape attempt had failed, Sharif doubted any of them would get another chance. "One of us got away," he pointed out in a low voice, further infuriating Orpheon, who lashed out and struck him in the face.

"Lyssandra was useless, anyway." He motioned to a cluster of merlon guards, who dispersed at his command. "Continue the search. When you find the girl, kill her."

"You will not find her," Tiaret said, sounding entirely confident.

"She must be long gone by now," Vic added.

"Either way, the rest of you are prisoners," Orpheon said.

Sharif managed to sound simultaneously haughty and bleak. "My people have a saying: Though the body is captive, the mind roams free. You and Azric must understand by now that you will never break our spirits."

"Really? Destroying your little djinni was only a first step." Orpheon's dark eyebrows went up and his lips curled in derision. "But now you have presented me with an interesting challenge."

The prince did not cower at Orpheon's threat. "What more can you do — kill me?"

The other man shrugged. "Only if need be. But why would I, when there are so many other creative options to explore? Mental pain, for example, seems to be quite a suitable chastisement for you. Make the great prince small and helpless. I've already warned you that because you're a leader, your actions have repercussions for others. Your mind may 'roam free,' but I'm sure I can reach it. Whether the punishment is direct or indirect, you can still suffer."

Sharif felt a knot of concern tighten in his gut, though he did not show it. Orpheon seemed to relish the fact that he was finally getting a response from the proud young man. With a triumphant laugh, he swam toward a simmering crack where molten lavaja flowed to the surface. Somewhere down there, Piri had vanished. Sharif stared at the crack, as if a part of him still expected to catch a glimpse of her.

"Bring me the beast," Orpheon snapped at several merlon guards. They swam away like a gang of thugs bent on vengeance.

Sharif was startled, then dismayed as Blackfrill and his undersea warriors returned, leading the captured great jhanta toward them. They jabbed it with their spears whenever the creature attempted to swim in another direction. Blackfrill carried a trident in one hand and Tiaret's teaching staff in the other. Anger welled up inside Sharif, but it did him no good to struggle pointlessly. He gritted his teeth and waited. Once the guards had the jhanta close enough to the edge of the lavaja cracks, they formed a protective ring around it, holding it with doolya ropes and threatening it with their sharp weapons.

With a cruel smile of anticipation, Orpheon went to a rack of metal rods the merlon workers had installed near the edge of the molten crystal. He selected one of the rods, looking with satisfaction at the flat piece of scrolled metal affixed to its tip, and plunged it into the bright, flowing lavaja. He waited while the scrolled end heated with blazing magic, then withdrew the instrument. A trail of small bubbles followed its movement, as if water were boiling around the scrolled metal. He held up the instrument, and the prince realized what it was. Sharif lunged, but the aquatic warriors held him tightly.

Casting a glance at Sharif, Orpheon swam with the sizzling rod past the wary ring of merlon guards. The tip glowed orange with heat.

"Observe, young prince. Another price of your disobedience." He rammed the burning branding iron against the great jhanta's left wing-fin. The gray flesh sizzled, and the creature flapped and writhed, making a shrieking sound that was simultaneously high- and low-pitched.

Guards yanked the ropes and jabbed savagely at it with

their spears, barely keeping the creature in check. Sharif's stomach clenched. He found it hard to watch the barbaric spectacle. The jhanta's shrieking set his teeth on edge, and still Orpheon did not let go of the branding iron. Finally, the fiend pulled the hot iron from the jhanta's wing, and Sharif could see that the brand had burned deep into the poor creature's flesh, deeper than he had seen on any other creature marked by the merlons. Beside him, Gwen shuddered.

With a taunting look, Orpheon swam out of the group of guards and casually thrust the branding iron back into the flowing lavaja. "Shall I continue?" he asked Sharif. "How does it feel to know that the beast will never be free again and will die in service to our master?"

"*Your* master," Sharif corrected. "I serve no one."

"Not even Sage Rubicas?" Orpheon taunted.

"We are apprentices to the Ven Sage, not slaves. I give my assistance freely *because* I am free. I belong to no one."

"Is that so?" Orpheon nodded to the pair of guards who held Sharif's arms. "Hold him still." He withdrew the brand from the lavaja again. "You will have a different form of apprenticeship here, young prince, and you will learn."

Although Sharif knew that the traitorous assistant was cruel, he still did not expect what happened next. With a movement so fast that it was a blur, Orpheon thrust the branding iron forward and rammed it against the meaty part of Sharif's bare shoulder. The prince, who had not flinched until now, went completely rigid. A scream rose to his throat, but he clamped down to keep it inside even as the branding iron scorched his flesh. He felt all color drain from his face. As if from a great distance, he could hear Gwen and Vic both crying out, and Tiaret shouting in defiance and outrage, but Sharif could barely comprehend anything through the agony.

His pain-fogged gaze drifted toward his friends, all of whom struggled with their captors. Though unable to break loose, Tiaret lashed out with her feet and managed to kick the branding iron out of Orpheon's grasp. Sharif slumped forward and drifted unconscious in the water.

The mark of merlon slavery glowed raw and red on his shoulder.

26

LYSSANDRA WOKE TO A gentle rocking and realized she was being carried. So, someone had found her on the isolated beach! She felt comfortable, warm, dry, and safe for the first time since the kidnapping. But what if it was only another vivid prophetic dream? What if she opened her eyes to find that she was still a captive beneath the oceans?

She gingerly raised her eyelids and looked up into the hazel eyes of Vic's father. "You're safe," Sage Pierce said, both comforting and anxious. "Where have you been? We heard from Vic and Gwen and your other friends."

"Anemonites," she rasped, finding it difficult to speak, both because she was exhausted and sore, and because it seemed so long since she'd made words in the open air. "Escaped merlons. The others . . . did not arrive? Not here?"

She turned her head to see that Ven Rubicas was walking

beside them, hurrying Lyssandra back to the city and the Hall of Healers. "An aquit arrived two days ago, telling us that the merlons had captured you apprentices, and that all of you had attempted to escape."

"Aquit?" Lyssandra couldn't remember seeing any of the small undersea messengers anywhere close to the merlon cities.

"Yes, Gwen sent it," Sage Pierce said. "She and Vic explained what happened, and we're putting together a full-fledged rescue operation."

"Alas, none of the others has made it to Elantya — only you. We have been patrolling the waters and beaches around the island," Rubicas added. "We must assume your companions were recaptured."

Or worse, Lyssandra thought.

"Anemonites," she managed to repeat. "Brought here."

Rubicas was grinning. "Yes, we saw them when we found you. It is wonderful that you freed them, and they have volunteered to help us with our defenses. Sage Polup is already with them."

"Thanks to them, we'll be able to respond to the merlon provocation within a day or two," Vic's father said. "Those merlons won't know what hit them."

The sages must have said more as they carried her along, but Lyssandra, with a real sense of relief this time, fell asleep.

IN THE HALL OF Healers, Lyssandra was fussed over, cleaned, fed, and told to rest. The healers helped her change out of her now-ragged brevi into a loose, comfortable gown. They were most fascinated by the gill slits on her neck.

Her family had rushed to the building, breathless and flushed with excitement. Kaisa had insisted on bringing food and a pot of her most potent greenstepe. Lyssandra's father hovered at her bedside, while her little brother Xandas chattered about how glad they were to have her back.

As soon as she felt the energizing effects of her mother's greenstepe, Lyssandra tried to get out of bed. "I must see the Pentumvirate. They must hear what I have learned."

The Healers clucked like hens, but Lyssandra's parents understood the urgency. Her mother seemed proud of Lyssandra's resilience.

"The Virs are in session. They have been meeting almost every waking hour since they received word from the aquit," her father said.

Kaisa turned to the Healers. "I know full well how to take care of my daughter. At any other time, I would insist she stay in bed for a week, but she is right. We will take her to the Pentumvirate chambers ourselves."

Lyssandra took her mother's arm and got to her feet. "Any delay puts my friends, and Elantya, at greater risk."

She had survived, had made it back to her home and family — which placed a greater burden on her shoulders. Though her other four friends had not been born in Elantya as she had been, the island was now their home, too. Vic and Gwen had Sage Pierce for their own family, and even Tiaret and Sharif had friends and Ven Rubicas to care for them.

A fresh current of guilt rippled through her that she had been the one to escape. Why couldn't it have been Vic and Gwen — the children of the prophecy? Or even Tiaret or Sharif? Their skills were superior to hers at fighting and leading. It wasn't fair for her to relax, safe and cared for, while her fellow apprentices remained in such peril. It was selfish, and she owed it to them to keep pushing herself, as tired as she was. She would see that they were rescued. She would tell the Pentumvirate everything they needed to know. She had to put every drop of strength she possessed into doing whatever it took to free them.

When they reached the governmental hall, Lyssandra stood before the five Virs and told them in great detail everything she and her friends had endured. She described the merlon city, the capricious and slightly mad King Barak, and the dark sages, Azric and Orpheon.

"These plans against us are grave, though not unexpected," said Vir Helassa. "The merlons have long resented Elantya."

"Azric is provoking them," Lyssandra said. "I think he has convinced King Barak to mount an all-out war. They have bombs made from pure lavaja."

"Yes, the freed anemonites are meeting with our best sages to explain the destructive power of these bombs," said Vir Questas. "Together they will develop a defense. Ven Rubicas believes his protective shield could save us all."

"Worse, though," Lyssandra continued, "Azric believes Gwenya and Viccus are seal-breakers. He intends to force them to break open crystal doors and set loose his armies of immortal warriors."

"Then why did he want you and the other two apprentices?" her father, Groxas, interrupted from behind her. "Were you simply captured by accident?"

At this, Vir Etherya grew pensive. "Lyssandra, do you know the children's song about the island of Elantya?"

Lyssandra nodded. "The fingerplay? Of course." She recited, adding the hand movements that went with each part of the rhyme.

Raised from deep beneath the ocean,
Five required to be complete,
Prophecies are set in motion,
Leaving evil no retreat.
Forming bonds from worlds divergent,
Pledged to serve and to protect,
At the time when need is urgent,
Ancient powers intersect.

On the final line, she interlaced her fingers and folded her hands. Only when she was finished did Lyssandra pause to wonder at the Vir's curious request.

"What does this game have to do with rescuing my son and Gwen and their friends?" Sage Pierce asked.

"That song is thousands of years old," Questas said.

In his precise, clipped voice, Parsimanias added, "Every Elantyan child learns the rhyme. It is a tradition."

"Until recently, we believed it to be a quaint verse about the formation of Elantya, but recent events have caused us to question that assumption," Helassa said. She gripped the rose decision crystal on the arm of her stone chair. "The Pentumvirate now believes that this song is not a history but a prophecy — a prophecy about the *five apprentices* of Ven Rubicas."

Lyssandra gasped as alternative meanings for each phrase in the song rushed through her mind. *Five required to be complete/Prophecies are set in motion.*

Questas smiled at her shocked reaction. "So, you see, we cannot allow the merlons to hold or injure *any* of you. Or to employ your powers to work evil deeds, as they did with the anemonites."

Sage Pierce stood up, clearing his throat. "I know I'm not objective about this, but I'd say that rescuing the kids is more important than anything else at the moment. We need to get Vic and Gwen and the others away from Azric, so he can't use them."

Sage Snigmythya wrung her hands. "We had hoped that Sharifas would use his flying carpet to aid you in your escape. His carpet . . . Did the summoning rune not work?"

Lyssandra shook her head. "He tried to call it, but the carpet never came. We thought it could not fly under water."

The five Virs looked at each other in consternation. White-robed Etherya finally asked, "Was the carpet with you when you were captured?"

Lyssandra frowned, trying to remember. "No, Sharifas left it in his chambers when we went to swim."

Helassa whispered to a young red-robed neosage beside her, who ran from the meeting hall. A few minutes later, he came back, accompanied by Ven Sage Rubicas, the two of them struggling mightily with something that they carried between them: Sharif's magic carpet, still rolled up and bound with a length of cord!

"It was there all along," Lyssandra said. "Trying to break free to rescue us!"

"Hmm, yes. Sealed in a cupboard beneath the prince's bed," Rubicas said. "After Orpheon stole my most valuable spell scrolls, I had many of our doors and cupboards inscribed with runes of protection to prevent them from opening for anyone not working with me. I never thought anything might need to get *out.* Hmm, I must work on that."

The Ven Sage removed the cord and was startled by the vehemence with which the rectangle of embroidered fabric snapped itself flat and sprang free. As if indignant, it hovered in the air, tassels trembling, then shot out of the hall.

Lyssandra grinned. "If you mean to mount a rescue operation, we had best hurry. Otherwise the flying carpet may make the attempt all by itself."

SIMULTANEOUSLY EXHAUSTED, ANXIOUS, AND grateful, Lyssandra allowed herself several hours to recover. Her mother fussed over her, making a fine restorative meal, and the ravenous escapee finished off every speck of food her mother brought, then fell into a heavy sleep. The moment she awoke, Lyssandra insisted on going to check on the preparations Ven Rubicas, her father, and Sage Pierce were making against the merlons.

"At least drink some more greenstepe," her mother said.

"I promise, Mother, once my friends are rescued, we will rest as long as you want us to." Lyssandra accepted the cup from her mother, gulped it, and rushed out of their home. As she sped on sandaled feet down the steep, cobblestone streets past whitewashed buildings, she saw people hurrying in all directions.

Like a stirred-up anthill, the harbor swarmed with activity. Multicolored smoke wafted from the chimneys of various buildings run by the sages, as well as the large laboratories in the Citadel. Everyday activities had been suspended as soon as the aquit delivered its message, and the Elantyans turned their focus toward the war. Now the entire island was on alert.

Lyssandra panted as she ran, feeling the air burn in her lungs — a strange sensation after spending so long under the sea, breathing water. When she made her way to the sheltered cove where the friends had gone swimming, she discovered a small group of neosages peering into the water, hurriedly scribbling documentation and taking notes. The group of escaped anemonite scientists had taken refuge here in the large sheltered lagoon.

Next to the diligent neosages stood a tall, hulking, manlike form made of metal and crystal, its arms and legs operated by pulleys, pistons, and tubes — Sage Polup's mechanical walking form. But the transparent head-tank in which the anemonite normally floated was empty. Polup had been removed and now burbled about in the safe, tranquil cove with his fellow anemonites.

Out at the breakwater barrier that sheltered the cove from the open sea, Elantyan engineers wearing heavy weights to help them sink, breathed through long hoses as they filled in the breach the merlons had made. Two sages, looking bedraggled and uncomfortable, splashed about and sank beside the engineers, working to scribe protective spells on the stone blocks of the breakwater, so the merlons could not open up another passage.

Lyssandra knelt by the water's edge, enjoying the exuberance of the jellyfishlike creatures and feeling warm in the knowledge that she had helped rescue them. The anemonites puttered to and fro, swiveling their rings of eyes to observe everything at once.

One of the creatures swam to the edge of the water, and the copper-haired girl heard the bubbling voice of Sage Polup. "Lyssandra, thank you for freeing my people from the terrible merlon masters. Even though these are dire times, I have not experienced so much hope since I first came to Elantya."

She bowed her head. "It was necessary, Sage Polup. The anemonites were enslaved. My friends and I only did what had to be done, as any Elantyan would."

Other anemonites began clustering around Polup. Some of their kraega steeds remained with them inside the cove. Two of the jellyfish scientists worked with the sharp antenna scribes to draw patterns on flat slates covered with a glowing algae.

"Elantyans should not need to leave friends behind," Polup said. "My people and I will not let them be sacrificed for us."

Gedup, the anemonite Blackfrill had threatened to kill as an example to the others, added in a higher-pitched voice like the whistling steam from a stepekettle, "You did more than free us from the merlons. You deprived them of our knowledge — which we now offer freely and enthusiastically to Elantya."

The neosages finished copying patterns from the underwater slateboard the kraegas were scribing. "They have provided remarkable designs. Look." The young neosage wiped sweat from his forehead and extended the sheet of parchment to Lyssandra. "This must be delivered to the laboratory of Ven Rubicas immediately. Shall I summon a skrit?"

"No." Lyssandra took it. "I will run there myself. Perhaps I can help them." She saw a drawing of a propulsion system adapted for use on a small, swift boat on the water's surface. "Who will use this?"

Gedup was still bobbing on the surface of the tide pool. "Sage Pierce has insisted that his speedboat vessel from Earth has the most suitable design. Its motor has no fuel. This can help."

Polup added, "More submersible bubble ships are being assembled, like the one presented to me at the great celebration. I call them bubletts. With these, we anemonites will not be slow and helpless under the water. We can swim faster than a shark, and will help you to rescue your friends."

Lyssandra felt a sense of relief. "Wonderful. I was afraid I might need to do it alone."

"You are never alone, Lyssandra. No one in Elantya is."

MUCH OF THE FURNITURE had been removed from Ven Rubicas's laboratory and study rooms, to be replaced by enormous tables, boxes of scrap metal, pipes, cloth, and a clutter of spell scrolls. Lyssandra smelled bitter fumes and the tang of molten metal and mixing chemicals.

Her father was there, hunched over a deep basin of water, his bushy beard tangled and smeared with either ash or chemical powder. He had large stone bowls in which he mixed fine-grained crystals of different colors. Groxas dipped a fingertip into one bowl, touched it to his tongue, frowned at the recipe, and added a handful of one powder, then another.

Rubicas looked extremely preoccupied as he paced from table to table. Including the assembly of the bubletts, Lyssandra counted seven entirely different projects taking place, all under the Ven Sage's supervision.

Vic's father was there, too, his eyes looking shadowy and hollow, his dark hair disheveled as he contemplated sketched designs from spell scrolls on the table. In front of him raised up on supports was the purple boat he had brought with him from his world — one of the strangest vessels Lyssandra had ever seen, filled with even stranger equipment.

"Ahh, Lyssandra, you are here," Ven Rubicas said. "We can always use another intelligent mind, an extra pair of sharp eyes, and two more skillful hands."

With a smile at her father, she hurried to the Ven Sage and handed him the drawing the anemonites had made. He skimmed it curiously and his eyes lit up. His bushy eyebrows rose up on his forehead. "Fascinating — and practical, too. Perhaps someday it can be expanded to work with large ships, just as I am working to expand my smaller shield spell to protect all of Elantya. I am glad to see that the anemonites are more than just thinkers in this great conflict."

"They feel responsible," Lyssandra said. "Some of them have volunteered to use the new bubletts to participate directly in the rescue operations."

With a flash and a puff of smoke, a miniature volcano of bright sparks erupted from where her father was working. He cried out, stepped back, and flung a thick cloth onto the blazing mixture of powders, smothering it. "There!" Groxas said, grinning at his daughter. "I think that is precisely the right mixture."

"Are not preparations for a victory celebration premature, Father?" Lyssandra asked in a bewildered voice.

"Oh, these are not *sky* fireworks, Daughter. I have been working with Sage Polup on a new concept. Did you notice I did not throw water on that blaze to extinguish it? Water would only have made it burn brighter. These are *sea* fireworks, specially formulated with a chemical and magical composition to blaze brilliantly under water — our most beautiful weapon. We will give those merlons a blinding show such as they have never seen before." Her father chuckled and Ven Rubicas grinned.

"But we cannot destroy the merlon city," she said. "We would risk hurting my friends."

With a grim and determined expression, Sage Pierce stepped away from the engine of the purple speedboat he was working on. "We have no intention of letting Vic, Gwen, or your other friends come to harm. But we're going to need a diversion to keep the merlons occupied so we can sneak down and rescue them. With this new propulsion system, my speedboat should get us to the right spot quickly."

Rubicas continued, "At dawn, Vir Helassa launches a full fleet of Elantyan war galleys. Between that show of force and a hundred or so sea fireworks in the water around the merlon city, we should have enough of a diversion to allow some anemonite bubletts and Sage Pierce to find them — with your guidance."

"Sage Pierce? Should he not stay —"

Vic's father reached into his boat and hauled out an odd rubbery suit and a heavy tank. "I'm the only one who can use this scuba gear I brought along. If Vic and Gwen need my help, then I'm going down there."

"Hmm, yes. It seems there is little point in arguing," Rubicas said.

"I would do the same," Groxas agreed, looking at Lyssandra.

Sage Pierce gave Lyssandra a meaningful, questioning look. "Tell me, how are Vic and Gwen holding up? Do you really think they're all right?"

"I cannot know for certain, Sage Pierce. I believe they are alive and strong — I *feel* it — but Azric does have evil plans for them. They need our help, so we must not delay." She looked around the bustling chamber and saw everyone using their abilities to help in the wartime preparations. All of Elantya was working together on this single operation.

"The aquit's message granted us a head start, and we will work through the night if necessary," said Ven Rubicas. "No matter what, we depart with the war fleet at dawn."

27

FOLDING HIS HANDS AND pressing his steepled forefingers together, Azric greeted Vic and Gwen with a sad smile. "I thought you understood the importance of this project to me. I truly did. I informed you that your friends' lives would be in danger should you prove uncooperative."

Separating them from Tiaret and Sharif yet again, refusing to answer what he would do to their friends, the dark sage had taken the two away from the merlon city. The water seemed murky and cold, as if a thick storm were gathering overhead above the sea.

Azric continued in his silky voice, "Yet I failed to recognize that you perceived an equal or greater threat to your friends *in Elantya,* as well. Such a perception would naturally figure into your decision on whether to escape. In addition, I held back information from you, hoping to use it at a later time to secure your goodwill. This was foolish, of course. I blame myself."

Gwen tried to jerk away as the deceptively handsome dark sage, the very model of congeniality, slipped an arm through hers and then through Vic's. "Allow me to show you something that cannot help but interest you. It will change your whole perspective on the idea of assisting me."

She and Vic had dreaded the moment when they would have to talk to Azric alone after their attempted escape and after Lyssandra had gotten away. The cousins were sure that the telepathic girl was still alive, that she had escaped after all. They *sensed* it. A strange and undeniable link had developed among the apprentices. They could not hear each other's thoughts, but Vic and Gwen felt an absolute, gut-level certainty that all of their friends were safe.

At the moment, Gwen shuddered for herself and for Vic, anticipating Azric's fury. Would he stain them with further agonizing tattoos? Or brand them the way Orpheon had marked Sharif and the hapless great jhanta? Would he hurt or even kill Sharif and Tiaret, just to make his point? The young man from Irrakesh had certainly taken the brunt of the punishment for their two escape attempts thus far.

Gwen knew that she could not let herself cooperate with Azric's evil plans. The consequences would simply be too devastating.

The dark sage guided them along. He sounded so reasonable. She was convinced he had hatched some sort of scheme to manipulate the cousins. After leaving the city far behind with his fast-paced swimming, they soon arrived at an enormous upcropping of volcanic rock completely surrounded by wild coral growths.

With a firm nudge, Azric pushed the cousins into the ink-dark maw of an underwater cave. With a sharp fingernail, he traced a rune in the wall just inside the entrance, and an eerie puce-colored glow began emanating from the walls above, below, and around them. By this unsettling light, they were able to see that the reef cavern was round, with a perfect domed ceiling. Tunnels led away from the chamber in several directions, including straight up and straight down; all of them had smooth, shiny walls, obviously cut by merlon magic. A pair of electric eels emerged from the tunnel above them and swam along behind Vic and Gwen like intimidating sentries.

"Excellent. All is ready for our visit! Vic, you'll be especially glad I brought you here." Azric swam forward with undulating movements of his body. With the electric eels close behind them, the cousins had no choice but to follow.

A faint tingle started at the soles of Gwen's feet, ran up her legs, tickled its way along her backbone, and spread to the tips of her fingers. "This must be a place of great power," she said. She could see that Vic sensed it, too. The deeper they swam, the stronger the sensation grew.

By the time they emerged into an enormous cavern filled with bright yellow light and very warm water, Gwen felt as if every nerve ending on her body had awakened. Azric led them straight toward the source of the brilliant glow. "Come along, it's just up here."

The curved floor of the cavern formed a basin into which

hundreds of golden ovoid objects had been heaped, throwing off heat and honey-colored light.

"Sheesh!" Vic muttered. "Either we found the lair where the goose lays its golden eggs, or we're somewhere near the hatching grounds on Pern." Gwen knew she should reprimand him for making jokes in their dire situation, but she actually found it comforting. Vic turned his aquamarine gaze toward the dark sage. "Is that what it is? Dragon eggs, I mean?"

Azric made a slight moue with his lips. "No dragons — not even sea serpents, I'm afraid. They're bombs. Lavaja bombs, to be exact. Designed for me by your friends, the anemonites. Go ahead, you can pick one up. Since they can only be detonated by a spell, you're in no danger."

Gwen bent down and pretended to examine the heap of magical high explosives. Vic put a hand on one, then picked it up. "What are they for?" Gwen asked, though she knew the answer before the dark sage spoke.

"Elantya," he said in a casual voice. "We learned our lesson after our previous attempt to invade. But we haven't stopped working beneath the water, excavating tunnels, undermining the very foundation of the island."

Gwen suddenly remembered the unexpected earthquake that had struck while they filled the aquarium in Ven Rubicas's laboratory.

Azric reached down, picked up one of the golden bombs, gently tossed it higher in the water, then caught it as it drifted down again. "We've been planting these explosives throughout the catacombs, right under your feet. When all is finished, I will speak the detonation spell." He tossed the bomb upward again. "Elantya will be severed from its foundations and sink forever beneath the waves. Proud fools." He caught the egg-bomb again and Gwen was reminded of Piri's transparent sphere.

Poor Piri. Poor Sharif. Azric, Orpheon, and the merlons already had a great deal to answer for. And now they were trying to kill everyone in Elantya. Gwen gritted her teeth. "Why would you tell us about this if you're still trying to win our support? You're not exactly making us want to help you."

Azric spread his hands. "Why, of course I'm showing you this to demonstrate that there's no point in going back to your doomed island. Very soon, there will be nothing to go back *to.* And the sages of Elantya have only themselves to blame. They dared to build an island in a world where there was no dry land without asking the native inhabitants for permission." He gave a short laugh. "By the laws of magic, this world belongs to the merlons, and they have the right to protect it from intruders."

Even though Azric was probably twisting the truth, Gwen had an uncomfortable feeling. Did she really know everything there was to know about this situation? Could Azric actually have a point? Were the merlons just defending what was theirs? That was probably how King Barak saw it.

"That's no excuse for murdering everyone," Vic said.

"To be sure," Azric said. "To be sure. I have considered saving the brightest and best. Such as two talented seal-breakers like yourselves."

"We won't help you kill anyone," Gwen vowed.

"Nope," Vic said. "And why did you think *I* would be especially interested?"

"I've saved the best for last," Azric said with a friendly, almost mischievous smile. "Come along."

Gwen wanted to scream or punch him or choke him, but what good would that do? And how *did* one choke an immortal wizard who could breathe underwater?

One of the electric eels butted her from behind, giving her a nasty shock. With a resigned sigh, she followed Azric out of the cavern.

AZRIC GUIDED THEM TO another cavern in the mounded reef. Now, the water grew cooler, which Vic found refreshing. He didn't trust the dark sage as far as he could spit — which, under water, was very difficult to do anyway — so he stayed alert, trying to expect the unexpected. The youthful-looking dark sage obviously had something up his sleeve.

A trio of eels guarded the second cavern. After Azric traced the light rune, the cousins followed him into a long tunnel, which was narrow and lined with sharp, clear crystals. Vic and Gwen had to be careful not to touch the walls as they swam. The familiar tingle was here again, indicating magical power, but the water grew colder and colder. Even so, Vic wasn't uncomfortable. For some reason, the power tingle along his arms and legs and back kept both the heat and cold from being anything more than interesting. He glanced around him at the jagged crystals on the tunnel walls.

Gwen gasped, and he snapped his head up to see what she was looking at. Before them was a cavern almost too beautiful to comprehend. The entire chamber seemed to be filled with cut crystal, as if they had ventured into the heart of a giant chandelier. Bright white light radiated from every direction. Millions of sparkling stalactites dangled from the ceiling, while corresponding stalagmites jabbed upward from the floor.

"Whoa. Are those aja crystals?" Vic asked.

"Not precisely," Azric said, folding his hands and pressing his steepled forefingers together. "This is more of a hybrid. I call it ice coral. A very useful substance, for my purposes at least."

"We have ice coral on Earth," Gwen pointed out, demonstrating her knowledge of aquatic life. "But it doesn't look anything like this."

"Completely different things, young lady. Somehow this species of coral managed to incorporate aja crystal into itself, producing this. Orpheon and I have not yet explored all of its uses, but it has an amazing cooling capacity and therefore quite useful preservative properties."

"It's . . . beautiful," Gwen said.

"Come this way. I have something you've been searching for." He beckoned them toward a sheet of ice coral several meters in diameter mounted over an alcove in the wall of the grotto. The ice coral here was as flat and shiny as a mirror.

With his finger, Azric drew a rune on its surface and murmured a word. The surface turned clear as water, becoming a window.

"Mom!" Vic cried, overjoyed at first, then concerned, then furious. He rounded on Azric. "You killed my mother!"

The dark sage's expression did not change. "I assure you,

she's quite alive. She's just in . . . storage, in a place where she can't harm my plans."

"You had her here all along and didn't tell us?" Gwen said.

"I had hoped I wouldn't have to use her as a threat, or an example. But, alas, you two have proved quite intractable."

"What happened? What did you do to her?" Vic demanded.

"I merely asked your mother to break the seal on a crystal door for me, to . . . liberate a world that is of particular interest to me. As I explained before, seal-breaking is a process that requires vast amounts of magical energy, far more than simply *opening* a crystal door. In fact, afterward a seal-breaker needs to recharge for five years or more before attempting it again. Sadly, Kyara tricked me. Instead of unsealing a door to free one of my immortal armies, she managed to shake off my guards long enough to reach the sealed crystal door to a perfectly useless place, a barely inhabited world with scrubby plants and only a squalid village or two. She wasted her energies on breaking the seal, and rendered herself unable to try again for five years!" His mismatched eyes narrowed, but he quickly composed himself. "I was quite displeased with her."

Vic swam closer to the clear enclosure that held his mother's body and pressed himself against its frigid surface, trying to see better. She wore a flowing gown of diaphanous green layers and her dark hair rippled in the water. Around her neck on a fine chain hung a five-sided xyridium medallion, inscribed with a strange symbol, just like his and Gwen's. He pounded his hand against the ice coral, hoping to wake her up. "Mom! Mom!"

Azric sighed. "As I mentioned, ice coral has potent preservative qualities. It would have taken a cadre of well-trained merlon guards to keep constant watch over Kyara, and that would have been a waste of resources. Therefore, I deemed it wisest to allow your mother to sleep until her powers recharged themselves."

Vic looked up at him. "Can I talk to her?"

The dark sage nodded pensively. "You'll have to earn that privilege. For now, dear Kyara will be quite safe, *as long as the two of you do as you're told.* Perhaps once you've broken a seal for me, I will let you speak with her."

Vic's heart sank. In order to talk to his mother, he or his cousin would essentially have to help Azric recover his armies and possibly conquer worlds. "What if we don't?"

Azric gave an eloquent shrug. "Being revived from ice coral is quite a sensitive process. In addition, ice coral is extremely delicate. If it should be accidentally jostled or broken, or if perhaps an aja bomb were to be detonated nearby, I'm afraid Kyara would not survive."

Vic pressed his cheek against the ice coral. He finally had an answer about his mother: She was alive, but caught within powerful sorcery. For more than two years he had wanted to see her, had wanted his family back together.

It was still possible, of course. Visions of an idyllic future danced in his mind: *A family picnic on the beach. He and his parents would sit on the soft sand talking and soaking up the sun, while Gwen frolicked in the surf, playing fetch with a golden retriever named Orson.* Vic wasn't sure why he had imagined a golden retriever, but it seemed like a family dog, and therefore rounded out the picture. His father was in Elantya now, but with his mother trapped here, frozen underwater, would they ever be together as a family again?

He and Gwen were in an impossible position. They had to protect his mother, and they had to find a way to save Elantya from the merlons' destruction. It was a fine line to walk. How far would they have to go?

He gave the dark sage a bleak look. "What do you want us to do first?"

THE ELANTYAN WAR GALLEYS, led by Helassa and Admiral Bradsinoreus on the *Bright Warrior,* glided out of the harbor and cut like sharp swords through the sea. Golden sunlight from the eastern horizon glinted off the polished armor of their prows. Protective designs were painted in glittering aja pigments along the sides of their curved hulls.

With war drums setting the cadence, like hearts pounding before battle, muscular soldiers pulled the oars while sages stood on the decks, reading from spell scrolls to add a nudge of current and wind, increasing their speed.

Accompanying the galleys, Sage Pierce's flashy speedboat from Earth zipped along, propelled by its new magical motor. Lyssandra rode with Vic's father in the glossy purple boat, looking across at the warships, anxious over what they were about to attempt. She had slept restlessly the night before, again troubled by mystic and disturbing dreams. Lyssandra rubbed the almost invisible cuts at the base of her neck, where Orpheon's spell had given her gills.

The speedboat's deck was already loaded with the equipment that Sage Pierce intended to use in their rescue efforts. Copying the original vessel designed for Sage Polup, the hard-working teams in Rubicas's laboratory had completed three more of the small bubletts. Each was made of silvery metal topped by a clear bubble tank of water, in which the volunteer anemonite scientists waited, ready to launch.

By noon, with the aid of Elantyan spells, they all arrived in the vicinity of the submerged metropolis, which Lyssandra and the anemonites had pinpointed. The speedboat scouted the area, while the warships made ready. With the hulls of numerous galleys prominently obtruding beneath the surface, the merlons would pay little attention to such a small boat. Or so they hoped.

The water around them was glass-smooth, like a mirror reflecting the blue sky. Everything seemed peaceful and calm. Not even a breeze ruffled the ocean. The war drums on one galley after another stopped, the soldiers lifted their oars from the water and locked them into place, and the ships coasted to a halt. The final drumbeats faded into silence.

Surely the merlons had heard the vibrations and seen the dark predatory shapes of the galleys slicing through the water. Even now, King Barak must be summoning his generals, rallying his aquatic warriors. Perhaps Azric himself would join in the battle. And that, Lyssandra was sure, would give them a chance to find Vic, Gwen, Tiaret, and Sharif.

Beside the copper-haired girl, Sage Pierce stared toward the blue horizon, shading his eyes. Perhaps he held out a faint hope that Vic and Gwen and their friends had escaped after all and were even now swimming toward them, which would make this entire operation unnecessary.

On the prow of the lead galley, Vir Helassa raised her hands, and shouted to the commanders on all of the ships. "Prepare to face our enemy! Ven Rubicas, Admiral, Sages Groxas, Polup, and Pierce — are you ready?"

From their various locations, all of them indicated their readiness. Fighters ran about the decks, gathering their weapons. Lyssandra's bearded father directed brawny workers to position small barrels filled with his special sea-fireworks mixtures.

Sage Pierce touched her arm. "Let's get ready, Lyssandra. We never know when the merlons will show up."

Working the controls of the new motor, he inconspicuously guided the speedboat away from the main cluster of war galleys. Lyssandra checked the four small bubletts, prepared to deploy them when it was time. The anemonites drifted contentedly inside their bubletts, testing the controls, getting used to the release mechanisms of their simple weapons. Fingering the gills on her neck, Lyssandra hoped she could remember how to breathe under water.

As the speedboat withdrew from the Elantyan ships, Sage Pierce moved methodically, pulling on the rubbery wet suit, gloves, socks, swim fins, mask, and tank. Despite the urgency he obviously felt, Lyssandra understood why he could not afford to rush. Deep underwater, any mistake could become a disaster for someone without gills. Vic's father refused to do anything that would hinder his chances of rescuing the captives. When he was done, he looked almost like a strange sea creature himself.

Looking up to the deck of the *Bright Warrior,* Lyssandra watched her father roll some of the waterproofed barrels filled with his special powder to the edge of the deck. The barrels were sealed with spells designed to release the aquatic fireworks as soon as they reached the appropriate depth. Groxas waved over at her, and she waved back with a bold assurance she did not feel.

"This is too quiet," Lyssandra said uneasily. "The merlon king hates surface dwellers. He cannot ignore this war fleet. And I do not trust Azric either."

"They must be preparing something, then," Vic's father said as he checked his diving suit, and put on the weight belt. "But they can't possibly know what we have in mind. We'll see how they respond as soon as —"

The glassy, smooth surface of the sea shattered like a breaking mirror. First, five scaly merlon heads broke the surface. Then twenty. Then a hundred. The snaking forms of sea serpents also split the water, displaying their brand marks, polished metal spikes, armor, and harnesses.

King Barak appeared among the warriors in a mother-of-pearl chariot drawn by two large sea serpents, and Azric was beside him. Both looked confident, as if *they* had lured the Elantyan war galleys into a trap.

From the *Bright Warrior,* Helassa shouted orders, and the war drums began to beat again. Oars dipped into the water, and the galleys shot forward, ready for battle. Groxas prepared to launch his explosive sea fireworks. Admiral Bradsinoreus and his sailors and soldiers lined the decks holding long harpoons.

Seeing the merlon king and the dark sage working together on some sort of spell, spilling blazing lavaja in rune designs on top of the water, Lyssandra cried, "Azric and the merlon king are working magic together. This is worse than I had feared!"

"Or better," Sage Pierce said. "The fleet came out here to divert the merlons' attention so that we can slip under the water and pull off a rescue mission." His lips quirked in a smile. "Yup. This is shaping up to be the perfect diversion." The speedboat raced away from the center of the brewing battle.

Azric and the merlon king finished their lavaja spell, unleashing a strange magic. Already, clots of black cloud stained the sky overhead. The wind freshened, swirling, picking up water and stirring it into a vortex. Three separate focal points of the weather magic churned the ocean into a froth with invisible propellers, pulling funnels up into the air to form a trio of angry waterspouts.

The sea tornadoes danced and thrashed, kicking up spray and moving toward the Elantyan fleet as if they were living things that could tear the armored war galleys into splinters. Facing the approaching waterspouts, Vir Helassa and the sages on the galleys shouted counter-spells from fluttering scrolls into the rising wind.

As the purple speedboat slipped away, Lyssandra felt as if they were letting the other Elantyans down. But they had their own job to do. Watching the whirling tornadoes churn toward the war galleys, she knew Vic's father was right — this was going to be a spectacular diversion.

29

NOT RELYING ENTIRELY ON the waterspouts, the merlons began to attack the massed Elantyan ships directly. The female general Goldskin rode one of the lead sea serpents, raising a jagged trident into the salty air. Merlon warriors splashed and burbled, making a hooting sound of challenge, and all the giant serpents rallied. Goldskin bellowed a loud, vibrating call to her soldiers.

Massive black shapes as large as the Elantyan war galleys breached and then splashed down. The gigantic whales — also enslaved by the undersea people — were covered with barnacles onto which needle-sharp spikes had been fixed. The menacing creatures moved toward the ships. Human soldiers and sailors rowed frantically, trying to move the galleys out of the way, but the attack came from all sides.

The angry water tornadoes spun closer, sending up spray.

The ocean around them was choppy now. The galleys rocked and swayed.

From a distance, Lyssandra watched her burly father roll the first spell-barrel off the deck. It splashed on the surface of the water, then sank quickly. The approaching merlons who saw it paid little heed, continuing to swim forward. Groxas shouted, and three more spell-barrels were pitched into the ocean. From other war galleys, five additional spell-barrels plopped overboard and sank.

"The fireworks will begin in just a few seconds," Sage Pierce said. "Get ready to go overboard. Is this the right spot?"

"As near as the anemonites and I can tell."

Lyssandra pushed Sage Polup's bublett over the side. The bubble-topped vessel splashed into the ocean upside down, then righted itself. The anemonite activated the engines, and the miniature sub began circling the speedboat.

Lyssandra gave the second bublett a shove. Though they appeared small, the metal hull, engines, and water-filled tank made the vessels quite heavy. Pushing the bubletts overboard without help proved more difficult than she had expected. Fortunately, the deck of the speedboat tilted downward with a swell, and the second bublett dropped into the ocean beside Polup's.

Suddenly, booming reverberations rose from the deep water below. Lyssandra could see flashes of light and brilliant showers of sparks accompanying a swell of bubbles released by the underwater explosion.

Two more dazzling blossoms shattered the undersea calm, making the merlons on the surface frantic. Some dove deep to investigate, others pressed forward with their attack on the war galleys. The soldiers on the decks hurled their harpoons at the sea serpents. One jagged spear penetrated the scaly hide of an attacking monster, but the others bounced harmlessly off the serpents' armor.

Lyssandra hurried with her work, hopeful that they could free her friends now that the merlons were so preoccupied.

The first of the waterspouts circled the *Bright Warrior*, coiling like a bullwhip, then lashing toward the prow, where Vir Helassa and her best sages stood reading from their spell scrolls. The whirling water howled and splashed forward, only to strike an invisible barrier, like a wall of wind, that deflected the watery tornado.

The barnacled whales, however, were not so easily diverted. Diving deep beneath the surface, one of the rough-backed sea beasts shot upward to ram into the keel of an outlying galley, nearly capsizing the vessel. The rows of oars flailed like the tiny legs of a centipede in the air. The whale submerged again and grated its back against the bottom hull, as if trying to scrape off the clustered barnacles.

The damaged galley rocked and tilted. A dozen Elantyan soldiers fell into the water and tried to swim back to the ships as sailors tossed down rope ladders. But attacking merlons closed in on them with deadly speed, raising their scallop-edged scimitars and narwhal-tipped spears. Only two of the Elantyan soldiers made it back to safety on the deck.

Meanwhile, Goldskin led the sea serpents in a charge against two Elantyan galleys. Archers and harpoon throwers made a concerted defense against the slithering sea creatures.

The female general shrieked orders, and the merlons attacked. Seven of them jumped from the backs of the sea serpents onto the decks of the war galleys, where they threw themselves into direct combat with Elantyan soldiers.

Vic's father quickly helped Lyssandra push the last two anemonite bubletts into the water. Now all four of the small vehicles were in motion, circling, ready to submerge. "Time to go overboard, Lyssandra." He picked up his specialized face mask, tugged the air hose, and checked the regulators on his tank.

Another of the black whales swam inexorably toward the *Bright Warrior,* ready to ram it. Lyssandra looked up from her work, pausing out of concern for her father aboard that ship. She tried to shout a warning, but the speedboat was much too far away. Nevertheless, the men and women on deck had already seen the threat. Groxas rolled one of the spell-barrels to the edge of the deck, calling for Ven Rubicas.

As the whale picked up speed, coming closer and closer, the soldiers aboard the galley braced themselves. Some threw harpoons, but they were like tiny needles to the beast, not powerful enough to make it pause.

Rubicas swiftly altered the aja crystal rune on the side of the spell-barrel, and Lyssandra's father heaved the barrel over his head with both hands and threw it down into the path of the oncoming whale.

Only a second after the barrel struck the water, the bubble spell dissolved and the sea fireworks erupted right in front of the gigantic black creature. Rockets and feathers and horsetails of light in blue, orange, red, and yellow splashed in all directions. The whale reared, spinning so that one wide fleshy flipper splashed up. Then the creature dove deep under the water, blinded by the flash as sparks continued to sizzle in all directions.

Lyssandra had been unable to tear her eyes away, but Sage Pierce tugged on her arm. Startled by an ominous howling sound, she turned to see one of the waterspouts racing toward them, whipping up spray.

"I guess they noticed us after all!" Sage Pierce gunned the magical engines and the speedboat circled, dodging through the water. He steered the boat on a zigzag course, and the sea tornadoes gave chase, though the merlons could not move the waterspouts so accurately. They had much larger concerns with the Elantyan war fleet.

The bubletts were already under the water, and Sage Pierce tried to circle around to get back to the right spot in the ocean. "Time to dive!" he called, pulling the full face mask over his eyes, nose, and mouth. The two of them jumped overboard, leaving the purple speedboat just as the waterspout glanced past.

Lyssandra plunged into the sea as the funnel of silvery white froth rocked and then capsized the boat like a toy, and spun it around. She felt herself being pulled by the current, sucked back toward the surface. She couldn't breathe. Her gills flapped, but her lungs still held air. Finally, she expelled the bubbles, coughing and choking, trying to reset her lungs to accept seawater. But she wasn't strong enough to swim against the maelstrom.

Sage Pierce, with his weight belt, sank rapidly. He moved

his arms and flippered feet to swim, though he was already out of the current's clutches. Then, unexpectedly, Polup's bublett streaked in front of Lyssandra, and she grabbed the metal fin at the back of the teardrop base. As the little vessel dove, she held on, letting the anemonite sage pull her deep out of harm's way. Finally she drew a swift rushing breath through her gill slits and felt energy flood into her bloodstream again.

The tornado churned past, rumbling like thunder under water.

Flashes of color showed that the sea fireworks bombardment was continuing. The four anemonite bubletts, towing Lyssandra and now Vic's father, as well, streaked downward toward the fairy-tale structures of the merlon city.

30

THREE MERLON GUARDS WERE stationed just outside the scalloped windoor, again. The cousins had been taken back to the undersea tower to wait alone while Tiaret and Sharif worked at Lavaja Canyon alongside the rest of the slaves. With a growing sense of dread, Vic feared that he and Gwen would soon be forced to cooperate.

Now that Azric had shown them Vic's mother frozen in ice coral, the dark sage seemed confident he could bend them to his will. Vic felt miserable. He no longer had any idea how they could get out of this.

Thinking about his mother, he wondered if there might not be some way to free her from the ice coral. Doctors sometimes saved people who had died of hypothermia, but he wasn't sure how it was done. And this was tied to some kind of spell. Simply smashing his mother out of the ice coral could be deadly if he didn't know what he was doing.

Gwen stared out the guarded windoor to the open undersea expanse. "Hey, Taz! Something's going on out there!" Her voice carried equal measures of concern and hope.

Vic joined her, saw undersea warriors moving about the merlon city in a flurry. They swam in squads, summoning packs of trained sharks, rallying sea serpents, all of them rushing up toward the distant surface. They even saw King Barak riding with Azric in a strange seashell chariot drawn by serpents.

"Somebody must have sounded an alarm," Vic said, craning his neck and trying to see up through the shimmering depths.

"Do you think it's the Elantyans coming for us? Maybe if Lyssandra got through . . . ?" Gwen turned her violet eyes toward him with a small hopeful smile.

Two of the guards outside the windoor consulted each other, barked orders for the remaining merlon to stay, then swam off to join the fray. Something big was happening. Through the black seashells in their ears, Vic and Gwen heard angry chatter, shouted orders, a call to arms. Vic grinned. Something told him that his dad was up there, trying to rescue them. Dr. Pierce was not the type to give up.

The fireworks started. The first flash of light was only a distant flicker, then a brighter burst accompanied it. They could hear thumps and rumbles reverberating through the water. "Those sound like depth charges," Vic said.

"They won't try to blow up the merlon city if they know we're down here," Gwen said.

"Nope. The explosions aren't even coming close — but they're sure creating quite a disturbance."

Agitated fish swam past the tower. The lone merlon guard outside the entrance thrashed about, glaring in at the cousins, then looking up toward the continuing display. He seemed angry to be stuck down here while a great battle was going on overhead.

Fireworks exploded in repeated flashes of color. Two branded sharks streaked past. The guard at their windoor shook his spear in frustration.

Vic looked at Gwen, wondering if they might somehow be able to overpower the guard. With all the warriors gone up above and the remaining people in chaos, the merlon city seemed almost deserted.

"Doc, this might be our chance," he said as quietly as he could. Gwen's hand clenched into a fist, but they had no weapons.

Just then, a teardrop-shaped craft flitted outside the tower's windoor entrance, a self-contained vehicle that zoomed in circles. The merlon guard, suddenly on the alert, jabbed at it with his spear. A second bubble vehicle drove in, as if to taunt the guard. Vic's mouth dropped open in surprise when he saw an anemonite inside the craft. "It's Sage Polup's minisub!"

The guard left his post and pursued the bubletts. Vic watched through the mesh of one windoor, wondering if they dared to take a chance.

Now, a swimmer entered through the open windoor on the opposite side of the tower chamber — a human form with flippers, rubbery skin, and scuba tanks! Lyssandra swam in beside Dr. Carlton Pierce. Vic saw his father's bright eyes behind the full-face diving mask, and watched a trail of silvery exhaust bubbles spill from the air hose.

Lyssandra spoke through the shells in their ears. "Come with us. Are you ready to escape?"

THEY STREAKED OUT OF the tower, swimming as fast as they could. After leading the merlon guard on a wild-goose chase, the anemonite bubletts circled around to join the four swimmers.

"We cannot leave without Tiaret and Sharif," Lyssandra said. "Are they out at the lavaja cracks?"

"Yup. But there's something else — something we have to show my dad first." Vic didn't know if they could free his mother from the ice coral, but he couldn't leave without giving his father the chance.

Gwen hastened to support him. "It's more complicated than you think." Seeing Lyssandra's expression of surprise and anxiety, she added, "And very important. We have to go there."

The copper-haired girl gave them each some items she had brought along for the rescue, the crystal daggers from Vir Helassa, the finger suntips from Sage Polup, and even Snigmythya's handkerchiefs, all neatly stored in the leather pouches Vir Questas had given them. "I thought you might find these useful."

As the furious battle continued on the surface, sea fireworks flashed and boomed through the water. All the merlon warriors seemed to relish a good fight. Vic didn't think King Barak and Azric suspected that the purpose of the attack was to provide an opportunity for the prisoners to escape.

The bubletts pulled them along like underwater scooters. Vic and Gwen directed the anemonites toward the reef mound that held the ice coral grotto. Despite their speed, Vic felt that the journey took an eternity. He hoped that his father, or Lyssandra, or the anemonites could free his mother.

"Whatever this is all about, kids, we need to hurry," Dr. Pierce said, sounding muted inside his full-face mask. "I don't know how long the diversion will last."

When they reached the cavern mouth at last, Gwen got out her finger suntip to help Vic find the rune Azric had activated on the wall. Vic traced the rune while his cousin muttered the syllables that they had heard Azric use — though they contained a ridiculous number of consonants, and Vic wasn't sure she pronounced everything correctly. The walls produced only a faint glow.

"Suck it up, Pierce," Gwen muttered to herself. Closing her eyes, she spoke the syllables again, though with a slightly different inflection and tone.

"Cool," Vic said as a bright, clear light blazed from every wall and tunnel. "Let's go."

Before they could move, though, the trio of guardian electric eels darted in to block the way. "Look out!" Vic knocked the closest anemonite bublett to one side just before it could touch a deadly eel.

The bublett Lyssandra grasped, however, extruded a pair of slender grappling arms and powered forward toward the serpentine guards. The sharp pincers grabbed two of the eels, the first one by its midsection and the second by its head. As the grapplers clamped down, the eels released simultaneous bolts of energy, short-circuiting the bublett's controls. Lyssandra, close to the burst, went rigid, shuddering from the pulsing shocks.

Vic cried out.

Fortunately Dr. Pierce had insulated gloves. He grabbed the girl and pulled her free of the bublett and the discharging eels. Although the anemonite inside the bublett struggled to restart the self-contained vehicle, the unresponsive craft drifted toward the floor of the cavern, its circuits dead. One of the drained eels wriggled its way free, but the other was still held by the grappling claw.

Vic's father grabbed the escaped eel, pulled it by its tail, and snapped it like a whip against the cavern wall.

The three remaining anemonite bubletts ranged themselves around Vic, Gwen, and Lyssandra in a protective cordon. Holding the motionless Lyssandra, Vic saw that the gill slits were taking in water. "Still breathing. Pulse is regular, but slow." He turned to Gwen. "Stay with her."

"Where do you think you're going?"

"To help Dad!" He launched himself toward the remaining eels.

Seeing a fresh target, the uninjured eel darted toward Vic, ready to blast him with repeated shocks. But his father seized it with his other gloved hand, grabbing its tail and holding on. Vic snatched the drained eel that was trying to wriggle out of the pincer of the fried bublett. Already discharged, it could only jolt Vic with faint zaps, and he grimly held on.

Together, like Zorro and son, Vic and his father cracked their eel-whips against the wall. By the time they finished, Lyssandra had revived, though she was still a bit dazed.

One of the anemonite bubletts landed beside the disabled one. "Imbra is my daughter. She may ride with me," Gedup said, opening the canopies of the bubletts, so the two jellyfish-brains could occupy the same crowded tank. They left the ruined bublett on the floor of the cave.

Now, when the miniature subs zipped forward, Vic and Lyssandra shared a bublett, each holding on with one hand, as Gwen led the way down the narrow tunnel filled with jagged crystals. Though the encounter with the eels had lasted only a few minutes, Vic felt an acute urgency. He needed to get to his mother, to break her free from the ice coral. His dad would know what to do. The water grew chilly around them, and he knew they must be close.

Once they entered the marvelous chandelier-like chamber, he and Gwen wasted no time. They swam straight toward the flat, broad patch of ice coral and traced the rune on it. "Over here, Dad! She's here."

"Who is?" His father hurried over just as the pane of frozen coral turned transparent to reveal Kyara, motionless behind the protective barrier. Watching the look of hope, joy, and astonishment on his father's face, Vic felt his throat tighten.

He had to swallow several times to ease the constriction. Through the diver's face mask he could see tears well up in his father's eyes. "Is she . . . is she . . . ?"

"She's alive, but Azric used the aja in the ice coral to cast a spell to hold her frozen like that."

Dr. Pierce didn't waste any time. "Gwen, Vic, help me get her out of there." He placed his hands against the transparent frozen barrier.

"We can't," Gwen said. "It's a tricky spell, and we don't know how to break it. We can't just smash her loose."

"Azric said she could die, and I don't think he was bluffing." Vic felt the dismay well up inside him.

"Doctors on Earth can do things like this," Cap said. "There must be a way."

Vic found that he had forgotten to breathe and he drew in several deep breaths of water. "I was hoping you knew."

"Perhaps the anemonites," Lyssandra suggested.

The anemonite bubletts floated in front of the preserved woman, intrigued. Sage Polup, Imbra, Gedup, and Ronra conferred briefly. "Yes. Yes, it can be done," they said. Vic's heart leapt.

"We will need to build the proper equipment, of course," they continued, obviously unaware of the hope they had created and then dashed.

"How, uh, long would that take?" Vic asked.

"Twenty days," they said. "Perhaps less, if the sages in Elantya have the proper materials and offer us their assistance."

Vic's father pressed the faceplate of his mask and both of his gloved hands against the ice coral and stared at his wife, speechless for a long time. "We'll come back for you, my Kyara," he said at last. "I promise. But we need to help others, too —" His voice caught. It tore at Vic to see his parents so close together — a sight he had dreamed of for two long years — and yet impossibly separate.

"Come on, Uncle Cap," Gwen said softly.

But Dr. Pierce could not bring himself to leave.

Vic didn't want to go either. For a moment, he wanted to tell the others to go on without them, to leave him and his dad behind. Didn't the two of them belong here with his mother? But he could not abandon his friends. Vic put a hand on his father's wet-suited shoulder. "Azric won't harm her. Without me and Gwen, she's his only bargaining chip and his only hope for breaking a crystal door seal."

Gwen took her crystal dagger out of its pouch. "Right now we have to go rescue Tiaret and Sharif, who are in immediate danger. If there's going to be a fight, we'll all need weapons."

The somber group headed back up the narrow tunnel, towed by the anemonite bubletts. When they emerged from the treacherous tunnel and swam past the mangled electric eels, Vic and Gwen pointed the way toward Lavaja Canyon. Overhead, the bright flashes and rumbles of sea fireworks showed that the battle was continuing. Far, far above they could see the dark shapes of war galleys, swimming creatures, and massed merlon warriors.

They did not, however, see two branded sharks streak toward them like fanged torpedoes.

Lyssandra grabbed Vic and pulled him back as a shark raced in for a vicious attack. Gwen slashed instinctively with her knife hand, then released the bublett so she could swim out of the way.

Dr. Pierce in his strange scuba gear seemed to attract the sharks, which dove toward him. Vic foolishly darted toward the predators, jabbing his small crystal dagger into one tough gray hide. When Gwen also rushed to protect Vic's father, they temporarily startled the sharks away. The anemonite subletts rammed and harassed the sharks, chasing them off before they could do more damage.

But the sharp fangs had done enough. One of the attackers had torn a hole in the scuba air hose, and bubbles streamed upward from it, like white foamy blood.

Vic's father let out a cry of dismay. Water began seeping into his mask as he grasped the damaged hose, wrapping his gloves across the gash to seal the leak.

"He can't stay down here!" Vic shouted. "He's got to get to the surface, or he'll drown!" Gwen was already at her uncle's waist, unhooking the heavy weight belt that kept him down at the depths. Dr. Pierce seemed to be trying to say something, but he could not form words.

Working quickly, Gwen took her handkerchief out, wrapped her leather pouch around the split hose to hold it together, and tied the leather in place with the hankie. Vic's dad put his hand over the "patch" to hold it in position.

"We will take him," Gedup said from the bublett that he and his daughter Imbra now shared.

"I can't let . . ." Dr. Pierce managed to say.

"Dad! Live now, argue later." There was no way Vic was going to lose either of his parents, if he could help it. He placed his father's free hand on the fin of Gedup's bublett.

"Don't worry, Uncle Cap. We'll handle the rest," Gwen said. "We're getting good at this sort of thing."

Shaking his head, Dr. Pierce looked longingly back toward the cavern where his wife waited.

"We'll find a way, Dad," Vic said. "But there's no time now. You've got get to safety." Vic patted the side of the bublett, and Gedup threw the engines to maximum. Within seconds, the two anemonites had hauled Vic's father out of sight, racing toward the dubious safety of the ocean's surface before the last scraps of his air gave out.

31

AT THE LAVAJA CRACKS, Sharif continued his endless, grueling work, scooping up molten crystal. Since the horrific branding incident, neither Orpheon nor General Blackfrill had let him work with the captive jhanta, obviously worried that he would try to escape again. Sharif had a genuine connection with the undersea creature. As he'd had with Piri . . .

Nearby, Tiaret and the other slaves were tethered to their work areas, laboring near the burning fissures and unsettled seabed. Sharif also had a seaweed rope tied to his ankle, keeping him in his work zone so that the guards could more easily patrol the slaves and make sure they remained in line. The brevi Sharif wore — barely more than a loincloth — offered no protection from injury. Too close to the hot fissures, both he and Tiaret already had numerous scorches and heat scars on their skin from the spurting lavaja. The brand mark still burned on the skin of his shoulder.

Trapped out here, Sharif had a great deal of time to dwell in deep thought. Stripped of everything he owned, Sharif saw clearly what all the riches of his world could not buy for him and the merlons could not take away: friendship, true friendship, undeserved and unearned. The kind his fellow apprentices and the jhanta and Piri had shown him. In fact, in their efforts to break his spirit, the merlons and Orpheon had shown Sharif what he truly was inside. As the people of Irrakesh said, "Adversity illuminates the soul."

He fingered the raw, painful mark on his shoulder and smiled faintly. He was not ashamed to be branded, for it had taught him something very important. Pausing in his tedious work, he stared into the bright lavaja for a time, letting the light fill his mind.

Sharif looked over to where Orpheon was browbeating a merlon slave, who had accidentally spilled a full crucible of lavaja into the mud. Orpheon actually seemed to enjoy bullying anyone who was not in a position to resist. Maybe it made him feel important.

Seeing this, and remembering how he himself had often felt superior, Sharif promised silently that if he ever escaped from this place, he would be a different person. He would not look down on those who were not noble-born, but instead admire them for their accomplishments and thank the Air Spirits of Irrakesh for the work they did.

Sharif would not demand his people's loyalty and respect.

He would earn it. And those gifts the Air Spirits saw fit to grant him, he would use to help those who needed it and to fight against tyrants, slave masters, and anyone else who robbed others of their dignity for their own selfish gain.

He vowed to strive to be worthy of those who had so freely offered him their friendship: Vic and Gwen, Tiaret and Lyssandra, the jhanta, Piri, even his flying carpet. They were all so different, yet bound by one thread. They were all his *friends.*

Suddenly, far above the undersea city, there were flashes and booming explosions, causing a stir among the workers and their slave masters. Sharif looked up and tried to assess what he saw. Distant rumbles echoed through the water.

For Sharif, the implications sank in almost immediately. The Elantyans must have come for them, at last! To a distant part of his mind, the colorful flashes felt like fireworks celebrating the epiphany he'd just experienced.

In a frenzy the remaining merlon guards sounded a call to arms. General Blackfrill, working beside Orpheon as he often did, seemed agitated that he could not go and fight with Goldskin against the Elantyans. He snarled at Orpheon, clearly resenting his lowly responsibilities.

As if in counterpoint to the overhead show of sea fireworks, the lavaja fissures burned brighter, blazing in front of Sharif and drawing his gaze again. He had changed and now saw himself in a completely different light. The loss of so much — Piri, his friends, his position, even his faithful flying carpet — had completely altered his perspective. The incandescent molten crystal burned a bright spot on his retinas, and he seemed to be staring into dazzling potential.

And something more. The lavaja pulled at him, and he sensed a seething magic much more powerful than the mere heat of the lavaja.

Gradually, like a minuscule buoy rising from the darkness of a bottomless ocean, a tiny bubble of hope formed within Sharif and drifted upward. At first he thought it was just imaginary. Then the feeling became solid and real — unlike anything he had ever experienced before. The vows he had just made to himself could not be empty ones. He would make good on his promises even if he had to give up his life to accomplish it.

While merlon warriors rallied and swam off to join the fight at the water's surface, a flicker inside the flowing crystal of the fissure caught his eye. The heat and bright fire inside the lavaja increased, like the hope inside him. It seemed to be connected to his own thoughts, his own resolve. Something was definitely happening!

A split second later a strobing dome of furious red broke the surface like an inflating bubble — then rose up until it hovered above the lavaja crack. A real blazing sphere, a crystal globe brighter than he had ever before seen it, floated at his feet in a brilliant rebirth. Sharif knew exactly what it was, though he could scarcely believe it.

"Piri, you are alive!"

At the sound of his voice, Piri's eggsphere shot upward, dripping a few sparkles of the molten crystal. The throbbing ball changed from the dark red of anger to the deep purple of love. Moving away from the thermal fissure, the nymph djinni began flashing a rainbow of colors: the white of pride, happy pink, friendly yellow, worried green, and urgent orange. Her orb spun in circles around him from head to toe and back again as if she were examining him for injuries. When she reached the brand on his shoulder, her glow turned back to a fiery red.

Piri had survived. Somehow, enduring the blazing heat of lavaja, she had been transformed, growing stronger rather than being destroyed. She had undergone a magical metamorphosis in the inferno.

Tethered to the work area, Sharif reached out, caught her orb, and pressed the superheated curved surface against his cheek, but her touch did not burn him. Magic. "It is all right, Piri. I am fine." His throat was clogged with emotion. "But you, Piri — look at you. You are alive and you can fly — or float — by yourself! You could not do that before!"

Her orb twinkled pink with laughter, and he heard a faint, soft voice in his head, tiny and high-pitched. *Yes.* He had never heard Piri's voice before, and now she spoke to him in one- and two-word bursts of thought.

Fly. Float.

Aja change.

New magic.

Amazed, Sharif held his breath and stared at the delicate female form inside the protective walls of the orb. His eyes burned. "You . . . you can talk?"

Just you, said the tiny voice in his mind. *For now.*

"Piri, I missed you so!"

I know, the tiny voice replied.

"I love you, too. I have so much more to tell you, but we

must escape immediately." Even though Orpheon and Blackfrill remained among the slaves at Lavaja Canyon, during the unexpected attack, their minds were elsewhere. Neither had noticed Piri yet, but the dazzling bright djinni sphere was sure to draw attention soon.

He looked warily around and saw that a wide-eyed Tiaret had noticed what was going on. In a hushed voice, Sharif quickly said, "Stay low, Piri, close to the bright cracks. After we free Tiaretya, we will go back for Gwenya and Viccus."

Friends here, Piri said.

"They are back in the merlon city, with Azric," Sharif corrected. "We have to find —"

No. Here, Piri said emphatically. She blazed white with pride.

Sharif turned and caught a glimpse of Vic and Gwen coming over the ridge of the canyon. He saw his friends — including Lyssandra! — holding onto silvery bubble contraptions that scooted them along at great speed. Farther down the edge of the blazing fissure, he saw Tiaret's eyes come alive with anticipation.

"All right, Piri. I will not doubt you again."

32

SHARING THE TWO REMAINING anemonite bubletts, Vic, Gwen, and Lyssandra streaked toward the simmering orange glow of the lavaja cracks.

"This isn't going to be easy, you know," Gwen said. "General Blackfrill will still be there, and probably Orpheon, too."

Ahead, the roaring fissures of lavaja crystal blazed brighter as if in angry response to the battles going on overhead. Blackfrill and all the workers had surely seen the fireworks. Many merlon warriors had already gone to join the fight above.

"We must take advantage of the confusion," Lyssandra said.

"All we have to do is free Sharif and Tiaret," Vic said, as if it would be a simple thing. "Then we can get out of here."

When they approached the glowing, scabbed landscape, they saw shadows playing around the ocean bed, flares and flashes from unstable eruptions of magical crystal. While the tethered merlon slaves resentfully toiled, Blackfrill moved back and forth, waving Tiaret's teaching staff, warning them not to be distracted by the battle.

"How are we going to approach them without being seen?" Gwen said.

"Who says we have to do it without being seen?" Vic asked. "It's time to try it my way: leap now, look later." He urged one of the bubletts forward. "There's Tiaret."

"Wait!" Gwen shouted.

The other anemonite craft followed as Lyssandra and Vic zoomed toward the tethered workers. Vic spotted Sharif at the bottom of the canyon on the opposite side of the bright fissure from Tiaret. They both looked ready to fight!

The two bubletts swung in like miniature wrecking balls as they pulled the cousins along. They transmitted a quick message. "Let go. We will distract them while you help your friends."

From the expression on her face, Gwen was clearly skeptical about the wisdom of the supposed "plan" — such as it was — but it was too late for her to stop anything.

The anemonite bubletts streaked in front of the tethered merlon slaves. In the turmoil, a crucible disengaged from its chain, fell from the crane, and tumbled into the seething lavaja. Several slaves broke free and scrambled about in a panic, which was increased by their natural resentment toward the dominant guards. Even the remaining merlon warriors became frantic, jabbing with their spears or throwing tridents at the racing anemonite vessels. A jagged-tipped weapon struck one hull, but bounced harmlessly off.

Blackfrill loomed up in front of Ronra's craft and swung

the dragon's-eye end of Tiaret's teaching staff at it. The downtrodden jellyfish scientist was all too happy to launch one of the two small quarrels built into her bublett. The stubby metal arrow struck the outraged merlon general in the shoulder plate and dug in. Blackfrill roared and grabbed for the bublett with one clawed hand, but the anemonite dodged out of the way.

Still tethered, Tiaret attacked the nearest merlon guard, grasping his spear without pausing to consider her own safety. She got the weapon away from him, slashed at her bindings, and freed herself. Yelling, the girl from Afirik swam over to Sharif and cut his ankle tether, freeing him just as Gwen, Vic, and Lyssandra reached them.

Now Orpheon joined the fray, looking furious at his loss of control. Five more guards, intent on their duty, brandished their spears and tridents to block the escaping humans and slaves. One warrior drew a curved scimitar.

Suddenly, unexpectedly, a floating globe swooped in front of Sharif, dodging and weaving. Like a fireball, the crystalline bubble throbbed a deep, dull red that flared into a nova of scarlet and orange that blinded the guards. A petite cannonball, the resurrected Piri smashed one of the merlon guards in the forehead, making him drop his weapons as he tried to flee from this unexpected enemy.

Meanwhile, Blackfrill had ripped the metal quarrel out of his shoulder. Brandishing the unbreakable teaching staff, he swam toward the five apprentices. The general, who had been looking for any excuse to get revenge on the young human captives, did not care about Azric's sorcerous plans. He only wanted to serve the merlon king.

Blackfrill charged straight toward Tiaret, the sharp end of the teaching staff extended and murder in his eyes. But unlike the other slaves, Tiaret was not easily cowed. She dove directly at the general, surprising him. "You have something of mine."

He jabbed the spear point at her, but she did not shrink away; instead, Tiaret seized the teaching staff and yanked. Blackfrill turned the staff, straining to bring its sharp point against Tiaret's side, then slashed with his other hand, raking sharp claws down her ribs. Though the cuts weren't deep, the pain caused Tiaret to recoil momentarily and lose her grip on the teaching staff.

Enraged, Blackfrill twisted the weapon out of her grip and drew it back, ready to plunge the sharp tip into her heart.

Close to her, Vic fought against another merlon warrior, who slashed with a narwhal-tusk spear. Seeing Tiaret in trouble, Vic instinctively reacted with the *zy'oah* reflexes his mother had taught him, moving with unexpected speed. While the merlon general closed in on Tiaret, he snatched a trident abandoned by a fleeing guard and kicked out at his own opponent as the sharp narwhal tusk came at him. Knocking the other merlon guard away, he paid no further attention to him, gripped the trident shaft as tightly as he could, and swung it toward Blackfrill.

He only intended to knock the merlon general away, to protect his friend as she had protected Vic so many times. But Blackfrill lunged forward, truly intending to kill Tiaret, just as Vic thrust the trident with all of his strength. All three points of the jagged underwater spear plunged deep into the general's chest.

Vic's own shock at what he'd done absorbed all his

concentration. Then he experienced a sensation that was strange — and *wrong*. It took him several seconds to realize that the other merlon guard had actually jabbed him in the thigh with the narwhal-tusk spear. In his urgent rush to save his friend, Vic hadn't even noticed the wound. But, without doubt, the pain would come.

Stunned, Vic held onto the trident, with Blackfrill skewered on it. The general twitched and thrashed, clutching at the tines of the weapon embedded in his chest until he went limp. Dark merlon blood drifted in the water, mingling with bright red from Vic's thigh.

Now the other guard, taking advantage of Vic's surprise, tried to attack him again. But Tiaret wrested her unbreakable teaching staff from Blackfrill's loosening hands and swung it at the guard, snapping his spear, then swung again to crack his skull. She looked at him, satisfied with the result.

"I guess we're even then," Vic said.

"For today."

Finally letting go of the bloodstained trident, Vic stared in disbelief at what he had done. "I . . . I killed him. I killed Blackfrill!"

When he and his friends had fought the merlons on the *Golden Walrus* and in Elantya, they had been nameless enemies, all alike to him. He hadn't seen where they lived, hadn't spoken their language. But Vic had *known* Blackfrill — had heard the sound of his voice, had hated him. The general had meant to slaughter Tiaret and probably would have killed all of them, unless they fought back. Logically, there was no reason to feel guilty.

Gwen swam toward him. "Taz, you're bleeding!" She took the handkerchief and pouch from his belt, pressed the leather pouch to the narwhal spear wound and tied it in place with the hankie. He didn't want to admit it, but the gash was really starting to hurt, and he could see how much he was bleeding.

Now Orpheon, enraged at the defiance of the human captives, took up a place near a wide fissure in Lavaja Canyon. The traitorous apprentice drew a rune in the water and muttered a string of unfamiliar words, summoning the power contained within the molten crystal flowing through the fissure. Tongues of lavaja flickered from the rift. The cracks blazed brighter.

In the water, Vic felt the tingle of burgeoning energy about to be released.

Sharif felt it too, and realized what Orpheon was doing. "No! You cannot possibly hope to control so much magic once you unleash it."

Orpheon barked a laugh. "The powerless prince doubts my powers? Perhaps that fool Rubicas is too feeble to control such forces, but I am not so weak. It seems I have yet another lesson to teach you." He spread his arms, hands pointed downward, fingers splayed.

Lavaja began to boil and plume upward from the fissures all around, awakened by Orpheon's dark magic.

Sharif moved closer to the former apprentice. "Wait. At least give the slaves and animals and slave masters time to leave the canyon first."

"They are of no consequence to me," Orpheon sneered. "And you are even less important. I am your master. Perhaps if you kneel to me I will consider your request."

Swimming forward, Sharif shook his head. "You may be powerful, but you are no master. You are still Azric's lackey, unable to make your own decisions." The water closer to the cracks scalded the prince's bare skin, making the brand mark on his shoulder throb.

"I do not need Azric's permission to kill you," Orpheon snarled, lunging toward Sharif. In that moment, he lost control of whatever magic he'd been working. Orpheon quickly shouted more words in the ancient language, trying to continue his spell.

The prince dove to one side and snatched up a coral-encrusted staff dropped by one of the slave drivers. He felt the resistance as he swung it as hard as he could through the water and struck Orpheon's knees a hard blow.

The dark sage stopped in mid-syllable, drifted a moment in shock, then caught himself. He spun and charged at Sharif, who swam backward toward the fiery cracks.

Suddenly Piri was there, flashing and dodging. When Orpheon had thrown the nymph djinni into the lavaja as a means to punish Sharif, he had never anticipated her return — or her amazing metamorphosis.

The crystalline djinni sphere smashed Orpheon in the groin, making him curl up and sink toward the ocean floor. It was too late to stop the process the dark sage's spell had set in motion, like an avalanche of magic.

Howling curses, Orpheon grabbed for Sharif with one hand and caught hold of his leg, but the prince spun, yanked the leg free, and kicked the dark sage in the mouth.

Piri flashed in Orpheon's face again. He struggled to see where he was at the edge of the fissure.

"I can still destroy you," Orpheon raged, snatching for the eggsphere. The crevice split open wider. Sharif kicked out at the dark sage with both legs at once. The traitorous apprentice jerked backward as a large plume of molten crystal splashed up, engulfing him in the incandescent lavaja. Just as quickly, the plume of superheated liquid crystal receded into the crevice, and Orpheon sank with it out of sight.

Even that didn't end the spell. The reckless unleashing continued to build.

The two anemonites circled Vic in their bubletts, sending urgent signals. The body of Blackfrill, with the trident still sticking out of his chest, drifted in the swirling, hot currents. Vic pressed his hand against his own wound.

"We have to go, Taz!" Gwen said, unclasping his heavy belt.

"We are in danger here," Tiaret agreed, grabbing his arm. In her other hand, she held her teaching staff. The slashes on her ribs hardly seemed to bother her.

Master Polup's bublett dove in front of Vic, forcing him to tear his eyes from the general he had killed. "Come, Viccus. If ever two creatures deserved their fates, they were Blackfrill and Orpheon."

Vic knew Sage Polup was right. He looked down into the seething molten crystal, but saw no sign of the former apprentice. The ocean began to grow hotter all around them as the pressure of the seething lavaja continued to build.

33

PIRI'S VOICE WAS URGENT in Sharif's mind. *Lavaja. Now!*

Exhilaration from the fight, from seeing Orpheon meet his end at last, still coursed through his veins. Several globs of lavaja belched up from the thermal vent, as if swallowing the evil man had caused it indigestion. All of the seabed around Lavaja Canyon cracked and split, and the water at the edges of the molten aja fissures boiled, producing clouds of tiny bubbles.

Now Sharif understood the djinni's warning. The lavaja was going to surge out in a great eruption. They had to get away — now!

With furious strokes, Sharif retreated from the work zone while Piri kept pace just beside him, glowing brightly. Lavaja began to bubble and rise, oozing out of the cracks and spewing higher. It was going to get very uncomfortable here soon.

Sensing the impending disaster, the other merlon slaves

scrambled to tear the tethers from their ankles. Once they freed themselves, the captive merlons dropped their lavaja-harvesting equipment where it was and swam away in all directions. The few remaining warriors and slave masters could not control them, especially with both Orpheon and Blackfrill gone.

Far overhead, the sea fireworks and the battle continued.

Lavaja soon, Piri said frantically in Sharif's mind. *Much more.*

Sharif took off his seashell belt and called out, "Piri says Lavaja Canyon is going to erupt. We need to get to the surface now. As you would say, my friend Viccus: Do now, talk later."

Polup understood all too well and did not wait for further plans or discussion. With Vic's free hand on the fin of his bublett, the anemonite sage shot upward so quickly that Vic, whose mouth had been open to argue, did not have a chance to utter a word before he was out of range. The wounded young man left a trail of bright blood in his wake from the bandaged spear wound.

A low sound rumbled through the water and a moment later curtains of lavaja spewed up from several thermal vents at once.

Freed of their heavy belts, Gwen and Tiaret also swam upward with all possible speed. Tiaret was a respectable swimmer by now, but her teaching staff slowed her despite her strong strokes. She would not let go, however, even though it meant she lagged behind. Ronra in the remaining anemonite bublett circled back so that the girl from Afirik could grab hold with her other hand and be towed forward.

Lyssandra sensed the brewing eruption and turned to swim toward the corral and pens where the animals were kept. "I will set the sea creatures loose. Do not wait."

Sharif turned, looking frantically for Lyssandra, but the petite girl dove downward, racing off to the undersea corrals. He called after her, but when the sea temperature noticeably surged, he had to swim as hard as he could, with Piri bobbing and flashing next to him. At least Lyssandra was swimming away from the widening fissures.

Below, the ocean floor cracked and split open as more uncontained lavaja boiled up, burning brighter, spewing feathery jets into the water. The warmth they felt was no longer just magical. Geothermal heat shot through the water.

"Swim — unless you want to be boiled alive!" Gwen cried, but none of them needed prompting. The water currents billowing up were hot enough to scald skin.

The two anemonite bubletts had climbed far ahead, pulling Vic and Tiaret. With the nymph djinni bobbing ahead of him, flashing an urgent yellow, Sharif strained to swim even faster. Beside him, Gwen was also pumping furiously, but he doubted they would get away in time.

Faster, Piri urged. *Now.*

Unable to resist the terrifying temptation, Sharif stole a glance back down into Lavaja Canyon, still concerned for Lyssandra. Rainbow plumes of molten aja now unfurled from every vent and crack in the sea floor, as spectacular as any fireworks Sage Groxas had ever unleashed.

But Sharif could not savor their beauty while fleeing for his life. His arms felt heavy and his legs were growing stiff.

Though he was utterly exhausted, panting water through his gills, he could not pause, even for a moment. A fresh burst of searing current scalded their feet and legs.

Then in a flash, something dark struck them, pushed them. In a scramble he reached out, grabbed on. A soggy tassel? At first Sharif could barely grasp what was happening. In his mind, Piri's gleeful voice sang, *Yes! Better!*

He clutched the edge of something that felt like wet fabric — his flying carpet! The carpet had returned, responding to his summons after all! Sharif caught Gwen's arm in mid-stroke and pulled her to the carpet with him.

"Where has it been?" Gwen asked in astonishment, wrapping her fingers around the edge and letting herself be drawn upward as swiftly as the embroidered rug could work its way through the water.

As they gained speed, rising away from the welling heat, Sharif had a chance to take a good look at the rich purple rug. The once-fine embroidered fabric was now quite a bit worse for the wear. Loops of seaweed were tangled in its fringes, a glowing streak of slime marked its center, and several large tooth punctures at its edges gave evidence of how much difficulty the loyal flying carpet had encountered on its journey to find him.

"We will never know what happened to delay it," Sharif said, "but I have never seen any *thing* so beautiful in my life."

Piri, glowing bright orange, darted ahead of the tangled tassels of the carpet, lighting the way toward the surface. The flying rug canted at a sharp angle and headed almost straight upward while Gwen and Sharif clung to it.

Gwen sighed with relief. Sharif couldn't see Vic or Tiaret anymore, and he feared that Lyssandra was entirely lost.

Suddenly, Piri blazed bright red again. *Shark,* was the only word that blared through Sharif's head. Then, *Sharks! Many!*

Noticeably slower under water, the carpet might not be able to outrun these deadly creatures. Sharif cast about, trying to see them, and realized that the predators were coming from above, streaking downward to intercept them. Sharif's heart pounded in his chest. He had no weapons.

"Sharks ahead of us," he said to Gwen. She surprised him by drawing her crystal dagger with one hand while holding onto the carpet with the other.

The carpet whipped around to evade the gray torpedolike shapes, but there were too many and they swam too fast. There must have been twenty at least. Blazing an angry battle red, Piri rocketed forward to pound one of the beasts repeatedly on its snout until it retreated. Then she shot out after another.

Meanwhile, several of the stealthy predators had doubled back and approached from behind. Gwen shouted a warning, and with her incredibly quick reflexes, she kicked the nose of the closest shark, which briefly retreated.

Fighting with one hand, Sharif thrust his thumb into the dark eye of a shark that darted too close, its teeth flashing. The beast thrashed furiously, more surprised than blinded. He and Gwen continued to lash out with a flurry of one-handed punches, kicks, and jabs, as they clung to the edge of the ascending carpet.

Too many, Piri said, and Sharif knew she was right. They would never be able to fight off all of these predators.

Something enormous now swooped up from underneath and careened in among the sharks. Sharif's strength was nearly spent, and he wondered desperately what could be coming after them now. A sea serpent? A small kraken?

Forcing himself to keep moving, he swung his arm to punch at another shark. His fist only succeeded in grazing the shark's flank — and he realized that it was swimming *away* from him and Gwen. In fact, all of them were. Piri glowed dazzlingly bright.

Now, Sharif could see what had drawn their attention: the great jhanta — with Lyssandra riding on its back!

Their petite telepathic friend rode the graceful creature, which swam furiously among the startled sharks, ramming them with its snub head, battering them with its heavy fin-wings, striking at them with its tail.

Soon, all the sharks had been driven off, scattered or stunned. The predators retreated, while Lyssandra, Sharif, and Gwen raced the rest of the way to the safety of the surface, where they hoped the Elantyan war fleet would be waiting for them.

34

BY THE TIME VIC broke the surface, the spear wound in his leg was hurting badly. He could tell he was still losing a lot of blood, and he pressed his hand harder against the bandage to slow the flow as he coughed out seawater and gasped for air.

He was surprised to see that the anemonite bublett had brought him directly to the capsized purple speedboat — where his father now rested on the waves. The boat still floated and might even be salvageable.

The capsized craft could only be a temporary island of safety, though. Vic had almost forgotten that an equally titanic battle was taking place with the Elantyan war fleet.

Not far away, they saw sea serpents and angry merlon warriors. Most frightening were the whipping pillars of waterspouts that continued to circle and harass the powerful war galleys. To his relief, however, the furious blue-and-white tornadoes smashed into an invisible wall as they approached the galleys, battering again and again against a smooth, impenetrable bubble.

Vic could see the sages on the prows of the galleys reading from spell scrolls. "Look, Dad! Ven Rubicas got his protective spell working. He's covered the whole fleet."

All the war galleys were carefully protected under a clear dome, and the merlons' sorcerous energy was dissipating. The waterspouts seemed to be weakening, tumbling into disorganized spray and steam.

Deep beneath the surface, the light from the furious lavaja tempest brightened as hot crystal continued to erupt, flashing like a giant lightning storm on the ocean bed.

"Where are your friends? Where's Gwen?" Dr. Pierce said, coughing again. His skin looked gray and he seemed to be quite ill.

"They're coming. They were right behind me, swimming as fast as they could." Tiaret surfaced holding Ronra's bublett, looking satisfied with the battle she had just finished, and clinging to her teaching staff as if she would never let go again.

On the opposite side of the boat, Sharif's bedraggled flying carpet sprang out of the waves with a loud splash. Gwen and Sharif both clung to the edge, but as they were pulled out of the ocean, they could no longer maintain their grip and they dropped, panting with their gills, back into the water. Vic tried to swim to them, but the pain in his leg was too great. The bleeding had increased.

Then Lyssandra surfaced, riding the graceful gray jhanta.

Sheltered by the capsized boat, they all continued to watch the last gasps of the waterspouts strike ineffectively against the shield spell that protected the galleys. Lyssandra dispensed refreshing greenstepe from the inexhaustible tiny vial at her throat. Vic had never found anything so delicious before. He tried to maintain his optimism.

The massed merlons and their combative sea creatures seemed to be in a flurry. King Barak, in his mother-of-pearl chariot, was waving his clawed hands and ranting in a loud hissing voice. Beside him, Azric looked concerned as merlon sentries swam up to deliver their reports.

The merlons had seen the brilliant holocaust of the erupting lavaja canyons down below. Goldskin sounded a retreat, and all of the merlons ducked under the water, leaving the battle behind.

Blinking her eyes, Gwen said, "It looks like Azric just got the news that we all escaped."

"Or that his whole lavaja operation just went belly-up," Vic added. "Good thing he didn't notice us over here."

When the merlon armies were gone, Ven Sage Rubicas dropped the protective spell from the war galleys.

Still applying pressure to the wound on his leg, Vic said, "Not to complain, but I think my dad and I need to get some first aid here."

Sharif quickly got them onto his flying carpet. "I will take you to the ships swiftly. There will be healers waiting there."

Lyssandra, still astride the jhanta, said, "I can take a rider, too."

The anemonite bubletts circled, offering their assistance as well. With Sharif's carpet zooming above the waves like a tasseled ambulance, they all headed for the war galleys.

AFTER THE HEALERS HAD applied a salve and bandaged his injury, then read a spell to help the wound heal, Vic tried to take a nap in a bunk on the war galley. But the pounding drums and the swaying deck made it difficult for him to sleep. His father had been treated with a spell for what the Elantyans called "depth sickness," and seemed to be recovering as well.

"In other words," Gwen said, "they have a spell to cure the bends."

Vic nodded. "Lucky for us, since we don't have the Seaview and its decompression chamber handy."

None of them had emerged unscathed from their fights with the merlons and their close call with the lavaja. They each had cuts, bruises, and burns, but they would all heal.

"I think we taught the merlons a lesson or two. Maybe King Barak won't be so quick to come after us again," Vic said.

"I wish we had been here to see the battle," Tiaret said. "It must have been quite a spectacle. It appeared that the merlons suffered a great many losses."

"That's not the best part," Vic said. "Orpheon's gone now — one less big bad guy to worry about."

Lyssandra's brow furrowed. "Do not be so certain, Viccus. Orpheon was one of Azric's immortals."

Vic snorted. "Immortal is one thing — but being swallowed up in a sea of lava? It would be quite a trick for him to swim up out of that without a scratch."

"Sorry, Taz," Gwen said, "but I saw the evidence for myself. Tiaret put a spear right through his heart. He didn't even blink, and he healed immediately."

Sharif sat next to them, cradling the shimmering djinni globe, then rolled Piri's eggsphere down his forearm and across to his other elbow. "I thought Piri was destroyed, too, but she was undergoing a metamorphosis in the lavaja. My people have a saying: The fire that destroys may also cleanse, heat, and shed light. I believe magic has similar contradictory aspects."

He had already washed his flying carpet, and now gave the rug soothing strokes as he surveyed the tears, tooth marks, and unravelings it had suffered during its unknown adventures to come rescue them. By the light of Piri's sphere, the prince from Irrakesh lovingly began to make his repairs.

35

THE MAIN EXPERIMENTAL CHAMBER of Ven Rubicas's laboratory swarmed with activity. The skirmish out on the sea was over, and the merlon king and Azric had shown their destructive strength. Simply by escaping, Vic and Gwen had removed a powerful tool from the dark sage: No longer could he coerce them into breaking the seals that would unleash his legions of immortal warriors.

But the Elantyans could not rest. Their defenses now needed to be stronger than ever.

Dozens of the island's best sages and engineers fabricated new underwater suits modeled after Dr. Pierce's scuba gear. Teams of apprentices assembled many more anemonite bubletts, enough for each of the jellyfish-brains to use. Meanwhile, the Ven Sage locked himself in his chamber, surrounded by numerous spell scrolls he had borrowed from the Cogitarium. He worked tirelessly to expand his shield spell to protect all of Elantya.

Vic had a hard time keeping up with it all. He still limped from the wound in his leg, which had received further treatment in the Hall of Healers. Although the cut from the merlon spear hurt, he considered it a small price to pay for their lives. Blackfrill had paid much more dearly.

"I know we're in the middle of a war," Vic said to his father, working close beside him, "but what can we do about rescuing Mom?" Since their return from captivity, he and Gwen had not left Dr. Pierce's side, except to sleep.

His father, watching a neosage tinker with the tiny engines of an anemonite bublett, warned, "Don't seal off that circulation system. Anemonites breathe water, not air." Then he turned back to his son. "Azric will have to keep her safe, son. If what you told me is true, she's his only hope to break the seal on another crystal door."

"But we can't just wait here and do nothing," Vic said.

With all the racket and bustle around them in the laboratories, Gwen laughed. "I wouldn't exactly call this doing nothing, Taz."

"I've got a plan, don't worry," Dr. Pierce said. "We won't let Azric keep your mom. Everyone is working to come up with a way to free her."

Gwen groaned. "What about all those lavaja bombs they were planting in catacombs under Elantya? How will we ever find them all?"

"Ven Rubicas and I met all night with the Pentumvirate, explained to them about Kyara, talked about the merlons' stockpile of lavaja bombs, and discussed how far Azric got training you and Vic to break crystal door seals."

"Sheesh," Vic said, "that's a lot to hit the Pentumvirate with all at once."

His father nodded. "But it's surprising how fast a bunch of bureaucrats can make basic decisions when the reason for their very existence is threatened. They started making emergency duty assignments right away."

Vic glanced around the room at all of the workers and nodded. "Looks like a lot of us apprentices are gonna be learning our skills on the job."

His father obviously admired the great efforts being made. "And we've got three times this many people assigned to us, working in shifts round the clock. A journeysage and a neosage are out collecting materials for the equipment the anemonites think we'll need to rescue your mom, but it may take a week or two. Meanwhile the whole island's on alert."

Beside him, Gwen stared through the curved clear aquarium wall into the microcosmic ocean. The tanks were completely restored now; during the time when the five friends had been held prisoner by the merlons, neosages had restocked the aquarium with plants and fish, careful not to disturb Ven Rubicas. At the moment, the anemonite Imbra was testing her new bublett, playing hide-and-seek with the five aquits who now lived in the tank.

Vic limped his way along the side of the workbench. "And this time they're attacking us from beneath the water. We apprentices still have our gills, so we can breathe under water. But if we don't get these suits and bubletts and Ven Rubicas's shield spell working, Elantya has no way to protect itself from undersea attacks."

"Hmm, perhaps not," Rubicas said, overhearing their conversation. He was bleary-eyed from all the work he'd done on his spells. "But we have made a good start. Sage Pierce has helped us immeasurably, as have the anemonites."

"They feel a personal responsiblity for helping design weapons for the merlons," Gwen said, "even though they were forced to do it."

"Just like we could have been," Vic said, wondering uncomfortably how long they could have lasted against Azric's threats and pressure. He thought of the terrible things Orpheon had done to Sharif, and how much more pressure the dark sages could have brought against the cousins. If he and Gwen had been held captive by Azric for another week or month, he wondered how long they could have lasted. Would they eventually have been coerced into breaking a crystal door seal for the dark sage?

"They didn't have a choice," he said in a low voice. "If they hadn't cooperated, they would have been killed."

Rubicas tugged thoughtfully at his fluffy, white beard. "Nevertheless, they bear responsibility for the consequences of their actions."

"I'm afraid he's right, son," Vic's father said. "The old I-was-just-following-orders defense is just an explanation. It doesn't pardon anyone's guilt."

"But it's not fair to blame someone when they don't really have a choice," Vic objected.

"Mmm," the Ven Sage said. "A choice may be unfair, unbearable, unreasonable, dishonorable, painful, awkward, complex, unethical, or impractical. It may even seem impossible. But there is *always* a choice, even if it is a bad or painful one.

"In any case, *we* did not cast blame on the anemonites. They themselves understood their responsibility and have vowed to make amends if they can. You, your father, your cousin, the anemonites, and your friends are all allies of Elantya for one reason or another, and we are proud to have you."

"Speaking of which, Sage Polup and several other anemonite scientists went on a mission to scout at the base of the island," Dr. Pierce said. "Would you two please see if they've found anything out yet?"

Still deep in thought, Vic left the laboratory, limping along beside Gwen.

THE WATER SURROUNDING THE island was deceptively calm today, as if there couldn't possibly be any threat lurking beneath it. The cousins found Lyssandra installing a wind crystal in one of the watchtowers that Vir Helassa had ordered be erected on the shore.

A score of anemonite scientists were in similar watch stations well beneath the waves, keeping an eye out for any merlon scouts. If an aquatic warrior came close to the shore, the anemonites would light the sea crystals in their towers, which would alert the Elantyan watchers, who would in turn light their beacons and sound an alarm.

"Hey, Taz, look what the cat dragged in." Gwen pointed

toward the ocean. Vic saw Tiaret's head emerge from the waves. Their friend from Afirik swam toward them and then walked as the water grew shallower, carrying an anemonite under one arm. Tiaret still had splotches of angry-looking lavaja burns on her skin from their escape, but they were healing nicely.

"Ironic, is it not," Lyssandra murmured, leaning against the crystal watchtower, "that Tiaret has become such an excellent swimmer. That is one good thing that came out of our captivity."

"Yup. Gives a whole new meaning to the phrase 'immersion method' of learning." Vic fingered the faint slits at the base of his neck. "Plus, the gills help a lot."

Gwen nodded. "I doubt that Azric or the merlons meant to help us by doing that, but on a world that's mostly water, it's certainly an advantage."

Vic called out to Tiaret, "So what's the news from down there?"

"A good many interesting chapters are about to be added to the Great Epic here in Elantya," Tiaret replied, sloshing up onto the shore.

"Yup, and I think we've been responsible for adding, uh, more than our share to the epic recently," Vic said.

The girl from Afirik quirked an eyebrow at him. "Perhaps our 'share' of the epic is larger than we wish to believe."

"In other words, it's like that old Chinese curse: May you live in interesting times." Gwen said. "None of us has had much of a chance to get bored recently. Our lives have been a bit *too* interesting, I think."

"But I got my dad back . . . and learned that my mom is still alive," Vic said. "That's certainly good news to make up for all the bad stuff that's been happening."

"Indeed, my friends," Sharif said, landing his newly repaired purple carpet beside them on the beach. The boy from Irrakesh also had several lavaja burn marks on his skin, but most prominent was the angry and indelible mark of the brand Orpheon had pressed into his shoulder.

Sharif stood, stepped off of his flying carpet, and tossed Piri's eggsphere into the air. The nymph djinni caught herself and hovered in the air beside his ear, glowing pink. "From my scouting flight, there is little evidence of merlon activity."

"Gedup tells me the merlons have not finished creating their catacombs or deploying the lavaja bombs," Tiaret said, setting the anemonite back in the shallow water of the cove. "Sage Polup concurs. We have some time to disrupt their plans, if we can locate all of the explosives. Gedup and Sage Polup do not believe that even at their fastest pace the merlons will be able to carry out their plan for at least ten days yet."

"So we've got time to find the aja bombs, maybe even evacuate the island if we have to." Vic grinned as his ever-present optimism took hold. "That sounds doable, don't you think?"

"*Evacuate* Elantya?" Gwen said.

"Why not? Aren't there plenty of crystal doors to choose from?"

A low rumble produced a strange, ticklish feeling in their feet that started to grow stronger. The island began to shudder beneath them, and the ocean suddenly grew choppy.

Gwen recognized it first. "Earthquake!"

Tiaret scowled. "The merlons are at work again."

The ominous rumbling increased, and the ground beneath them gave a strong jolt. One of the half-built watchtowers down along the beach teetered and fell over with a loud clang. Then, abruptly, the ground stopped shaking.

"I believe, my friends, that much of the future of Elantya will depend on us," Sharif said. Piri flashed orange. "So does Piri."

"Because of the prophecies?" Vic asked.

"I am beginning to think that the prophecies indicate more than only you and Gwenya," Lyssandra said. She sang the children's fingerplay song for them and explained that the Pentumvirate now considered it a prophecy. "The Virs believe that all five of us are involved."

Gwen found she was almost relieved at this revelation. Other people had prophecies about them now, not just the cousins. In fact, everything was beginning to fit together like the pieces of a puzzle: two sisters, twin brothers, "twin" cousins, five apprentices. "Then it's a good thing we work well together," Gwen said. "I can't deny that there's something special about the connection we all have."

"Yup," Vic chimed in. "And I'd sure hate for Gwen and me to be in this prophecy thing all by ourselves."

Sharif put an arm around each of the cousin's shoulders. "No, we are all in this together."

Piri gave off a friendly yellow glow, brighter than the afternoon sunshine.

About the Authors

REBECCA MOESTA (pronounced MESS-tuh) is the daughter of an English teacher/author/theologian, and a nurse — from whom she learned, respectively, her love of words and her love of books. Moesta, who holds an M.S. in Business Administration from Boston University, has worked in various aspects of editing, publishing, and writing for the past twenty years and has taught every grade from kindergarten through college.

Moesta is also the author or coauthor of more than thirty books, including *Buffy the Vampire Slayer: Little Things*, and the award-winning *Star Wars: Young Jedi Knights* series, which she cowrote with husband and *New York Times* bestselling author Kevin J. Anderson. A self-described "gadgetologist," Moesta enjoys travel, movie-going, and learning about (not to mention collecting and using) the latest advances in electronics.

* * *

KEVIN J. ANDERSON is the author of more than eighty books, including *Captain Nemo, The Martian War, Hidden Empire, Of Fire and Night*, and many popular *Star Wars* and *X-Files* novels, as well as bestselling prequels and sequels to *Dune*, cowritten with Frank Herbert's son Brian. He has also written dozens of comics and graphic novels for Marvel, DC, IDW, Wildstorm, Dark Horse, and Topps. He has over seveteen million books in print in thirty languages. His work has appeared on numerous "Best of the Year" lists and has won a variety of awards. In 1998, he set the Guinness World Record for "Largest Single-Author Book Signing."

* * *

For more information on
Rebecca Moesta or Kevin J. Anderson, see

www.wordfire.com
or
www.elantya.com
or
www.myspace.com/rebeccamoesta
or
www.myspace.com/kevinjanderson

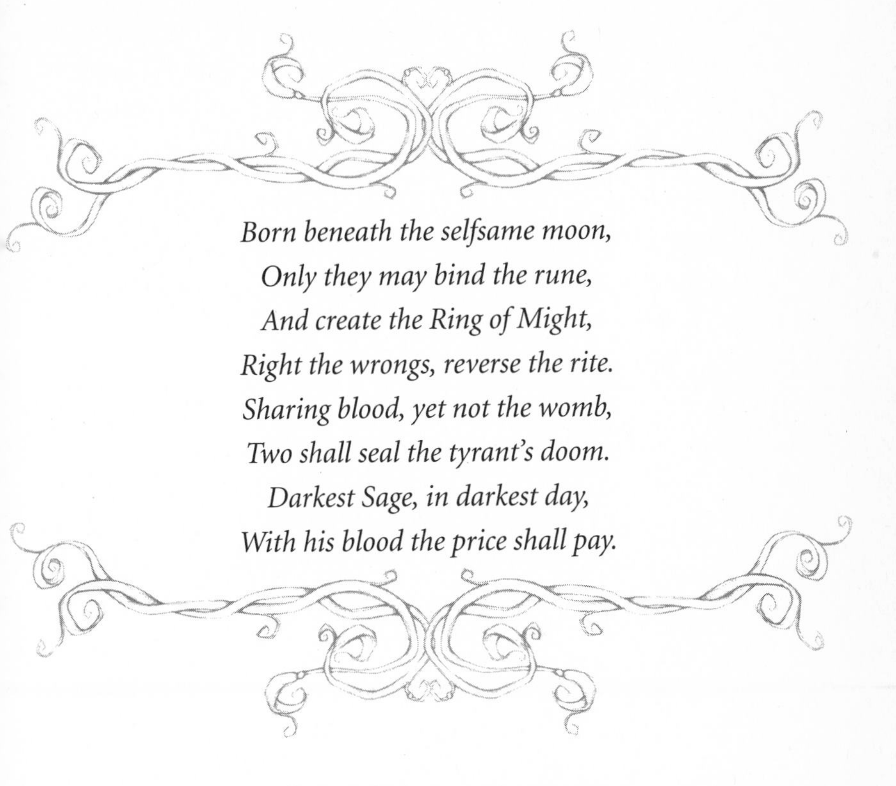

Born beneath the selfsame moon,
Only they may bind the rune,
And create the Ring of Might,
Right the wrongs, reverse the rite.
Sharing blood, yet not the womb,
Two shall seal the tyrant's doom.
Darkest Sage, in darkest day,
With his blood the price shall pay.